AFRICAN WRITERS SERIES

Chaka

D0109102

CHAKA

Thomas Mofolo

New English translation by Daniel P. Kunene

HEINEMANN

Heinemann Educational Publishers
Halley Court, Jordan Hill, Oxford OX2 8EJ
A Division of Reed Educational & Professional Publishing Ltd

Heinemann: A Division of Reed Publishing (USA) Inc.
361 Hanover Street, Portsmouth, NH 03801-3912, USA

Heinemann Publishers (Pty) Limited
PO Box 781940, Sandton 2146, Johannesburg, South Africa

OXFORD   MELBOURNE   AUCKLAND
JOHANNESBURG   BLANTYRE   GABORONE
IBADAN   PORTSMOUTH (NH) USA   CHICAGO

© This translation Daniel P. Kunene 1981
First published in English by International Institute of
African Language and Cultures 1931
This translation first published 1981

British Library Cataloguing in Publication Data

Mofolo, Thomas
Chaka. – (African writers series).
I. Title   II. Series
896´.39   PL8689.9M57C5

AFRICAN WRITERS SERIES and CARIBBEAN WRITERS SERIES
and their accompanying logos are trademarks in the United States of
America of Heinemann: A Division of Reed Publishing (USA) Inc.

ISBN 0 435 90229 6

Printed and bound in Great Britain by
Cox & Wyman Ltd, Reading, Berkshire

99   00   01   13

CONTENTS

ACKNOWLEDGEMENT

I wish to express my sincere thanks to Ms Leah Mookho Lekhehle, Secretary to the Assistant Registrar at the National University of Lesotho, who typed this manuscript for me. I was fortunate to have a person of her competence, who insisted on producing a word-perfect copy, to do this project. The extremely difficult circumstances under which she worked for me called for a sense of dedication which she amply demonstrated.

ACKNOWLEDGEMENTS

INTRODUCTION

Some highlights concerning the history of the 'Chaka' manuscript

The history of the 'Chaka' manuscript is discussed in some detail in my forthcoming book, *Thomas Mofolo and the Emergence of Written Sesotho Prose*. I shall therefore confine myself here only to some salient points which may be of interest to the reader of this translation.

There seems to be no doubt whatsoever that the 'Chaka' manuscript was completed by around late 1909, certainly before March 1910. It was on this latter date (on the 23rd March, to be exact) that Mofolo left Morija rather suddenly, as first stated by Gérard[1] and now amply confirmed by evidence I later obtained at the Paris Evangelical Missionary Society (PEMS) archives in Morija. Mofolo returned to Lesotho in 1912, but not to Morija.

The decision to leave Morija for good was an extremely painful one for Mofolo. He had established himself well at Morija by this time: he had published one book, namely *Moeti oa Bochabela*[2] which had been very well received by the missionaries and by many Basotho readers; the serialization of another book of his, *Pitseng*,[3] spread over one year in the *Leselinyana*[4] was nearing completion, and the work was to be published in book form less than a month after his departure; he had been a member of the *Lekhotla la Tsoelo-pele* (Council of Progress) (given the English name of *Basutoland Progressive Association*) since its inception in 1907; he was a reporter for the

[1] Albert Gérard, *Four African Literatures: Xhosa, Sotho, Zulu, Amharic*, Berkeley: University of California Press, 1971, p. 131.

[2] Thomas Mofolo, *Moeti oa Bochabela*, Morija, 1907.

[3] Thomas Mofolo, *Pitseng*, Morija, 1910.

[4] The full title is *Leselinyana la Lesotho*, first published in 1863, and still being published today.

Leselinyana, and had just covered a meeting of the *Lekhotla la Sechaba* (Basutoland National Council) in February and March, just prior to his departure; he was a proof-reader at the Morija Sesuto Book Depot; he also did occasional reviews for the *Leselinyana*. To leave a place where he had so much going for him was, no doubt, an act of tremendous sacrifice.

We know that the 'Chaka' manuscript was in existence by the time he left because it is mentioned in the *Livre d'Or de la Mission du Lessouto*,[5] a commemorative volume published by the PEMS to cover the first seventy-five years of the Mission's work in Lesotho, that is 1833 to 1908. The *Livre d'Or*, published in 1912, states that 'A fourth manuscript dedicated by the same author to describe the customs of the Zulus is at this very moment in the hands of one missionary from whom Mofolo has asked for criticism and advice.'[6] What made 'Chaka' a 'fourth', rather than a 'third' manuscript was the existence of another manuscript, also mentioned in the *Livre d'Or*, submitted by Mofolo very likely in 1908 and rejected by the missionaries. It is referred to by a French title, namely 'L'Ange déchu' (the fallen angel).[7] As regards the 'Chaka' manuscript being 'dedicated to describe the customs of the Zulus', Thomas Mofolo jr (Mofolo's son by his second wife, also known as Mofolo Mofolo) states that the original manuscript contained at least two chapters which described in some detail the history and customs of the Zulus, as well as their military system which had apparently impressed Mofolo very highly during his researches in Natal. Mofolo Mofolo states that these chapters had to be left out of the final manuscript as published in 1925 in order to reduce its size, since in those days authors were expected to pay the costs of producing their own manuscripts, and the less bulky a manuscript was, the less costly it was to produce. The two-plus chapters were left out for those reasons, says Mofolo Mofolo, and this was done in consultation with the author. According to Reverend Albert Brutsch, Archivist at Morija, while it is not quite accurate to say that authors were expected to pay to produce their manuscript, there were neverthe-

[5] Paris, 1912.

[6] *Livre d'Or*, p. 509. The original French reads: '*Un quatrième manuscrit, consacré par la même auteur à décrire les moeurs des Zoulous, est en moment entre les mains d'un missionaire auquel Mofolo a demandé des critiques et des conseils.*'

[7] *Ibid*, pp. 508–9.

less cases where, because of the excessive bulk of a manuscript, the author had to bear part of the cost. He cites Germond's *Chronicles of Lesotho* as an example.

The question of these omitted chapters naturally interested me a great deal, and I more than once put the question to Mofolo Mofolo whether there might not have been other reasons for this action. He was, however, quite unequivocal on this point, insisting that the chapters were left out solely for the reasons mentioned above, and not because they were considered to be in any way offensive and/or detrimental to the teachings of the missionaries.

There is evidence that the first time Mofolo gave any further attention to the 'Chaka' manuscript since 1909 or 1910, was in the early 1920s, which coincides with the return to Lesotho from France of the Reverend A. Casalis who was the one person who constantly advised and encouraged Mofolo in his efforts as a writer. This revision of the manuscript was finished some time before July 1922, the time when Mofolo told Zurcher that he (Mofolo) 'had just finished writing the book Chaka'.[8] When this is taken together with the fact that, as Gérard asserts, 'the records of the "Conférence des missionaires du Lessouto" clearly show that Casalis was solely and entirely responsible for the publication of the book',[9] the conclusion is inevitable that the revisions of the early 1920s were done with Casalis's direct assistance, and probably at his suggestion. Casalis would then have, quite understandably, strongly supported publication.

In terms of the delay in the publication of *Chaka*, then, the problematic period is three years, that is 1922–5, and not the entire fifteen or sixteen years beginning 1909/10. Which means that there are still unanswered questions suggesting a hesitation in the publication of this book. This seems to be supported by the failure to serialize the book in the *Leselinyana* before publication, a time-honoured tradition which was still being practised at that very time. In the absence of evidence to the contrary, these facts suggest an attempt to suppress the manuscript. However, the major controversies around this book took place *after*, and not *before*, its publication.

[8] J. Zurcher, private correspondence with me, February 1979. Zurcher came to Morija from Switzerland in 1920 to take charge of the Printing Works.

[9] Gérard, *op. cit.*, p. 129.

Translations of Chaka

By translating *Chaka* into English in 1931 (published by the International Institute of African Languages and Cultures, now the International African Institute), F. H. Dutton made an important contribution to world literature, and performed an invaluable service to the dissemination of Sesotho culture through literature. Through Dutton's translation, not only Europe became aware of, and benefited from, Mofolo's masterpiece, but indeed Africa itself. We often lose sight of the fact that translations of this nature facilitate communication within Africa as well. It is through translation, to take just one more example, that the present writer came to enjoy p'Bitek's beautiful lament, *Song of Lawino*, which he could not have read in the original Acoli. Dutton's translation of *Chaka* inspired non-Sesotho-speaking Africa to heights of creativity as exemplified by the works of Senghor, Badian and Mulikita.

After Dutton's translation, *Chaka* was translated also into French. Then abridged versions were published in English, German, French and Italian. More recently an abridged version has been published in Swahili, very likely translated from Grenfell Williams's English abridged version. And even more recently still, the unabridged version has been translated into Afrikaans. Unfortunately the translator, Chris Swanepoel, has marred an otherwise good translation by leaving out portions of the original without any explanation whatsoever. Some of these omissions are quite extensive.

The merging of history and fiction in Mofolo's Chaka

By his own testimony, Mofolo, in writing this book, did not intend to tell *the truth, the whole truth, and nothing but the truth* about the Zulu king; but neither did he intend to tell nothing but 'exaggerations produced by a facile pen' as suggested by N. R. Thoahlane, a Mosotho reader writing in the *Leselinyana la Lesotho* in February 1927. In responding to a letter written by Reverend S. M. Malale, a Sesotho-speaking Shangana, in July 1928, in which Malale questioned the accuracy of certain historical facts concerning the establishment of the Shangana nation, Mofolo, having admitted that Malale was a better judge than he regarding that particular aspect of the history, went on to say:

Ke a kgolwa diphoso tsa mofuta wona di ngata haholo bukeng ya Chaka;
empa ha ke a di tsotella haholo hobane ha ke ngole histori, ke ngola tshomo,
nka re ke ngola nnete, empa ee ekeditsweng haholo, ya fokotswa haholo, ha
tlohelwa tse ding tse ngata, ha ngolwa tse ding tse ngata tseo e seng nnete, e le
feela ho phetha morero wa ka ka buka ena.

I believe that errors of this kind are very many in the book Chaka;
but I am not very concerned about them because I am not writing
history, I am writing a tale, or I should rather say I am writing
what actually happened, but to which a great deal has been
added, and from which a great deal has been removed, so that
much has been left out, and much has been written that did not
actually happen, with the aim solely of fulfilling my purpose in
writing this book.

A similar statement is found in the book itself, at the beginning of
Chapter 23, where Mofolo says:

mme ere ka ha e se kgopolo ya rona ho bolela ditaba tsa bophelo ba hae
kaofela, re ikgethetse lehlakore le leng feela, lee lokelang morero wa rona
mona . . .

but since it is not our intention to recount all the affairs of his life,
we have chosen only one section which suits our present purpose . . .

This unspecified 'purpose' leaves one curious, and it is with a view to
at least partially satisfying this curiosity that the following com-
ments are made in order to identify some of the more important
areas where fact and fiction are at variance with each other. In just
about all of these, the effect is to build up greater intensity in the plot,
and to increase dramatic tensions by creating new juxtapositions of
highly volatile events and situations.

Firstly, the spring of action in Mofolo's version of Chaka's life is
that Senzangakhona, though having three or four wives, has no son
and therefore no heir. To correct this situation, he decides to take
another wife. He therefore arranges a feast to which he invites the
young people from the neighbouring villages. Having fallen in love
with Nandi, he persuades her to engage in complete intercourse with
him in the fields on her return home. She becomes pregnant, and in

spite of hurried marriage arrangements, she is at least two months pregnant by the time she joins Sensangakhona's household.

While the above makes for an excellent plot which is simply chock-full of potential dynamite, the historical Senzangakhona did not have the problem of lacking an heir, and did not engage in the actions narrated by Mofolo. But since the historical Chaka had a truly Achillean stature, Mofolo's artistic triumph is scored not so much in making Nandi give birth to Chaka, but in creating attendant circumstances which complement that stature. Thus Chaka's alleged 'illegitimacy' becomes his Achilles's heel, and Mofolo capitalizes on this triumph by making the senior wives soon get sons of their own, and thus have a stake in the succession.

Senzangakhona's meeting with Nandi is remembered differently in other accounts. According to A. T. Bryant in his *Olden Times in Zululand and Natal*, Senzangakhona was travelling when he saw Nandi bathing in a stream, was attracted to her, and asked for *amahlay' endlela* (the fun of the road), but he lost his head and, instead of the customary external intercourse called *ukuhlobonga*, he destroyed her virginity. R. R. R. Dhlomo, a Zulu author and historian, states that Nandi herself, having heard about Senzangakhona and his handsomeness and tall stature, went to find him and declare her love for him.

The pregnancy resulting from this first encounter is the subject of moral judgement by Mofolo. Firstly, he states that according to Zulu custom in those days, a young couple involved in such an act were killed, together with all their peers who shared the same sleeping quarters. But this is not true. While considered a disgrace and a devaluation of the girl, the accident of premarital pregnancy was nevertheless always regarded as a possibility, and law and custom provided for the normalizing of the situation by as quickly as possible moving the people involved towards a reincorporation into normal relationships. No one was killed for this act.

Secondly, Mofolo introduces the concept of illegitimacy as a powerful motivation to action: it is the threat which Senzangakhona's senior wives hold over his head when, having born male children of their own, they demand that Chaka be disinherited and he and his mother banished. And it is also for that reason that Mofolo's Senzangakhona reacts to this threat with such a sense of fear that he capitulates. The historical Senzangakhona took the whole thing in his stride and proceeded to normalize the situation by beginning marriage negotiations. Illegitimacy is a concept that can only be legitimate in certain societies, for example an individualistic, monogamous society. Add to this the Christian concept of morality, and you have the element of guilt introduced, and inevitably a strong motivation for the man involved to deny paternity. This is why Mofolo's Senzangakhona tries to camouflage the fact of Nandi's premarital pregnancy. But in Zulu society paternity would be a pride and the child would never suffer a lack of identity or of care.

Nandi's expulsion from Senzangakhona's household is another area of Mofolo's variance with history. According to Mofolo, Senzangakhona was still very much in love with Nandi, and it was only because of the pressure from his senior wives that he banished her. But other accounts emphasize Nandi's temperament as the cause of her expulsion. She is said to have had an evil temper, was domineering, and generally intractable, making life for Senzangakhona utterly miserable.

Next Mofolo creates the powerful magician, Isanusi, whose name means 'Diviner'. When, at their first meeting, Chaka wants to know his name since *isanusi* only names his profession, Isanusi declares, with a self-assurance bordering on arrogance: '*I* am "Diviner" both by name and by deed.' But such a person never existed. Isanusi is the result of Mofolo's transformation of Chaka's ambition into a man. Yet, a man who was also a doctor, a herbalist and a diviner, whose composite powers made it possible for Chaka to obtain his highest ambition through war and with the aid of magic. Ndlebe and Malunga, Isanusi's aids, are similar physical manifestations of Chaka's personality traits—vigilance and prowess respectively.

Isanusi is both the originator and the instrument of many of Chaka's desires. One of these, which again is contrary to historical fact, is the choice of a new national name. Historically, the name AmaZulu (meaning the descendants of Zulu), was in use long before Chaka's time, and was derived from their ancestor uZulu kaMalandela (Zulu son of Malandela). Mofolo, on the other hand, makes Chaka choose this name, which literally means 'people of the sky', in response to Isanusi's suggestion that the new nation deserves a better name than the one they now have, namely AmaFenulwenja

(People of the Male Organ of a Dog). Mofolo uses this opportunity to underscore Chaka's megalomaniac view of himself: 'Mazulu! It is because I am big, I am like that same cloud that just rumbled, before which no one can stand.' He claims to be a messenger of Nkulunkulu, sent by him to make the Zulu people the greatest nation on earth by teaching them the art of war and rendering them invincible.

But perhaps the most notable deviation from history which Mofolo exploits to the full to attain dramatic tension, is his creation of Noliwa, Dingiswayo's sister with whom Chaka falls in love. No such person existed. Yet Noliwa is the instrument for bringing to the surface that 'last spark of humanity still remaining in him', namely his human tenderness and his capability of loving. And there is no question about the genuineness of this love which makes Chaka dance for joy, and whose kindling and nurturing by Ndlebe is in sharp contrast to its ruthless sabotage and banishment by Isanusi at the time when it is at its highest peak. Chaka's murder of Noliwa who is now pregnant with his child, is another artistic highwatermark for Mofolo. It is symbolic of the murder of both love and life in one swift stroke. Thus the 'spark' is extinguished and 'a beast-like nature took possession of him'.

Then there is Chaka's alleged murder of his mother, Nandi. While artistically this helps to hasten Chaka's descent into a moral limbo, there is conclusive evidence that this is not what actually happened in history. According to Bryant, Chaka not only loved his mother, but he adored her. Bryant, who relies heavily on Henry Francis Fynn's diary, tells how Fynn, a close friend of Chaka, was out hunting elephants with Chaka when a messenger came with the news of Nandi's illness at her royal village of Emkindini sixty miles away. Chaka immediately stopped the hunting and though it was a late hour, ordered a march to Emkindini which they only reached at noon on the following day, having travelled through extremely rough terrain throughout the night. Chaka asked Fynn to go in and administer medicine to his mother to make her recover. Fynn came out announcing that Nandi was suffering from dysentery, and that she was not likely to live. When Fynn emerged a second time to announce Nandi's death, Chaka went and adorned himself in his best war attire and then came and stood before the hut in which his mother's body lay. Fynn goes on to say: 'For about twenty minutes he stood in a silent, mournful attitude, with his head bowed upon his shield, on which I saw a few large tears fall. After two or three deep sighs, his feelings becoming ungovernable, he broke out into frantic yells, which fearfully contrasted with the silence that had hitherto prevailed.'

One comes away with the impression that Mofolo strove for historical accuracy in some areas of his narrative with the same deliberate determination with which he distorted history in other areas, either by omission or by addition, or by bold shifts of emphasis. One reason for this is, as has been stated above, obviously the artistic one of enhancing the dramatic impact of the narrative which, after all, is a history-based fiction. Yet one wonders, at the same time, whether this constitutes the entirety of the 'purpose' stated by Mofolo. After all, the image of the historical Chaka, the empire-builder the mere mention of whose name struck terror into the hearts of lesser kings, who set entire communities to flight rather than face his armies, the hero of millions—this image could be, and probably was, hurt by some of the distortions when taken literally as historical fact. It must remain an unanswered question, yet a nagging one, whether or not Mofolo intended to achieve this latter effect.

Problems of translation

The challenges of translation are many, and they are sometimes insuperable. Because of the culture-specific nature of language, the speaker is able to withdraw behind it to barricade himself away from the outsider. Yet there is an ambiguity here, namely that the more effectively he excludes the outsider in this way, the more thoroughly he reveals the richness of his own culture. The translator comes in as a kind of cultural go-between who provides his good services to pass on, as best he can, the benefits of one culture to the practitioners of the 'other' culture.

One of the most difficult things about translation is that you have to determine your loyalties before you embark on it. You have constantly to ask yourself whether your translation does justice to the original, whether in fact it says what the author intended to convey. Then, on the other hand, you have to make sure that by trying to be faithful to the original, you do not then travesty the idiom of the receiving language. Often I have found translating Mofolo not only difficult, but indeed also agonizing. Having decided that my first loyalty was to the original, my first draft, especially in the more difficult areas, was almost always atrocious. I always had to come back to it without the original, to iron out its crudities, so that in the end I split my loyalty virtually equally between the donor language and the recipient language.

Secondly, one has to decide what the purpose of one's translation is. Is it for the purpose of revealing the style of the original? Is it in order to convey the idiom of the original through a distortion of the receiving language if that be necessary? Is it to find the closest equivalent idiom in the receiving language? If one's translation is trying to reveal the style which the writer makes manifest through his intimate knowledge of the structure and idiomatic versatility of his language, then the receiving language almost invariably suffers. So too if the translation seeks to jolt the reader into an awareness of the idiom of the original, which gives an exotic flavour to the translation. I suppose that one could say that the best translation is one which blends all these together according to the translator's poetic sensitivity.

Specific translation problems encountered

1. *No dictionary equivalent in English*

This involves culture-bound words, and has been handled in different ways. First, and perhaps most common, is that the original Sesotho word is retained, immediately preceded or followed by a defining statement, which is woven into the narrative in as unobtrusive a manner as possible. Here are some examples:

a) Mofolo tells how, during the festivities in the feast called by Senzangakhona in order to find a girl he could take as an additional wife, the young men went to the young women and asked them to *kana*. There being no one-to-one equivalent between *kana* and any English word I know, I made the young men ask the girls '*to play the choose-a-lover game called* ho kana'.

b) Mofolo says that *ho kana* is like the *sedia-dia* of the Basotho. I have said that it is like '*the* sedia-dia *girls' dance among the Basotho*'.

c) Mofolo continues his comparison of the Zulu lovers' game with Sesotho equivalents by stating that it is closer to *ho iketa* than to the *sedia-dia*. I have handled this like the others by saying 'ho iketa *whereby a girl offers herself to a young man for marriage without waiting to be asked*'.

But even such definitions are not always adequate. For example, the girl who engages in *ho iketa* does not propose love to the young man as one has heard that women in Europe do during a leap-year. The Mosotho girl engages in totally non-verbal behaviour in which symbolic acts are performed, the most important of which consists in her going to the young man's home and sitting outside the courtyards in a certain attitude, thus demanding that her presence be recognized and certain rituals performed by her hoped-for in-laws.

2. *No equivalent idiom*

Sometimes I felt the original imagery had to be retained since it was so striking. But since a close (or 'literal') translation would make no sense in English, I often had to resort to a kind of paraphrase of the original. Here are two examples:

a) Mofolo describes the pain Senzangakhona felt when he had to expel his wife and son from home under the pressure of the senior wives by saying that Senzangakhona 'swallowed a stone' and expelled them, in other words he performed a most painful act. I translate this as follows: 'The pain was like swallowing a stone.'

b) When the woman doctor 'works' on Chaka to strengthen him, her aim is that the young man should 'have a liver', and that explains why the major ingredients in the medicines she uses are the livers of brave and ferocious animals, and the liver of a brave warrior. The liver is the seat of bravery and courage, and to reflect this I translate this as: 'in order that he would also have bravery in his liver'.

But again one does not always feel that such paraphrases and/or amplifications are either necessary or useful. So I am afraid some inconsistency is inevitable.

3. *The irrepressible stylistic feature*

I have also sometimes felt that the style of the original needed to be reflected in the translation. Where I have succumbed to this, the result has been to introduce an element of exoticism (not deliberate nor for its own sake), at the same time stretching the idiom of the receiving language. In these situations a 'free' translation would have smothered the freshness of the original. Here are some examples:

a) One of the hallmarks of Mofolo's style is the use of various forms of repetition, resulting in a whole variety of parallelistic structures. In the following example, the effect of the repetition is to convey Mofolo's admiration of his character, Chaka. It is Chaka's first battle since he was enlisted in Dingiswayo's armies, and he fights with adeptness, with courage, and with much grace, and he literally carves a path through the enemy's ranks. Mofolo says:

> a a b c
> *A sa kena,/ a sa kena/ ntweng,/ mora wa Senzangakhona*

and I attempt to retain the a, b, c rhythmic pattern by translating:

> a a b c
> No sooner had he entered,/no sooner entered/battle,/the son of
> Senzangakhona

The rest of the sentence is: *than he felled men with his short spear, and he opened up gaps in the enemy ranks.*

b) Another repetition pattern, perhaps even more difficult to translate, is one where Mofolo uses synonymy whose effect is to lend greater emphasis to the statement. In many cases I have refrained from attempting to carry this structure over into my translation. One of the few cases where I could not resist the temptation is where Mofolo describes how the tree Isanusi needed for one of Chaka's medicines, which bled when chopped, could only be cut by someone completely naked. The relevant sentence is translated:

The person chopping it had to be naked, totally nude.

4. *Second-language 'interference'*

Writing in Sesotho about a Zulu king, Mofolo could not help breaking into Zulu at certain appropriate moments. Where he has then gone on to provide a Sesotho translation, I have followed the practice of giving the original Zulu and then translating Mofolo's Sesotho into English. It has sometimes been necessary to correct Mofolo's translation of the Zulu. In that case I have translated direct from Zulu into English, placing my translation in parentheses; I have then translated Mofolo's Sesotho translation of the Zulu *as it is* in the open text. In many cases, however, including the long praise poem for Chaka at the end of Chapter 17, Mofolo has not translated the Zulu into Sesotho. In those cases I have given my English translation in parentheses.

In this context, I should mention that Mofolo's definition of the royal salutation 'Bayede', is highly impressionistic and emotionally coloured. It reflects the sentiment that the greeting was god-inspired, having been revealed to Chaka in a dream, and thus confirming the growing myth that Chaka was chosen by the gods to come and teach the Zulu people the art of war. He is cast almost in the role of a Christ. It is this sentiment which Mofolo conveys when he says, 'Bayede means "he who stands between God and man", it means "the junior god through whom the great God rules the kings of the earth and their nations".'

I must not leave the reader with the impression that the translation was nothing but problems. There were numerous passages, comprising the bulk of the book, where the translation flowed with amazing ease and grace, making one marvel at the close parallels in human thought in different cultures, and its conversion into the intricate system of sounds called language.

CHAPTER ONE
NANDI CHOOSES CHAKA

South Africa is a large headland situated between two oceans, one to the east and one to the west. The nations that inhabit it are numerous and greatly varied in custom and language. Yet they easily divide themselves into three large groups: the nations settled along the western seaboard are of a yellow complexion. They are the San and the Khoi. The ones in the centre are the Batswana and the Basotho. Those to the east are the Bakone or the Matebele. The boundaries between them are prominent and visible; they are boundaries created by God, not man, because the nations to the west are separated from the ones in the centre by great sandy waterless deserts, and those in the centre are separated from those to the east by a massive mountain range of towering peaks rising in the Cape Colony and running parallel to the sea, yet far, far away from it. These nations are markedly distinct from each other, so much so that a person travelling from the west to the east is immediately conscious of having come into a different country and among strange people when he arrives among the Sotho nations in the centre, and likewise when he descends towards the Matebele nations over there beyond the Maloti mountains.

Our purpose here has to do with the eastern nations, the Bakone, and it is fitting that, before we plunge into our story, we should describe how the nations were settled in the beginning, so that the reader may understand what will be narrated in the coming chapters.

The greater portion of the land of Bokone, which lies between the Maloti and the sea, is covered by forest. Besides, the crops there are never bitten by frost, for there are only light frosts because of the nearness of the sea. It is a land of lush greenness, and of extremely rich pasturage. Its soil is dark, and that means that it produces much food; its indigenous grass is the luxurient *seboku*; its water lies in marshes, and that means that its cattle grow very fat. There are numerous rivers, and that means that rain is plentiful. It is a land of dense mists which often clear only after the sun has risen high, and that means that there are no droughts since the moisture takes long to dry up.

In the early days, when the people were still settled upon the land, nowhere were there as many people as here in Bokone, because its villages were not only large, but also numerous. As regards their customs, we can say that they are a people more skilled in medicine than any other group in South Africa, and no wonder, since they live in the proximity of forests where medicinal plants are in abundance. None can equal their skill in medicines used for witchcraft, for bringing disaster on one's adversary, for love-charms, for charms to make one popular and bring good fortune and for dispelling one's enemies—not even the Khoi or the San who are so famous for their knowledge of herbs, can measure up to their excellence. They are also famous for their ability to communicate with their ancestors who died long ago, and to talk with them and thus obtain advice from the gods.

Water serpents are highly regarded in Bokone, and so indeed, are such little crawlers as the cobra and the puff-adder. A person who has seen a snake is considered to have seen something portentous which presages either good fortune or extreme bad luck accompanied by plagues that are coming to him from his ancestral gods. A snake is not to be killed in Bokone, and anyone who kills it is considered to have done a deed that surpasses all others in ugliness. Such a one will carry for the rest of his life the shame of having killed that snake. He who kills a snake is regarded as insulting the gods and showing them disrespect by killing their messenger because, in Bokone, a snake is a recognized messenger who conveys the wishes of the dead to their living descendants. If it should enter a house while the occupants are outside, they will never go back into that house, and will stay outside until the snake eventually goes out at its own pleasure, since its visitation means that one of the ancestors is longing for them. Or if a snake should enter a house in which some untoward event has recently taken place, this is regarded as indicating that the dead are unhappy, that they have been hurt by the way their descendants have handled their affairs, and that they will visit terrible afflictions on them, such as sickness or war. When a snake enters a house, the owners at once begin to express their thanks, or to ask for forgiveness from their gods who may be angry with them. Snakes are abundant therefore, since they are not killed. It is understandable, then, that the snake should be an ingredient in all the medicines of Bokone, because there is no way in which such an important thing could be left out.

When one travels downward between the sea and the Maloti, coming from the direction of Delagoa Bay, in the north, the first Bakone one comes upon are the Swazi nation. Across the Mfolozi-Mnyama River were settled the Ndwandwe people who were ruled by Zwide. Between the Mfolozi-Mnyama and the Mfolozi-Mhlophe, all the way to the sea, were the Bathethwa who were ruled by Jobe; or perhaps we may more fittingly mention the name of his son, Dingiswayo, who became more renowned than his father. Between those two, but a little to the north, was settled a small weak little nation which owed allegiance to Jobe, and which was known as the Fenu-lwenja. Later, however, that little nation was to gain much fame, till all the nations of Bokone were called by its name. Near to the Fenu-lwenja were the Mangwane led by Matiwane, who once invaded Thaba-Bosiu. There were also the Maqwabe, the Mafuze, the Bathembu, the Makhuze, the Mahlubi, the Bakwamachibisa, the Mathuli (where the city of Durban now stands). The reader must understand that we are describing how the nations were situated long ago, when the people were still settled upon the land.

Many small and weak nations who inhabited the area along the banks of the Mfolozi-Mhlophe, used to flee to Jobe, king of the Bathethwa, to beg him for asylum, since he was very kind to all people; and among these was the Fenu-lwenja (later to be called the Mazulu). In those days the Mazulu were weaker than most other little nations, and they survived only because of the kindness and wisdom of the great king Jobe. They were mostly famous for their trade in tobacco, carved wooden basins, and other artefacts.

There is no place in the entire world where wars are unknown. There comes a time when the nations hunger for each other and continually fight each other, sometimes over many years. But in the end peace returns once more, and the land is warm again. Sometimes while the nations are living in a state of peace, none bothering

3

the other, a male child arises among one of them and he, even though but one individual, creates so much unrest that peace is banished from the earth and much blood is spilt. But the sufferings which were occasioned by the *difaqane* were unknown in the olden days when the people were still settled upon the land. The nations were living in peace, each one in its own original territory where it had been from the day that Nkulunkulu, the Great-Great One, caused the people to emerge from a bed of reeds. In the midst of so much peace and prosperity no one thought, even for one moment, that the affairs of their lives were about to change, and that they would wander in the wilderness having no fixed home, and would be killed by the spear, by exhaustion, and by hunger.

The tiny nation of Mazulu was ruled at that time by Senzangakhona, a very young man who had three wives, or maybe four. However, he had no male child in any of his houses. He had girls only. For that reason he was dissatisfied and he lacked peace in his heart, fearing that his estate would be without an heir. Besides, for a king it was more painful not to have a male child than it was for a commoner, because a king was concerned not only about the wealth of his own personal household and his livestock which would have no one to inherit them, but also about the estate of kingship, which involved the land and the people.

That being the case, Senzangakhona decided to marry again so that he might obtain male children through his younger wives. He therefore organized a large feast where there was much dancing, and during the festivities he secretly kept his eye open for any young woman he might find attractive. Among the young women who had come to the feast, he was attracted to Nandi, a girl from Langeni who lived at Ncube's village in Senzangakhona's territory. Nandi was a great singer and dancer, and she was also skilled in clapping hands and carolling for the young men as they danced. Nandi stood tall and erect, had a well-rounded face and a light brown complexion like a cannabis seed. She had an impressive presence, and a dignity to which many people said she owed her beauty.

The dancing and the games ended, and the people now indulged in beer drinking. Then a group of young men left the others drinking and went to the young girls and asked them to play the choose-a-lover game called *ho kana*. When Senzangakhona saw this, he hurried to join them so that he should be there when the game was played. By then Nandi had already noticed that Senzangakhona had intentions towards her, and that he wanted to be chosen by *her*. The *kana* is similar to the *sedia-dia* girls' dance among the Basotho, but it goes beyond the *sedia-dia* because in one sense the *kana* resembles *ho iketa* whereby a girl offers herself to a young man for marriage without waiting to be asked. Since Nandi herself loved Senzangakhona, she did in fact choose him, and Senzangakhona was greatly pleased that he had been chosen by the one he loved.

The festivities being over, it was now time to disperse. But the young people, for their part, spent the night at Senzangakhona's continuing with their games, and going home only on the following day. Senzangakhona told the young girls from Ncube's to wait for him in the fields in the valley just below his village. That day Senzangakhona used strong arguments to persuade Nandi that the two of them should do an ugly deed that was against the law of nature and of man. Nandi had to walk away from him right there in the fields, greatly disappointed when she realized that the one she had chosen as her lover did not love her with pure love, and when she came to the other maidens, she told them what Senzangakhona had said.

In those days in Bokone, if a girl became pregnant before she was married, she was killed. So, indeed, were all her age-mates, both the young men and the young women, that is to say, all those who slept in the young people's quarters. It was said that the fact that one of their own peer group had done such a deed was a clear indication that they too were now familiar with the little path she had taken, and would therefore defile the nation, that is to say the young generation, by setting them a bad example. Those young girls were also greatly disappointed when they heard about Senzangakhona's evil scheme, but in spite of that they were afraid to report him because a king, among the black people, is above the law. Yet the proper thing to do is that such a young man should be reported at once, so that he alone should be killed, and the others should live. Senzangakhona easily convinced them with a lot of deceitful talk and with the promise that he would marry Nandi, till at last she bowed her head and Senzangakhona accomplished the evil design of his heart.

When Nandi missed her monthly period, she informed Senzangakhona and he, being afraid of the scandal, made hurried arrangements to marry her. He gave Nandi's parents fifty-five cattle, and quickly took her in marriage so that the people should not notice that she was already damaged. But in spite of all that Nandi went to Senzangakhona with her pregnancy already having advanced somewhat. When her time of delivery came, Senzangakhona sent her back to her people, and she gave birth to a boy child, for whom Senzangakhona had long been yearning, who occupied his thoughts night and day, and his joy was full to overflowing. When the messenger came to Senzangakhona he said, 'There has been born to you a boy, an ox of the vultures', and indeed there never was a child for whom these words were more fitting. He was a male child, and he was also an ox of the vultures, as the reader will see afterwards.

On that very day Senzangakhona sent a messenger to inform his overlord, Jobe, that on that day he had obtained a herdboy who would watch his herds, who would fight his wars, who would succeed him in the kingship. These words of Senzangakhona's too foretold great events which we shall see later. When the messenger arrived at Jobe's, the latter's sons were present also. He told the message of his errand in their hearing, and when he finished, Jobe said, 'Go and say to your master that I am thankful for his sake, and that I wish that the child should grow to become both a human being and a man of worth. There is the news, Godongwana. This person who is described by your subject will fight your wars, not mine, because as for me, I am now old, and he will reach the state of manhood when I am already gone.' Jobe too spoke like one who knew what this child was going to become in the world, and he did the proper thing too by placing the matter in the hands of his sons.

That child was given the name Chaka by his father, and when he reached the month of the *kuruetso*,[1] Senzangakhona asked Nandi to

[1] In the second month of a child's life certain rites, collectively known as *kuruetso*, were performed upon the child. We here summarize a description of these rites by Azariele Sekese in *Mekgwa le maele a Basotho* (The customs and proverbs of the Basotho). At the time of the first appearance of the new moon, if the child is a boy, other boys in the community are invited to play certain games, during which the following words are said to the infant: '*Kururu, kururu*, there is your age-mate over there', while the child's face is turned towards the moon.

Secondly, the child is given its first taste of meat from the hand of a man (if the child is a boy) or a woman (if a girl) who is well known for good character and exemplary behaviour, in the expectation that the child will grow up to be like the one who gave him/her the meat.

Thirdly, the child, whether a boy or a girl, is given milk milked by a young man who bring him to him for a while so that he should see him and get acquainted with him. After that Nandi returned once again to her own home with her infant Chaka, to keep him away from witchcraft, since it was rumoured that Senzangakhona's wives had been bewitched so that they would not carry male children.

CHAPTER TWO

SENZANGAKHONA DISOWNS NANDI

As an infant, Chaka was a lovable, bouncing little fellow with chubby cheeks who did not cry even when he fell. Even when he was chastized he did not often cry, or he might cry only once and then keep quiet. Children generally squall when they are given a beating, and they beg for mercy, at the same time telling how repentant they are; or else they run away. All those were things which Chaka never did. He said that pleading for mercy gave satisfaction to the inflicter of the punishment. As for running away, he said that that was cowardice for when a person is chastized for a wrong he has committed, he must endure the punishment that arises from his wrong-doing. Chaka was, nonetheless, a peaceful little lad who did not trouble his mother with anything. Those who knew him as a

---

has not yet known a woman, from a cow which has not been covered by a bull since it bore the calf responsible for its present lactation. The young milker must, besides, be known for his exemplary behaviour and general good character.

Fourthly, the child, who has hitherto not been exposed to rain for fear that, if touched by rain prior to this time, he/she will be given to stealing, is now deliberately exposed to rain. On the first rainy day during or after the second month (up to the third or fourth month) the child is laid down in the courtyard, face upwards; and as it cries the adults laugh mockingly and say '*Haiaha*, you thief! There's a thief for you!' Thereafter they remove it from the rain.

child told how, even as he played with other children, any person whose eyes met his, even without having known him before, could tell at once that he was of royal blood, and not the child of a commoner; they said that all who saw him described him with the words: 'He is the cub of a lion; he is the nurseling of a wild beast; he is a new-born little lion.' The people all acclaimed him in the same way.

Chaka, after his father saw him, returned to Ncube's; and even on the occasion of his weaning, only Nandi went to Senzangakhona's while Chaka remained behind, and was continually being sent cattle and goats which were called his food.

There was a woman doctor at Bungane's who was very famous for her knowledge of charms to make one popular, charms that brought good fortune, and charms that caused a king to be loved greatly by his people and by other kings. It happened that on the day Chaka was to be strengthened with potent medicines in accordance with the customs of his own people, this woman was fetched so that she should be the one to give him his first taste of meat. On arriving there, she said that Chaka was still too small, and was not yet ready for the strong medicines of kingship. Nevertheless she fortified him with medicines that brought good luck so that he should be successful in all his undertakings. To do that she took the bile of a yellow snake found in Bokone, which was highly respected by the Matebele, the very one through which they said the spirits sent their messages. She mixed the bile with some of her medicines and made him drink the mixture. She said that the child, Chaka, would, in the course of his life, receive great blessings such as had never been received by a human being.

She gave Nandi a medicine horn and said, 'Always when the moon is about to die you must bathe this child at the river very early in the morning, before the sun has risen, and then when he has finished bathing he must walk quickly back home, and when the first rays of the sun shine upon the village, you must take some of this medicine with your fingers and anoint his head with it. You must anoint only the centre of the head where the child's head throbs; be sure to anoint also this tuft of hair which is never to be shaved off. You must do these things before he eats anything. Bathe him in a large river, not a small one.

'When this child is already grown and knows how to bathe

8

himself, whenever he gets into the water, you must go away from him and wait in a place that is out of view, and you are never to go to him unless he calls you. He, on the other hand, must not shout when he calls you, he should rather whistle. If he should see something that frightens him while he is in the water, on no account must he run away, regardless of whatever may appear. You, for your part, must never, even on a single day, ask him what he has seen; rather let him volunteer of his own accord to tell you. Even when this child has grown to be a man, he must never be accompanied by another man when he goes to bathe, he must go entirely alone, or else go in the company of a woman if he wishes to be with another person.'

When Chaka had reached the stage when he was not only able to crawl and to stand, but was attempting to walk, his father, Senzangakhona had a son born to him by his second wife. That child was given the name Mfokazana. When Chaka was ready to be weaned, Nandi returned to her husband's home at Nobamba, and shortly after she arrived there Senzangakhona had another male child, named Dingana, born to him by one of his most senior wives. It was from that time that the lives of Chaka and his mother took a turn for the worse. Before that, Nandi was a precious thing at Nobamba, since the king's wives held her dear for having removed the shame from them all by giving birth to a boy, while Senzangakhona also adored her, for his part, because of obtaining through her the boy-child for whom he had been yearning so long. Nandi was given enough food so that her breasts should swell with milk for Chaka. She was the queen of the household, yet when Mfokazana and Dingana appeared, everything changed. The senior wives turned their eyes to the children born by them and declared that Mfokazana was the king-elect followed in seniority by Dingana. And even as matters stood thus, Senzangakhona once more became the father of a boy, named Mhlangana, whose mother was also senior to Nandi by marriage, and it was then that the affairs of their lives went completely to ruin.

No one was exactly sure about the circumstances surrounding Chaka's birth. Many people did not know that Nandi was married when she was already heavy. Only very few knew this, and none of them would dare to breathe a word because they would be in serious trouble. It is possible that some who watched her carefully noticed that her months did not reach the number of months of the preg-

9

nancy of women. Since Senzangakhona still loved Chaka and his mother a great deal, the senior wives took offence, and demanded that Senzangakhona should say openly what the order of succession of his sons was, so that the nation should know, and the boys too should know their status. However, Senzangakhona refused. The senior wives talked a great deal among themselves about this matter and even told the councillors to advise the king to arrange things for his children; but whenever the councillors tried to raise the matter, Senzangakhona would fly into a rage and tell them that they should get out of the affairs of his household, and that they were councillors in matters pertaining to the nation, not in private households. The senior wives therefore found a sorcerer who turned Senzangakhona's heart away from Nandi so that whenever he tried to visit her he would feel so afraid that he would go back at once.

After becoming pregnant again, Nandi went back to her home at Ncube's so that she should be delivered there; and while she was gone the senior wives came before Senzangakhona with anger in their hearts, and they demanded that Nandi should never again return to Nobamba. When Senzangakhona attempted to refuse, they said: 'We hope that you have considered well what you are saying because we, for our part, have come to the end of our patience. You refused to listen when we said you should tell the people that, even though Chaka was born first, the proper heir to the kingship was Mfokazana, followed by Dingana and Mhlangana, and today again you refuse to listen when we say that Nandi should never return to this place. We fail to understand why we should be disgraced by such a dog as Nandi who came to your house already pregnant when we ourselves were maidens, and in every way unblemished, when you married us. Besides, we have born you children, and have filled your houses, and the marriage cattle will come to you in herds and fill your folds at once. We have also born you boys. If that wasn't the case, we would understand. Now we are going to tell about you and Nandi, and will report this matter to the Great King Jobe.'

When Senzangakhona heard this, he was very frightened, and he trembled. It became clear to him that the shame he and Nandi bore would be exposed, that Nandi and her age-mates would be killed, and that he himself would be likewise killed since, in spite of being a king, he was teaching the people evil ways. He begged his wives to let the matter end right there; he declared that Chaka was no longer heir to the kingship, and that Mfokazana would instead be his successor. He also promised that Nandi would never again set foot in Nobamba. But his wives in order to satisfy themselves completely, demanded that Nandi be banished from Ncube's and be required to return to her own home at Langeni's together with her child, Chaka. Indeed Senzangakhona banished her, even though he did afterwards plead for them to be allowed to return to Ncube's. Senzangakhona's wives were, however, stupefied, and it did not occur to them to demand that Senzangakhona should explain the new order of succession to Jobe, and so Jobe knew only Chaka as the successor.

The pain which Senzangakhona felt in his heart when he had to part with Chaka, his child, and Nandi, his wife, was such that we are unable to describe it, for he loved them greatly. But he was mortally afraid of the scandal involving him and Nandi, and he did not wish that anyone should hear even the slightest hint of it. He therefore decided that by far the best thing to do was to give up Nandi and his son, to give them up and count them among those who were gone for ever. He also realized that, if he did not give up Chaka, not only would Chaka's mother and all her age-mates be killed, but his little kingdom would be torn apart when all those boys grew up. So he closed his eyes, and the pain was like swallowing a stone as he gave up his wife and son.

Gossip is not like bread, so no one withholds it from another. Therefore, even though Senzangakhona kept his scandal with Nandi a dead secret, it did get to be known, and though it was not publicly exposed, the people nevertheless knew it and gossiped about it. From the time they first heard it, they began to hate Nandi and Chaka with a fearful hatred, and they agreed with the royal wives that Mfokazana was the rightful successor to the kingship. They, however, went even further and wished that Chaka should be killed, for he was a child of sin, and they declared that it would have been much better if he had been the child of a concubine.

When Chaka was old enough to herd calves, he experienced untold suffering. The other boys harassed him, and always beat him up most severely, for no reason whatsoever. One day as they were herding, they singled him out to go and bring back some straying calves. When he came back he suddenly heard one of them saying: 'Grab him!' They caught hold of him and thrashed him until he was limp, and it was only then that they left him. He asked why he was being molested in that way, but he received no explanation; indeed it became clear that the more he asked the more severely they battered him. These boys were persecuting Chaka because they heard vague rumours that suggested it would be a good riddance if they killed him. One day in one of these constant fights, Chaka smashed one boy's eye. The next day that boy's father caught hold of Chaka and beat him up, causing him frightful injuries.

This daily fighting taught Chaka how to fence with his sticks, how to parry many sticks about to land on him all at once, how to fight both in attack and defence. It also helped him build up his running speed in case he had to run away from his attackers. He became fearless in fighting for he had become accustomed to it, and he never became short-winded when running. In fencing, he learned how to parry a blow just at the right time, how to crouch, how to stoop to avoid a blow, how to dodge to one side, how to jump, and how to land a blow at the right spot at the right time.

On the day the man had given Chaka a beating, his grandmother was very grieved by the life of suffering which Chaka led as herder of calves. So she withdrew him from that duty and made him a bird-scarer in the sorghum fields where he had to go at the earliest dawn carrying a glowing *towane*—a grass fire-kindler which burned his fingers even before he arrived where he was going. Besides, he walked through the chilly dew and was so cold by the time he arrived in the fields that he was not even able to scare the birds properly. Even though they did not beat him, the other scarers made fun of him, and spat in disgust whenever they talked with him, and they turned up their noses at him and generally treated him like a half-wit. And even as all these things were happening to him, Chaka did not know what wrong he had done. Truly there never was a child whose growing up was as painful as Chaka's. For a person to be disowned by his father is a painful thing indeed.

The calf herders now suffered from boredom because they had become accustomed to relieving it by torturing Chaka. Then they decided to go right there to the fields where he was. And as Chaka was sitting contentedly one day, he saw a whole gang of boys suddenly appearing right near him in the middle of the fields and the tall grass, and they surrounded him. In vain did he look this way and that, there was nowhere he could run. Worst of all, even his little stick was far away from him, in the shelter. They caught hold of him and battered and bashed him till he fainted, then they threw him in a ditch in the tall grass, thinking that he was dead. A certain person who had gone to inspect the fields saw them all the time, but was unfortunately too far away, and when he came to where they had thrown Chaka, he realized that the boy was not dead, but had simply fainted. Then he poured water on him and put him in the shade where it was cool, and Chaka quickly recovered. But he was so exhausted that he was unable to stand. The kind-hearted person informed Chaka's relations and they came and carried him home in an ox-hide.

That day Nandi came to the end of her endurance and she informed Senzangakhona about the hard life that Chaka was leading, but Senzangakhona did not answer. He too was sad in his heart, and it was as if every time he swallowed, his saliva was mixed with blood; yet he realized that if he intervened, he would give his detractors a chance to tell what they knew. When the wives saw the messenger, they told Senzangakhona to stop sending the cattle and sheep which were called Chaka's food, and even though his heart was truly sore, he stopped sending them, so that his shame would remain concealed. Oh, how bitter is the fruit of sin, for Senzangakhona has now become separated from his wife whom he loves and whom he married with fifty-five head of cattle, and he has become separated also from his child Chaka, through whom he first knew a son, and, to make it worse, he is forced to persecute them.

From then on, the old woman refused to let Chaka herd calves, and she also refused to let him scare away the birds in the fields, and this made him a laughing-stock, a stay-at-home.

When Chaka was getting to be a young lad, Nandi took him to that doctor of hers so that he should be strengthened with potent medicines which would protect him from these people who were intent on killing him. The doctor took some medicinal powder, mixed it with other medicines and gave it to them saying: 'The day the moon goes into darkness, Chaka must go to the river very early in the morning. When he finishes bathing, he must vaccinate himself with this medicine, and then he must go back to the village, and then smear his head with the one I previously gave you. As a result of that, even if his attackers should surround him in a large group, they will never defeat him, but instead he will scatter them with ease. He will kill rather than be killed. I want to state very firmly again that this child will receive blessings that exceed all expectations. Tell me, have you ever seen anything at the river, while you were bathing?' Chaka said he had not. Then that woman put her hand on a vein in Chaka's arm and listened, and then said: 'The events which will take place around the life of this child are of great importance; they are weighty matters. I shall hurry back from Zwide's where I am now being summoned, and if it is at all possible, I shall be back here with you on the tenth day from today. If I should be unable to come on that day, you must know that I am held up by work. But in that case I shall send someone to come and find out for me how things are going, especially since I know that tomorrow Chaka will rise early and go to the river, for that is his day.'

When she was already on her way the doctor felt concern lest Chaka was a coward because that would destroy the potency of her medicines. She therefore sent him two kinds of medicine, one for vaccinating and the other for drinking, whose purpose was to turn him into a fierce person, and make him long to fight; he would also have bravery in his liver, and be fearless. Among the ingredients in those medicines were the liver of a lion, the liver of a leopard, and the liver of a man who had been a renowned warrior in his lifetime. She mixed them all together. The medicine for drinking was constantly added to Chaka's food. She ordered that the vaccination should be done by a woman with a new-born child, who, besides, must be her first child.

The messenger brought the medicines, and Chaka was even vaccinated while he was still there, and then he went back. From that day on, Chaka had an uncontrollable desire to fight, and it had to be a serious fight in which heavy sticks and spears were used. He dreamt about it at night when he was sleeping; he dreamt about it during the day, with his eyes open; and whenever he saw a man carrying a stick or a spear his whole body would at once begin to itch, and he would wish to engage that man in a fight. He would dream that he saw hordes and hordes of enemy warriors come to attack him, and he would see himself putting them to flight all by himself, without being helped by any of his people. He began to love

14

only those conversations that spoke of war. Even before that Chaka was a very brave person, but he had never been the one to provoke a fight, and he was not quarrelsome, but now these medicines spurred him on and he even went to the pastures in defiance of his grandmother's orders.

The moment he arrived in the pastures the other boys would rush at him all at once, but he would give them terrible gaping wounds with his blows, till they fled. Soon all the herdboys gave up fighting him, and he became their leader. He watered his cattle first in the marshes, and he was the first one to graze where the pastures were rich. Always at the end of a fight he would feel a sense of happiness, and experience a wonderful feeling of relaxation, like a poisonous snake which, after biting a person, lies sick until that person dies, whereupon it casts its skin and begins to move about again. Chaka soon realized that he did not get tired easily even if he fought for a long time, and that by the time he became tired, he had killed or wounded many people. When he fought, his stick struck the defences of his opponent with such force that the opponent fell to the ground, while his enemies' sticks were so weak when they landed on him that they were no better than the dry maize stalks left standing in the fields by the reapers.

CHAPTER THREE

CHAKA KILLS A LION

One day when Chaka was still a young lad, an uncircumcized little bullock, he took the cattle out to the pastures very early in the morning, before they were milked. As daybreak approached, he and his herds were in the mountain pass which overlooked several fields which lay huddled together below. Little did he realize as he drove out his herds that a lion had raided one fold in the very village where he lived, taken a young calf and dragged it away. It appeared that, having eaten its fill, it had noticed that it was almost daybreak, and then decided to lie down right where it was, taking advantage of the extremely tall grass. Chaka went with his cattle, not aware that he was walking in the tracks of such a fearsome beast. Suddenly, in the twinkling of an eye, the cattle turned about and fled all the way back home. He remained there wondering what did this portend, or what they had seen. Seeing he had no other alternative, he followed them back to the village.

At that time the sun was about to rise, and the people at home saw the cattle scattering away from him, and they knew that the beasts had seen a lion because the owners of the fold which it had plundered during the night were busy narrating to the others the happenings of that night, at that very moment when the cattle fled. And even as they were talking to each other, they saw the lion moving away from a spot near where the cattle were, and gliding towards the forest, but, since the forest was too far, it lay down again in the tall grass, near a large bush.

Chaka arrived as the men were planning to go after it, and he went with them. They formed a large semi-circle and walked very close to each other so that the lion should be confused and not know whom to attack first. When they disappeared, it moved away from where it was, but far from running away, it came towards them, yet camouflaging its direction by moving in zig-zag patterns across their path. And then, when it was about to become exposed to their view, it crouched and waited for them to arrive. They came walking briskly, close to each other, and they were continually speaking words of encouragement to one another stressing that no one should slack behind, and that, if it jumped on one of them, the others should immediately rush to the rescue and help the victim. No one was to run away. They walked on, feeling extremely tense and cold with fear, their hair standing on end since they could feel that they were about to come face to face with a ferocious beast. And even as they were supporting each other with their words, they suddenly heard it roaring right there very close to them, and it was clear that it was leaping to the attack at the same time. It just went *hum-m-m*, and it was already in their midst:

O, Tawny One, brother of Mothebele, rise up,
O, Tawny One, fawn-coloured king of the wilds,

16

Why, you eat not what belongs to men,
But eat, for your part, the sleepers-in-the-veld!
A nephew bereft of uncles
Kills and lays claim to all the booty.

Gracious! They scattered in all directions and they ran helter skelter, most of them in the direction of the village. Many had not even seen it, but had only heard its roar. Each took his own direction, some running downhill, others uphill, others across, some direct back to the village. Indeed that very one who had been speaking encouragement to the others was the one to start running first, though in truth the poor man could not really be said to have been the first to run since they all took off at the same time. When it jumped, the lion caught one man, hurled him to the ground and stood on top of him. Chaka came running from one of the farther ranks. He tried to stop one man so that they should both go to the rescue of the victim, but it was obvious that this man had no speech left, and neither did he have time since he was so preoccupied with the business of running away. Chaka went running and shouting so that the lion should hear that someone was coming and not kill that poor man immediately.

As he came closer, but still being a long distance away, it roared once more, and that roar made those who were running away add more speed to their flight in the belief that the lion had been following them all the time, and was now close behind them. It roared so that the earth seemed to tremble, and that roar reverberated in the stomachs of the cowards as they fled. And as it roared, it was already leaping to the attack, the yellow calf, wild beast of the forests; it jumped with its mane bristling, its eyes staring, its tail taut, and its claws bared, ready to devour a man. It jumped once, and with the second jump it was already on him.

Chaka waited for it without fear. It came, it jumped. When it was in mid-air he shifted his position ever so slightly, and on landing it dug its claws into the ground where he had stood, having been unable to change its direction while in the air since it was not a bird. But, even while it was still in the air, before it reached the ground, just as it came close to him, he plunged his black-and-white spear into a vital spot just under its shoulder blade, and when it fell on the ground, it fell for good. At that moment, when it was in the final

17

throes of death, its roaring was something indescribable. Chaka looked at it without showing any fear, and it was not as if he was looking at a ferocious beast, one that was attacking *him* besides. When Chaka stabbed it, the vanguard of the men was already entering the village, and its blood-curdling final roar made them fling themselves into the houses without even looking back, and they pulled the doors shut and tied them securely, leaving the children and the women outside where they were standing. To them it was as if the lion was now in the middle of the village. The noise of the women outside was, to them, like the screams of those whom it was killing, and they therefore went on tying the doors even more tightly.

Chaka now went forward to see the man the lion had attacked first, but when he came to him he found that everything belonged to yesterday. This surprised him because he had not delayed. What had, in fact, happened, however, was that, in attacking him, the lion had snapped his cervical spine with its claws. Indeed the lion itself, as it stood on top of him, believed he was still alive, not realizing that his life was a thing of the day before yesterday.

The men's flight home was like 'he-who-has-no-speed-will-be-left-behind' and 'don't-pass-*me*-and-I-won't-pass-*you*', and they did not even know which one of them had been killed. The women were the ones who saw everything clearly because they were watching from a distance, and were not running away. When they saw that Chaka had killed it, they told the men in the houses and urged them to come out and help him carry it, but the men swore that the lion was hiding in the grass, since no young man of such tender years could have killed it. This they said because they saw Chaka still alive.

Chaka waited and waited. In the end, when he realized that no one was coming, he shouted and announced that the lion was dead. The men now began to believe that it was indeed dead. But now a feeling of shame overtook them, shame caused by their act of leaving a man in the claws of a wild beast, and the fact that that beast had been killed by a young lad whose chin was yet smooth, who had not yet fought in any wars. They found it difficult to go, and the women, particularly the younger ones, seeing that the men were not going, started on the path leading there. Only then did some men go, but others were overcome by shame, and they stayed in the village.

That lion was carried unskinned to Senzangakhona at Nobamba, and he in turn passed it on to his overlord Dingiswayo, since Jobe was already dead. He said, a hyena is eaten only in the royal village. He sent word saying that that beast had been killed by his son Chaka all by himself, after all the men had run away. He spoke those words without realizing that he was thereby cultivating goodwill for Chaka in the king's heart.

That lion brought envy into the village. The men and the young men were seized with shame when Chaka was being singled out for praise, and especially when it was said that they ran away and bolted themselves up in their houses. The young women composed a song on that day which said:

Here at our home, at Ncube's, there are no young men,
There is but one young man of worth;
Here at our home, at Ncube's, there are no men,
For all the men here are cowards
They ran away leaving their age-mate in the field,
Leaving their comrade wrestling with a wild beast,
Gripping a lion by its jaws.
Senzangakhona has no men, they will desert him and he will be
 killed.
O, Senzangakhona, come fetch your child and take him home,
He is a male child, a shield-bearer,
He will fight for you and conquer your enemies.

They always sang that song where there were many people, and this they did intentionally, with a purpose. The women, Nandi's age-mates, also composed their own song which ended:

True men are gone, we remain with strange beings,
We remain with men-like beings who are not men!
What can we do with Chaka, a mere child?
Women of Ncube's village behold, a wonder!
The women of Senzangakhona's house are useless,
A woman is Nandi, she alone,
For she has borne a male child in all respects.

The reader should read these words bearing in mind that there is nothing more humiliating for a man than to be sung about by the women in mockery and contempt, nor, on the other hand, is there anything as pleasing as when they sing about him in praise. We are talking about those days of our fathers, not these modern times.

19

Those two songs generated a bad feeling among the men and the youths when they realized that the young girls would be attracted towards Chaka and *they* would not receive any more attention. Besides, in those days the women were not attracted by a man however handsome he might be if he was a coward. A woman's aim was to find someone who was a man indeed in battle, a true brave when spears were being wielded, or when occasions of precisely this nature arose. Such a one, however ugly he might be, was loved, and songs were composed to praise him and deride the others. In a way we cannot blame them for being like that, because those were days of might. Woman who wanted to be well protected had to find herself a man of that calibre, who was feared by others, a truly tough fellow.

That evil spirit spread until it influenced people like Mfokazana, and all of them plotted to kill Chaka, no matter in how cruel a manner, perhaps at some feast where he might be present. Senzangakhona's senior wives, in their turn, alleged that the women of Ncube's village had insulted them with their songs, and they urged Senzangakhona to intervene on their behalf. While matters were in that state, a messenger from Dingiswayo came to Senzangakhona and said: 'Dingiswayo greets you. He wishes to know why you have not brought before him the young man whose birth you reported to his father, Jobe, so that he should see him and know him. He says that he is very thankful for the wild beast you sent him, and urges you to send Chaka to him so that he may also bring back with him the young bullock with which he wishes to thank you.'

This message from Dingiswayo blunted the anger of the wives and of the men of Ncube's village. They all realized that if Chaka should die, Dingiswayo would demand him from them. Chaka himself also heard about Dingiswayo's message, but for his part waited expectantly for word from his father, but his father remained silent till this very day that is shining above. In those days Chaka still trusted his father a great deal, and he was sure the day would come when he would straighten out his affairs for him. Little did he know that the sun would never rise to light that day. The affairs of his life eventually moulded themselves and took their own course, while his father maintained his silence. Indeed it was evident that, instead of working for Chaka's welfare, he was fanning the brush fire so that it should burn him.

CHAPTER FOUR

CHAKA IS VISITED BY THE KING OF THE DEEP POOL

It was once again Chaka's day for rising early and going to the water, and indeed he went at the earliest light of dawn. His mother, being conscious of the evil spirit among the people, went with him. There was not a soul who knew that there was a time when Chaka went to the river early in the morning. When they arrived at the river, the Mfolozi-Mhlophe, his mother hid near where her son was going to bathe. The reader should remember that it is not shameful in Bokone for a mother to see her son naked and bathing, because people hardly wear anything in Bokone.

Chaka washed himself. It happened that, as he was about to finish, the tuft of hair on his head shivered and shook, and the skin under it felt warm and it rippled very quickly; and just as suddenly as it began, everything was quiet again, dead still. It was very early in the morning, long, long before the sun was due, and he was bathing in an ugly place, where it was most fearsome. High up from the place where he stood was a tremendous waterfall, and at the bottom of that waterfall, right by him, was an enormous pool, a frightening stretch of water, dark green in colour and very deep. In this pool the water was pitch dark, intensely black. On the opposite bank, directly across from where he was, but inside the water, was a yawning cave, a dark black tunnel which stretched beyond one's vision, flooded by the water and sloping downward. It was not possible to see where that immense pool ended because, a little way down from where it began, the water was covered by a very dense growth of reeds which grew on both of the inner sides of the river; and on the opposite bank, a forest covered the flank of an adjoining hill, and came to brush against the river's edge. That forest was also dense, a veritable thicket where tree rubbed against tree in close embrace. This was an ugly place which instilled fear into one even in the daytime, where no one could ever dream of bathing alone, a place fit to be inhabited only by the *tikoloshe*. Chaka bathed alone in this place simply because he was Chaka.

Chaka once again splashed himself vigorously with the water, and at once the water of that wide river billowed and then levelled off. Then it swelled higher and higher till he was sure it was going to cover him, and he walked towards the bank. No sooner was he there than a warm wind began to blow with amazing force. The reeds on the banks of the river swayed violently to and fro, and shook in a mad frenzy; and just as suddenly as they began, they quickly stopped moving and were dead still, and they stood erect just as if no wind had ever blown. The water subsided and the wind died down. In the centre of that wide dark green pool the water began to ripple gently, and it was evident that there was something enormous moving under it.

Nandi saw all these things, and she was so frightened that she was trembling, and she almost went to Chaka, but was held back by the strict injunction: 'You are never to go to him unless he calls you.' And now she was crying within her heart for Chaka to call her. While Chaka was looking over there in the deep where the water was rippling, he saw the huge head of an enormous snake suddenly break surface and appear right here next to him. Its ears were very long like those of a hare, but in shape they resembled those of a field-mouse; its eyes were large, green orbs, and it was more fearsome than we can say. It rose out of the water to the height of its shoulders and came towards Chaka. Chaka, a man always ready for action, felt his body shudder when he saw that it was without doubt coming direct towards him. His first thought was to reach out for his stick and spear so that he could defend himself, but then he remembered the question he had been asked twice by his doctor: 'Tell me, have you ever seen anything at the river while you were bathing?' Then he stopped, and he surmised that it was being attracted towards him by the charms in his body, and that that was why he had been continually asked that question. And now he stood with his body tense and stiff, and he stared straight into its eyes, and oh, how fearful it was! And when it came close to him, it stuck out two long tongues and stretched them towards Chaka as if it wanted to pull him with them into its mouth which was so wide that he could enter it with ease. Chaka, when he saw those tongues coming towards him, was frightened, truly frightened and he trembled, and it was the first time that he experienced that kind of fright, the fright of someone with cowardice in his heart. He was so frightened that he almost turned tail and fled, but then he remembered the strict injunction: 'You must on no account run away, no matter what may appear.'

Stricken by fright, Chaka shut his eyes so that, if that snake intended to kill him, it should kill him with his eyes closed, avoiding looking in its face. Slowly he raised his hand and grabbed the tuft of hair which he had been told to hold tight if he was very frightened; at the same time he whistled gently in order to call his mother. Nandi, at that time, had also covered her face, afraid to see her son being swallowed by such a huge water monster. But when she heard the whistle, she uncovered her face and she was all the more frightened when she saw how close it was to Chaka, and so instead of going to him, she lay flat on the ground, and she watched from a distance, trembling so much, meanwhile, that there was not even time to cry aloud or to shed tears.

When eventually Chaka opened his eyes, when he realized that it had not touched him, he saw that snake, its eyes still gazing straight into his, but already about to disappear in the water and with its tongues already withdrawn. It was clear that it was returning back into the water, moving backwards, so that if Chaka had taken long to open his eyes, he would have found that it had already disappeared. When he opened his eyes, he looked direct into the pupils of its eyes, and it too looked at him in a like manner. They stared at each other, the snake in its own abode and the man come there to provoke it. They stared at each other in that manner with Chaka's hand refusing to leave the tuft of hair where the strong medicine was.

At last the snake came out of the water again, and it did so without making any noise, without splashing the water, but simply gliding out, so that the only indication that it was coming out was the fact that it was once again getting closer to him. He stared at it till it reached the point where it had been when he shut his eyes. It stuck out its tongues and wrapped them around his neck, and they crossed at the back of his head and came to join again in front. Then, supporting its weight on him, it drew itself out and coiled itself

23

around his entire body, and it unwound its tongues and started licking him from the head right down to the soles of his feet. When it finished, it raised its head to the level of his face and it looked at him at close range, and its hot, stinking breath engulfed him. Once again it licked him thoroughly all over his face, and then it returned into the water backwards, keeping a steady gaze on his face.

Chaka never saw where its body ended because it was all the time in the water, which is to say that even Chaka himself did not know its length. After it was once again completely submerged, the water once more billowed vigorously and swelled. A chilly wind blew and the reeds swayed and eddied. A small column of thick mist arose from the deep pool, it formed an elongated cloud which came and covered him so that he could see nothing, even quite close to him; and then out of the reeds over there something boomed with a heavy, stentorious voice:

Mphu-mphu, hail!
Kalamajweng, Kalamajweng!
Mphu-mphu, hail!
Kalamajweng, Kalamajweng!
Mighty monster in the water-r-r
Kalamajweng, Kalamajweng!
It is seen only by the favoured ones
Kalamajweng, Kalamajweng!
Is seen by those who will rule over nations
Kalamajweng, Kalamajweng!

It repeated those words twice and then was silent, and at the very moment it stopped, a very soft voice spoke and said:

Hail! Hail! This land is yours, child of my compatriot,
You shall rule over nations and their kings
You shall rule over peoples of diverse traditions
You shall even rule over the winds and the sea storms
And the pools of large rivers that run deep;
And all things shall obey you with unquestioning obedience,
And shall kneel at your feet!
O yes, oi! oi! Yet you must go by the right path.

24

Chaka only heard the words but did not see anything because of the mist covering him; and when the voices finished speaking those words which Chaka did not understand completely, the mist opened up and moved away from him, but it did not go back into the water from where it had come, but simply vanished and was no longer there; but more accurately we might say it seeped into his body. Nandi did not hear these words, she only saw the snake and the billowing of the water and the swaying of the reeds, but as for the voices, she did not hear them, which is strange since she was not so far away. We can only conclude that they were meant for Chaka alone. After these ominous happenings Chaka put on his clothes and went up from the river; and it happened that when he arrived home, the rays of the sun shone upon the village, and his mother smeared him with his medicines in the usual way.

Nandi sent a messenger to Zwide's on that very day to tell the doctor about these developments. The messenger came back and reported that the doctor was extremely busy and was unable to come, but that she would come at the end of that very month. Should she still be unable to come, then they should go to her at Zwide's.

The appointed month passed and the doctor did not appear, and when they were getting ready to go to her, there came a messenger with sad news to Chaka and his mother, telling them that their doctor had died. Nandi and her son were grieved in a manner that we are unable to describe. They felt abandoned and unable to decide what to do because they had put much trust in this doctor, for they saw that everything she predicted happened truly in the manner she had foretold it. Now they wondered where they would find a true, genuine doctor.

When the messenger saw this, he said: 'Your doctor said I should tell you that you should not worry because, when the sickness gripped her and she began to feel that she would not live, she sent someone far away to fetch the doctor who had taught her everything she knew about medicine, and she made a point of asking him to complete the work of strengthening Chaka with the help of her medicines, since she had been prevented by death. It is clear then that, if he who is coming is the one who taught your doctor about medicine, he must have knowledge and understanding of powerful herbs which surpass those of your doctor. Besides, he is not only a doctor, he is also a diviner who receives revelations through his head. She said you must not put yourselves to trouble looking for that doctor, for he will come to you of his own accord, since he will divine for himself where you are. That woman, your doctor, did everything she did with medicines only, whereas the one who is coming sometimes uses the divination of the head. He will see danger while it is still far away and you will have time to avoid it; he divines the wars before they are fought, and even before they have been contemplated, and even foretells which side will win, and these things all happen the way he has foretold them. Your doctor said I should urge you to calm down and not to torment yourselves, for your affairs are still going well.'

When Nandi and her son heard these words, their fears subsided, for they had been very anxious indeed; they told themselves that under the circumstances everything was as well as it could be, if only the one of whom they were told did not delay in coming till they found themselves in danger.

At just about that time Chaka's name was maliciously linked with all things evil. Those whom he had defeated in fighting talked all manner of ugly things about him. Some said he had been vaccinated by a *tikoloshe* and that explained why he was so skilled in fighting with his sticks, and why he never ran away. Others said he was actually fathered by a *tikoloshe*, and that that was why his father had without any compunction chased him away together with his mother even though he had married her with so many heads of cattle. It was rumoured strongly that Chaka was not at all a human being who resembled other people, for even his mother's months of pregnancy had not, according to those who claimed to know, reached the number of months of the pregnancy of women. They spoke these things meanwhile trying to devise a plan to kill him, yet also careful that the plan should not make Dingiswayo aware of the murder, and that it should appear that he had either died a natural death or had been killed by predatory beasts. Chaka's fame, on the other hand, continued to spread, till it reached Dingiswayo who, in his turn, had a growing desire to see him, and indeed not only to see him, but to enlist him in his regiments.

CHAPTER FIVE

CHAKA LEAVES HOME IN FLIGHT

In those days, long ago, wild beasts used to terrorize the people a great deal. On many evenings, while the people were sitting around or as they were about to turn in, a hyena, if it had found no goats to eat, would come into the village and grab a person and run off with him, with no one brave enough to go in pursuit and force it to abandon its prey. That poor person would scream continuously in the middle of the darkness, saying: 'It's picking me up! It's putting me down! It's picking me up again! It's putting me down! Now it's eating me!' He would shout these words in an attempt to raise the alarm so that the people would know where he was and come to his rescue. But in spite of all that, it would eventually eat him with no one coming to help him. Since there were no strong doors, very often children such as Chaka were placed near the door in the young people's hut, so that the hyena should take them and the others should escape. Chaka himself was made to sleep by the door there in the young men's hut, so that such hazards of the night, including those involving witchcraft, should begin with him. He had been turned into a barricade used to protect the others. But, in spite of all that, such dangers kept passing him by: a hyena would simply sniff at him and pass to the far end of the hut and grab someone there. Indeed, it appears that a hyena always avoids taking a person sleeping right by the door, just as if it knew that the ones who sleep near the door are the hated ones.

Twice or three times, Chaka had his hands tied right there in the young people's hut, and was made to sleep outside near the door tied up like that, so that the hyena should see him as soon as it came. This would be done on a day when a hyena had been seen near the village, and it was expected that it would catch some people after dark; but on those occasions the hyena would feast on goats and leave the people alone. Chaka's growing up was truly painful.

Such cases of people being eaten by hyenas happened in Lesotho as well, because we hear that a hyena ate one of Moshoeshoe's wives. It took her in the middle of the village, in the presence of other people, and she sang that painful song as it went with her in its mouth. Yet Moshoeshoe heard her all the time together with his warriors such as the Brave of Makoa, Makoanyane, and Mokolokolo of Thesele who were present and heard her; but all of them were afraid to go outside, saying that it was a hyena made from a lump of bread, a hyena of witchcraft.

One day a hyena entered the young people's hut at dead of night, when the people were in deep sleep right there at Ncube's. Mfokazana was there, together with some young men from his village. When it entered, there was utter silence, every one dead with fright, because it was dreaded in a manner we are unable to describe, even by the braves. It went in, sniffed at a person, and passed; it sniffed at another one and passed; it sniffed at another one whom it picked out and carried outside, and this happened to be the girl with whom Mfokazana was in love. Everyone pretended to be dead, they maintained absolute silence; Mfokazana himself did likewise, not simply imitating the others, but truly afraid, lying like a corpse, yet in fact he knew the identity of the person the hyena had taken.

When the hyena came outside, that girl screamed in a loud and painful voice which even woke up many people in the village who were fast asleep at the time and she began to sing the song of those taken by the hyena: 'It's picking me up! It's putting me down!' She cried in this manner, this poor child, in the midst of utter stillness, the sound of her heart-rending voice being heard throughout the entire village, and fleeting through the darkness of the night, and penetrating the forests and the neighbouring villages; and the people of those villages knew too that a hyena had attacked and they tucked their blankets more tightly around them, as if it had said that it wanted to eat many people in one night.

It was feared very much, the brown hyena, and the people trembled when they heard of its deeds,

The brown hyena, wolf with a brown-coloured forearm,
Little father of the lion and the spotted hyena,
Child with zig-zag tattoo, mark of brave warriors;
Brown hyena, you child who is a warrior-who-hunts-by-night,

What makes you fear to hunt by day?
I fear the guilt of attacking the people's herds.

Chaka was sleeping in a different hut with a few others, having left the young people's hut because of the way he suffered there, and the great hostility of the other young men, which made him fear that they might kill him while he slept. He heard that girl's scream in his sleep; the second time, however, he heard it distinctly, and he even recognized the voice of the person who had been taken by the hyena, and his sleep was immediately gone and he woke those with whom he was sleeping, saying: '*Vukani, madoda, intombi yemuka nencuka!*' ('Wake up, men, a girl has been taken by the hyena!') In a flash he was out of the house.

Because of the weight it was carrying, since this was a heavy person, the hyena had to rest frequently, and it took a long time to get out of the village.

Chaka, when he came outside, stood and listened to hear the direction from which the voice came, and just as he stood there he heard her: 'It's putting me down!' Then off he went, this young warrior, and he ran on his toes so that he should not make any noise; and when the girl said again: 'It's picking me up!' Chaka saw the hyena, and even saw the person in its mouth. Now he ran fast, knowing that the hyena would not hear his footsteps because of the sound of its own; also he was running so that he should reach it before it rested again. He came right up to it and stabbed it even as it ran foolishly with its stumpy ears bent forward. He stabbed it under the forearm with a mighty stroke and the spear went in and came out on the other side and pierced the ground, nailing it down. It fell down flop, and it let the girl slip out of its grip, and it lay prostrate kicking but twice or three times in its last efforts. It died in complete silence, like a dumb creature, without crying or making any sound whatsoever. Chaka said one word only, '*Nanso!*' ('There!'), and he kept quiet and proceeded to pull out his spear slowly, as was the custom when one had killed a fierce beast.

As for the young girl, her eyes were dim and she could not see well, not even where the hyena was taking her. When it sagged down, she thought it was simply resting. But when she realized that it was not picking her up again, she was at once on her feet, and she looked about, even though she could not see clearly. The first thing she saw

29

was an extraordinarily tall person standing next to her, near the hyena; and her eyes, whose sight was dimmed by fright, did not see properly, and she thought that the hyena had now reached the place of the witches who owned it, and that she was now going to be eaten. She let out two piercing cries with a voice far more painful than before, the voice of someone who is dying when all hope of being saved is gone and death stares him in the face at close range. And when she cried like that, the people continued to tremble in their houses, and the young people, in their hut, were like dead things, and among them Mfokazana was the most scared.

This young woman, when she let out this painful cry, even fell on the ground from fright. Chaka held her by the arm and helped her up, and he spoke encouraging words saying: 'You are safe, stop crying and rejoice. It is the hyena that has died. Get up and see it. It is I, Chaka.'

The young girl heard the voice, but it was like a confused noise. Chaka spoke again, and this time she heard and recognized his voice. She looked into Chaka's eyes and found that it was indeed he, Chaka, in person. She looked at the hyena and saw it lying prone on the ground. She cast a glance this way and that, her sight being quite clear now, and she saw the houses and the cattle folds of her village and realized that they were indeed the very ones she knew. She looked once again at the hyena, and she found that it was not just lying there, it was dead, completely and for ever dead. And once again Chaka encouraged her with his words saying she must put aside her fear since she was safe.

All her senses now came back, the sting and pain of death were gone; the light, the fullness and the joy of life were once again in full view; she yelled three times and she clung to Chaka, hanging on to him and kissing him, and doing all sorts of things, and she said: 'I knew it could never be any one else but you, Chaka, saviour of those in the grip of death, where all hope is lost! Mfokazana abandoned me even though we were next to each other, in the same hut!' And then she started to run at great speed, tearing across the village, shouting to all the people to get up and come and see a miracle, come and hear a miracle, the miracle performed by Chaka who had lifted her out of death, out of the jaws of a hyena.

The people were overwhelmed with joy, even though their joy was mixed with shame. They asked themselves, with much astonishment, how far were Chaka's deeds going to go in their beauty, their nobility and their praise-worthiness. The young people also asked themselves, with sadness and shame, how long was Chaka going to continue degrading them, since their feeling of unworthiness just kept growing. Why, just a few days before he had killed a lion after they had all run away, and now even today he killed a hyena that had run off with a person right from their midst with none of them ready to go to the rescue. The young girls whose age-mate had been taken by the hyena immediately came out of their houses to go and see their peer who had just returned from the dead, and also to see her worthy warrior, as well as the wild beast he had killed, which they feared so much that their food went down with difficulty; they went also to sing songs which would praise Chaka and despise Mfokazana.

When Mfokazana began to understand how matters stood, he at once left his house and started on the road to his home at Nobamba; however, he realized that it would not help to go there, because the news would reach there before the sun and his disgrace would be even uglier because it would be said that he was so ashamed that he ran away. At once he decided to kill Chaka in a cruel manner so that those who were praising him should be spited, and instead of a song of praise they should raise the sound of weeping; he said: 'I have already been disgraced too many times because of this dog of Nandi's, today I must remove it from my path.'

By that time the people had already run with great speed to go and tell Senzangakhona what had happened. A group of young men, among them Dingana, were on their feet at once to go to Ncube's. By the time Mfokazana arrived at the spot where the hyena had been killed, the people had already gathered there in large numbers, and Chaka was sitting on the hyena he had killed, slowly wiping off the blood from the handle of his spear; he was completely silent, and only his deeds spoke, only the people spoke. The young girl he had saved was now crying even more than before, for it was now that she began to see the horror of the death from which she had returned, when she realized that she was the first to have escaped from the jaws of that vicious animal.

When Mfokazana arrived there, he hit Chaka on the back of his head so that he fell forward on his face. Chaka, as he got up, reached for his spear and his stick, ran through the crowd and then turned around, and just as he did so he came face to face with Mfokazana pursuing him.

It happened that, as soon as they faced each other, Chaka struck him directly on the forehead and threw him down. The young men of Mfokazana's peer group came, but Chaka fought like a man: he smashed the skull of one of them and his little brain fell out, and he died belching like someone who had drunk too much beer. That stick, as it came up, split someone's chin apart so that his jaws were separated and his tongue dangled in space: what an ugly death that man died! And when Chaka swung it sideways, it crushed another man's head between the eye and the ear, and the eye was dislodged from its socket, and it fell on the ground a flat mass like the eye of a sheep. The last young man, even though his comrades were already on the ground, was now fighting in earnest. He kept trying to go round Chaka's back, and because of that frequent turning from one side to another, he stumbled and was thrown forward towards Chaka. Chaka moved slightly out of his way, and just as the man was about to pass him, he hit him in the back of the head, so that he went and fell on his face, and he died with his teeth dug deep into the ground, and with his wound in an ugly place, at the back of his head. Only then did Chaka find a little time to catch his breath and he sat down again on that beast of his. Blood came out of Mfokazana's mouth and nose and ears, and it flowed like that of a sheep whose neck had been severed, and it did not seem that he might live.

When Dingana arrived there and heard what had happened, and saw Mfokazana on the ground, he immediately attacked Chaka believing that he was tired so that the highest praise should go to himself for having killed Chaka, the bravest of all braves. But above all, he realized that the kingship would now be his once Mfokazana and Chaka were dead. A few people of Ncube's village took Chaka's side, and the battle was joined and great blows were exchanged. After a while, the brother of the girl who had been taken by the hyena inflicted an ugly wound on Dingana, and he was greatly weakened from the loss of blood and lay stretched out on the ground. At that time, the night passed completely, and Senzangakhona arrived together with his wives.

The people who told Senzangakhona had not specified that it was Chaka who had killed the hyena; they had simply said 'your son', and rumour began to say that it was Mfokazana, and that was why the royal wives came. They arrived just after the fighting had ceased, and they saw Chaka sitting on the hyena and this at once proved to them that he was the doer of the deed. And just as they began to look around they saw Mfokazana, Dingana and the others where they lay, all covered with blood; then the air was filled with crying when they saw that, even though the hyena was indeed dead, it had been killed together with their children, and by Nandi's son at that. They spoke with anger, saying Chaka should be killed. Senzangakhona then gave the order to all his people and the people of Ncube's saying: 'Kill him!' And it is here that we see clearly that Chaka had indeed become a hare-that-was-struck-on-the-ear, one-without-parents, a buffalo-standing-all-by-itself, because all those who saw him fought him without any reason at all.

Quite a few men of Ncube's village, as well as certain other young men, at that point offered themselves to die with Chaka. The women, Nandi's age-mates, sang a song of grief, a lamentation; they sang crying, with tears flowing down their cheeks, saying:

Alas! You gods, think of us,
Look upon us who are killed for a crime that is not there.
Alas! You spirits, you are our witnesses,
You are the witnesses of that day in the fields.
Alas! The King is without truth,
He is without truth, he is a chameleon
Even after we have born for him a male child,
A male child, conqueror of the mighty ones.
Alas! Senzangakhona is afraid of his equals,
And vents his rage upon the defenceless!

The battle was joined. Chaka now decided to fight in earnest since he had heard from his own father's mouth that he was to be killed; now he fought without any further restraint, without feeling a sense of respect for anything. He had thought, after all, that his father would first ask where the trouble had started; but now, since all he heard was the order his father gave, he fought in all seriousness. Up to this time he had only been fencing with his stick, but now he began to use his spear.

In that battle his spear broke, and eventually even his stick broke, and then he jumped and stood to one side to see where he might find

33

weapons, and he found that he was left all alone, every one on his side already lying on the ground. As he jumped, they were immediately in hot pursuit. He ran in earnest now, not simply running away from the sharpness of the spear, but determined to flee, to throw himself away, to give himself to the plains, and go to a place where he would never again be seen, from where he would never return. He ran until he entered the forest and hid himself there.

When Dingiswayo heard this, he imposed a fine of cattle on Senzangakhona, saying that he taught his warriors the ways of cowardice; he commanded him to search for Chaka at once and bring him to him alive, not dead.

In this chapter we find that it is indeed true that the fruit of sin is amazingly bitter, because we do not see any transgression on Chaka's part in these matters, yet, in spite of all that, his father commands that he should be killed. The real issue, the cause of it all, was that Nandi and Senzangakhona suffered from guilt, and Senzangakhona, fearing that his crime would be exposed, went to the length of plotting to kill his own son. Yet, if Senzangakhona had not committed this shameful deed in his youth, Chaka would have been at his home at Nobamba, a precious child, a child dearly loved by his father.

CHAPTER SIX
CHAKA MEETS ISANUSI

Chaka was in the forest when, at high noon, a heart-rending wailing arose in Ncube's village. He saw milling crowds, men and women, including those from the neighbouring villages, who had come, summoned by the screams they had heard in the night when the

34

hyena ran off with a person, summoned also by the second occasion of weeping which began when the night was beginning to clear away. The wailing which Chaka heard was that of the women who were crying for their men who had died, and those who were crying for their brothers and their lovers who had died. These were all crying for their dead, and were not concerned with Senzangakhona. But there were others who were crying for Chaka himself, asking themselves how great was the hatred of the person who had bewitched his father to make him abandon his child with such lack of concern, and for no reason whatsoever.

At mid-day the cattle and the goats cried in their folds because of hunger; the calves and the kids cried for being deprived of their mothers' milk; dogs howled in the middle of the village, crying for their masters who had died; and even the fowls added to the crying, even though *they* were simply carried away by the general din. When the noise of all these creatures came together, it became something never heard before, and the air was simply choked with sound, and it was like the day a great king had died because, when the great bee has died, even the animals know it. Chaka heard the wailing of all these creatures and, loving kingship as he did, he said: 'All these things are happening because of me, and yet I am still but a green sapling, a weakling. How will it be the day I become a man and I take over the kingship? How I shall take my revenge the day that sun of mine shall rise!'

He saw all the affairs of his life, from the time of his childhood, and he found that they were ugly and frightening, and made a man shudder. And when he thought of the day when he came back from rounding up the calves, and found that there was already a plot against him, and the day the boys surprised him in the fields, and about the lion and the hyena, he realized that here on earth people live by might only, and not by right; he decided that here on earth the only person who is wise and strong and beautiful and righteous, is he who knows how to fight with his stick, who, when people argue with him, settles the matter with his stick; and he decided that, from that day on, he would do just as he pleased, and that, whether a person was guilty or not, he would simply kill him if he so wished, for that is the law of man.

Chaka had always been a man of firm decisions who never gave up something he had started before it was accomplished according to his wishes; even when it was hard he persevered till things went the way he wanted them. But then his purposes, up to that time, had been good ones; today, however, he had only one resolve: to do whatever he wished, even if it might be ugly, and to avenge himself to the fullest extent, in a manner known to him alone.

When evening came, he left the forest, and he wandered in the plains, without even knowing where he was going. He crossed the Mhlathuze, the Thukela and the Mvoti, heading directly south; and in his flight he forgot the king who loved him, Dingiswayo.

One day, in the middle of the day, when the shadows crept underneath their owners, the heat of the sun overcame him, sweat oozed out of his pores, and the soil was hot as he trod on the ground, and he was compelled to look for shade. There were many trees, but they were widely scattered. As he looked around, he saw one straight ahead, far from the others; it had wide branches, and stood all by itself. Then he went to it. That tree stood tall from the ground, to a height which a person could not reach with his hand; the lower part of its trunk was bare and without branches, and the lowest branches began up there at that height, and they arched towards the ground, and were as full-leaved as those of the willow tree. The higher branches, on the other hand, stretched outward like the palms of a person, and they cast a big wide shade. At the tree's base was a little fountain with sweet cool water. Chaka came to it tired, weakened by running and hunger, his feet hard from the swelling caused by the dews he had walked through, his thoughts confused, and his head aching from pondering over his problems. He came there and drank from that fountain, ate the bit of meat which he had obtained from one of the villages he had passed on the way, and after eating he drank the water of that fountain again to wash the food down. Because of fatigue, he began to feel drowsy; so he got up and looked this way and that, examining his surroundings with great care. He looked up into the tree's branches, and even threw a stone up there. And then when he found there was nothing he could see, he leaned against the tree, and was instantly fast asleep.

When at last he woke up, when the shadows began to lengthen, he found a man doctor standing right there by him, looking at him in a strange way. Chaka's body shivered the moment he set eyes on him and, being always ready for action, he quickly grabbed his little spear, jumped up and stood to one side, afraid that he had nearly been murdered in his sleep; but he soon realized that this was not someone who would kill him; besides, it was clear that when he woke up, that man had already been standing there for some time, and could have killed him if he wanted to. When Chaka first woke up from his sleep, and their eyes met, he saw that the man's face was distorted with hate, and his lips were like those of a man sick with nausea, and right inside the farthest depths of his eyes he saw malice and unbounded cruelty, he saw someone who had more evil in his heart than any murderer, the very incarnation of malice, treachery and betrayal. His body shuddered, and he blinked his eyes. Then when he looked at the man again, he found that his face showed sympathy and pity, and was sad on his behalf; and when he looked deep in his eyes, he saw profound compassion and a heart that felt the grief of others, and had true love. The face he had first seen was completely gone.

He was a man of middle years, with just the first tinge of grey, and because of the many pouches he carried, as well as the porcupine quills and monkey skins on his body, and long tassels of unkempt hair, Chaka knew at once that he was a doctor. Then while he stood there full of suspicion, the man put down the things he was carrying and sat on the ground. He took out his nose-scoop and cleaned his nose, and then put it away again; he took out his snuff-box made of a gourd, tapped it sharply several times with his fingernail, poured out a small quantity of snuff which he sniffed up his nose, going *hlwi-hlwi*. He spoke with a contented voice because of the sweetness of the snuff and said: 'Greetings, then, you from the royal house. Come here and let us talk about things!' When he spoke those words, the sound of his voice was full of conviction and truth, and it was clear that it came from a heart that knew no guile; it was not the voice of a tempter, but that of an honest man. Chaka came near and said: 'Yes, I accept your greeting, even though I am not a person of the royal house, but one from a little village, and crawl before those who crawl before the king.' The doctor laughed and said: 'It would be a wonder if you were not of a royal house, because your appearance and the manner of your speech indicate that you are; besides, you are not a person of this place where you are now.'

'By what sign do you see that I am not a person of this place, when it is you who find me in it?'

'I see it by many things. I see by your feet that you have travelled a

37

very long distance, and that you covered most of it running. I see by your brow that for many nights you have not had enough sleep, and that you travel with a heart that is full of grief. The weakness of your eyes tells me that for days more or less numbering the fingers of one hand, you have not had enough food to eat. Speak the truth, isn't that so?'

Chaka took time to answer fearing lest this man should have been following him all the time. 'As regards all these things you have just mentioned, that is truly so. But where do *you* come from? Where are you going? Where is your home? How do you know my affairs?'

'The manner in which you speak tells me that you are not only of the royal village, but indeed the child of a king. I will answer your questions, but first I must finish mine. As I listen to you and examine you carefully, I can see that your right hand is tired from killing people, and that you are, at this very moment, in flight, and that is why you jumped high when you saw me, because you have reached a point where you are afraid of people; besides, the way you speak tells me that you are a child whose upbringing has been very hard indeed. Is that not so?' Chaka was now so surprised that he was unable to answer, and then the doctor said: 'You must look straight into my eyes as I talk to you,' and they looked at each other. 'The trouble which led to your being in this place arose in the night. You were fighting with a wild beast, and you even killed it. That beast was a hyena; I can see that by its fur which has stuck to your blanket. A few days before that you had killed another. Good gracious! I can see that you are rejected by your own father, and that he, in turn, is afraid of his wives. This time you escaped from a serious danger because you were meant to be killed.'

When the doctor finished saying those words, Chaka adjusted his blanket, and a large section of his belly was exposed, and so also were the vaccinations, and the doctor saw them. Chaka once more asked the questions he had asked before, and the doctor then said: 'As a human being, you might think that I heard of your affairs through someone else, yet it is not so. But, in order that you may believe in me, I shall tell you one small matter which is known to you alone. In your tuft of hair there is a medicine to bring you luck and kingship. When you adjusted your blanket I saw, I who have the power of vision, and I became aware, I who am wise, that you were once visited by the great master who comes from those who have departed, who are above, and that master was highly pleased with you. Besides, my eyes which see things which have already passed, can see that you were very frightened when the master was with you, so much so that your hand refused to leave this tuft of hair, in the manner you had been instructed by the woman doctor who is now gone.'

The reader can imagine for himself how great was Chaka's amazement as all the secrets known to him alone were being exposed. When the doctor mentioned these things, Chaka jumped for joy, and felt indeed like one dreaming. A light dawned on him from far, far away yonder, and it streaked across space till it lighted on his heart and shone there; joy and happiness also arose from that far-off place, and came and massaged his wounded heart. He said to himself: might this not be the *isanusi* who, it had been said, would come to him! And he saw, and was indeed convinced that, if this is he, then truly his affairs were going to take a new turn, because it was quite clear that this man could feel things with his head. Then he asked once again the question he had already asked two or three times, and said: 'I have asked you a question, but it seems to me it is a question you do not wish to answer: Where do you come from? Where are you going?'

The doctor took his stick and pointed up to the sky, and said: *'Ngivela kude le!'* ('I come from far away yonder!'), and he was quiet for a long time staring right up there where he was pointing, and he sighed.

Chaka: 'It seems to me you are pointing to the sky! Exactly where are you pointing? Do you come from the clouds?'

'No, by pointing upwards I am simply estimating for you the distance to the place from which I have come, because, if I pointed at those mountains, even if I were to say, far away on the other side of them, you would fail to understand the distance which I have travelled.' Chaka's face lit up, and it glowed; he remembered that it was said a doctor had been summoned from far away yonder, and once again he pursued his questioning: 'At this moment where are you going? You have not answered my question completely.'

'At this moment I'm going to ... I'm going to ... Look here, Chaka,' and now he called him by his name so that he should see without any doubt that he to whom he was talking was someone who knew him like the back of his hand, 'Look here, Chaka, I do not have much time to talk to you about trifling matters, the plains ahead of

39

me are wide, and the country I still have to traverse stretches far. There are many who are suffering, who are oppressed, who are unable to attain the desires of their hearts; the kings who await my coming, so that I might fortify them and smooth things out for them, are many. Besides, I want to return soon to my home, and my home is far away.' So saying the doctor once more was silent for a while and he stared longingly up to the sky where he had been pointing, and then he said: 'I have told you some of your affairs which are known to you alone; and if even now you still don't know who I am, or if you have now changed your mind, you must tell me so that I may pass on and go where they are waiting for me.'

When Chaka heard these things, he nearly went mad with joy, and he said: 'Tell me, is it you who are supposed to complete . . .', his voice trembled, and he was unable to speak because of the fullness of his heart when he saw that right there, in the wilderness, in the barrenness of the desert, in his state of forlornness, he met the one concerning whose coming he had long abandoned all hope, through whom all promises were to be fulfilled. The doctor was piercing him with his eyes as those thoughts were coursing through his mind, intent on peering right inside Chaka's heart, where all the confidences and the secrets were hidden; and in answer, he simply nodded his head. And then when he saw how Chaka was overcome with emotion, he said: 'Have no more doubts, I have already come.' When he said so it was clear that this was a man full of self-confidence who was talking, a man with the power to accomplish that which he promised. Those words struck Chaka right in the centre of his forehead, and they convinced him, and he entertained no further doubts. He felt the heavy load of a grieving heart loosening and falling to the ground, and he was light and buoyant. He also felt something like a ray of light streaking inside his heart and settling down where that load had been, and he saw clearly that his father's kingship was now his, that he had that day secured it, and it would not any longer slip out of his grasp as long as he was with this man.

The doctor: 'First, before we go into any details, I ask you whether you bind yourself to observe all my commandments completely? I am asking this because there is nothing I can do unless you so bind yourself.' It is the law of the profession that in matters of this nature, or of curing someone of sterility, or of surrounding a property with protective medicines, a doctor should lay down his conditions which the people have to abide by or refuse right at the beginning if those conditions are too difficult because, if they do not refuse at the very start, the doctor will still claim his reward even if, through their negligence, his labours have not attained any results.

Chaka: 'I bind myself to abide by your commandments in every way in which you will command me.'

'My commandments and my laws are difficult, but since you want kingship, a thing which is hard, it stands to reason that even the efforts to obtain it are difficult, and heavy, and demand complete self-submission.' Chaka swore once more that, no matter how difficult they might be, he would obey them, if it was within the power of an earthly person to do so. Then the doctor said: 'So be it. I said to you a while ago, lay your fears to rest, I have already come, and even now I still repeat that your hardships and your sufferings are now all things of the past; the blessings you were promised in your childhood will on this very day begin to fall upon you; you will succeed in everything you do. Now, tell me the desires of your heart, and the one thing on which, of all others, you want me to concentrate all my skills.'

'I do not have many wishes. My heart yearns for the kingship for which I was born, which will slip out of my hands simply because I have bad luck. I say to you, work on me so that that kingship should be restored to me.'

'I understand. All you want is your father's kingship, beyond that there is nothing you want, not even a kingship that surpasses that of your father. That is what you are saying, is that not so?'

'No, I do want that. If you can make me into a great king, one who is independent, to whom all lesser kings owe allegiance, I shall be very grateful. But, doctor, you must tell me the truth concerning what you are able to do; very often you doctors promise people wonders, things you know very well that you will never be able to accomplish.'

'You must believe in me, I will never deceive you. I believe that you have, in a small way, seen the affairs of this world, that people live by favouritism and bias, by hatred and by strength; and now you too must part with mercy from this very day, because mercy devours its owner. Besides, I shall not stay long with you; I shall simply work on you, and then go away, and while I am gone you will strive for the kingship which you desire.'

41

CHAPTER SEVEN

ISANUSI STRENGTHENS CHAKA
WITH MEDICINE

After Chaka had come to an understanding with the doctor in everything, the doctor began his work. He started by cutting off the tuft of hair under which the medicine had been placed, saying that that had been done because Chaka was still too weak for the powerful medicines of kingship. He made vaccination cuts around his heart, then rubbed in the medicine with his eyes shut, speaking as follows: 'Permitter-of-those-who-are-gone, permitter-of-those-who-are-taken-unduly, accept him, receive him, bring him all the blessings of those who are gone, that they may lie on him as the dew that lies upon the ground! Upon his tracks may there be mud and marshes of rains that fall in torrents! May all his enemies vanish when he appears, like mist that evaporates when the sun rises!'

When he finished, he washed the medicine off his hands with water, after which he clapped his hands together in the direction of the place where he had made the scarifications on Chaka's body, and when the droplets of water touched the cuts, Chaka's entire body was seized with smarting pains, and he felt numb; the cuts swelled into weals, but when the doctor stopped, the cuts also subsided at once and became the size they had been before. The doctor said that that was the one and only medicine of good luck, and that he would never be vaccinated again with one of that kind.

Secondly, the doctor made a cut at the hair-line on his forehead, lifted the skin and stuffed a powdery medicine in there, and he also put in one containing the brain of a crocodile. He did those things with his eyes staring fiercely, and he worked with extreme haste. He said that that was the medicine of kingship which would make all those who saw him tremble and kneel before him; when he was angry, the faint-hearted would die from fright. His command would be taken so seriously that, if the one commanded delayed in carrying it out, others would tear him apart even while Chaka kept his peace. In war, there would be none who could face him. The doctor said that the medicine which remained to be used was one which he did not have with him; he said it was a medicine associated with the spilling of blood, with killing: 'It is extremely evil, but it is also extremely good. Choose!' The doctor placed matters in Chaka's hands; he told him, without hiding anything from him, that that medicine was truly evil, then he, for his part, stood to one side so that Chaka could act according to his wish.

'I want it,' said Chaka. And now the final link has been cut, Chaka has deliberately chosen death instead of life. When he said so the doctor looked at him for a long time without saying a word, and then he said: 'Very well. Let's go and look for it.'

There was a tree in Bokone in those days which always stood all by itself in the plain, especially in deserts. It was said that before a person could cut it, he had to be strengthened with medicines, and then only could he go to it, because if he cut it without having strengthened himself, he would die at once. It was said that, when a person chopped it, it cried like a goat, and, besides, its sap was red like human blood. The person chopping it had to be naked, totally nude. It was a tree of witchcraft, because if a person placed it on the windward side of someone's house, all the people in that house would die. It was kept in the veld like the medicine for healing fractures. It was generally believed that once that tree had a section of it removed, it withered immediately, its life force going away with the medicine that had been taken from it.

The doctor vaccinated Chaka's right hand with the medicine made from that tree, mixed with other medicines as well as snake poisons. He made two cuts on the outside of the hand, opposite the middle finger, two more cuts at the wrist joint, and two on the thumb. He did the same thing to the left hand, except that there he did not actually cut, but simply feinted the cuts with his razor, and then he rubbed in the medicine; and the pain that Chaka felt as the medicine was applied where the doctor had simply been feinting with his razor was beyond description, and Chaka felt it in his heart, it even brought tears to his eyes. The doctor mixed the remaining medicine into an ointment and gave it to Chaka, saying that every time he returned from bathing in the river, he must anoint himself with it just as if it were an ordinary lubricating fat, and rub it especially into the areas with the cuts.

Lastly, the doctor went to look for another tree far away yonder by the sea, and cut two branches from it. From one of these he made Chaka a stick which he hollowed out a little at the thick end and put that terrible evil medicine into the hole. From the second branch he made Chaka a spear with a short handle so that it could not be hurled, and once again he stuffed that fearful medicine into a hole at the base, and then bonded the spear with fire, after which he stroked the handle of that spear with that same medicine, at the place where it is fixed to the blade, and then he tied them together securely with the binding skin. The colour of that tree, after the bark is taken off, is very beautiful indeed; it is dark brown and it glitters brightly when the sun shines on it, and has such a high gloss that it almost looks liquid.

When they had finished all those things, they retraced their tracks in order to go to Dingiswayo's. On the way the doctor advised Chaka very strongly to obey Dingiswayo with true obedience, to work happily for him, because it was through him that he would attain the kingship he wanted. In addition, he told Chaka that, because of his many responsibilities, he would not visit him often. 'If something should happen, and you need me quickly, when you go to the river on your appointed day, you must anoint yourself with the medicine I gave you, and then go into the water, and I shall hear at once that I am needed. But if you should need me urgently when that day is still far away, go to the river before the sun comes up, or for that matter at any time when you are confronted with danger, cut a reed from the river, peel off its covering, and then go into the water and bathe, after which you must stroke that reed with that same medicine, partly submerge it in water and call me in a whisper, speaking softly into the reed, saying "Isanusi", thereafter throw it into the middle of the river. You are to do all these things with your eyes shut. I will hear that I am wanted urgently. In battle, when you are sorely pressed by the enemy, and see that death is at hand, simply strike your forehead, where I have stuffed the medicine, with the base of your spear which also contains the medicine, that is to say that the medicines must strike each other, and then call "Isanusi!", and help will come to you in the twinkling of an eye, and your enemies will flee when they hear that name.'

'Doctor, we have already been together several days now, talking about one thing, but you have not yet told me your name. Who are you?'

'Neither did you tell me yours, I discovered it for myself with my own intelligence. When you call me, say "Isanusi".'

'But "Isanusi" is not your name, it simply describes what you are, whereas what I am asking is your name.'

'You speak the truth, but *I* am Isanusi both by name and by deed.'

'I was about to ask you, Isanusi, how many days it would take you to reach me, starting from where you will be when I call you?'

'That will depend on where your call will find me. If it comes to me when I am near, I shall arrive quickly; if it finds me far, it is understandable, of course, that I shall be slightly delayed. But don't ever fear that I might delay so long that you would be overtaken by danger, that will never happen. Besides, if I am held up, I can send one of my servants to you; as a matter of fact, my thinking is that the day you take over the kingship, one of them should come and live with you, and watch over you for me.'

'But doctor, will they also . . .'

'You must not say "doctor" when you speak to me, you must say "Isanusi". Be careful not to say "doctor" when you summon me, and thus make it impossible for me to hear your call.'

'But you are a doctor, aren't you?'

'Yes, I am, but my name is Isanusi, and that is the name I use in addressing the dead, and it is by that name that they know me.'

'I was about to ask you, Isanusi, whether those servants of yours will know where I am?'

'With precision.'

'How will they know?'

'How did *I* know? The way that I knew is exactly the way they too will know. One important matter which I want you to understand well, is that the great king who once visited you at the river is a person who loves war; if you do not spill blood, he will not be pleased with you. Also the medicine with which I have vaccinated you is a medicine of blood; if you do not spill much blood, it will turn against you and kill you instead. Your sole purpose should be to kill without mercy, and thus clear the path that leads to the glory of your kingship.'

45

'As far as that is concerned, doctor...'

'You must not say "doctor", you must say "Isanusi".'

'I say, as far as that is concerned, Isanusi, you must not worry yourself too much, because I have now thought about my affairs in a different way, for I have seen clearly how the affairs of men are conducted in this world, and I shall direct them in a way that will teach the people to live in a proper manner; indeed, if my spear had not broken the day I was attacked at my home, I would have made for myself a famous name, and people would have talked only of Chaka in the coming years; the old people would have told their grandchildren how I had fought on that day, putting an end to a great multitude all by myself. The youth would have been instructed with the words: "You must fight the way Chaka fought." My name would have lived after me, and been spoken long after I had turned to dust inside my grave. Oh, people, how that spear spited me!'

'I see that you do not crave for kingship only, you also long to be renowned to the very ends of the earth, to gather so much fame that when your deeds are told, they will sound like fairy tales; that is another thing which you yearn for, just like kingship.'

'Yes, fame is sweet; I would not be happy even though I were to be a great king, if I were not famous. Besides, the fame I want is that which comes when men are gripping their spears, and braves with stout necks fall dead on the ground, and all the fine young men come to their end. I would like my kingship to be one which I will reach out and grab for myself, so that my fame may grow.'

'Chaka, I tell you there is nothing that is too difficult for a man. If you are a *man*, and you know how to work with your spear, everything will happen the way you want it. It is through the spear that the brave acquire cattle, it is through it that fame is achieved, and it is through it that kings rule, for he who does not know how to use it, is ruled. The diligent cultivator of sorghum is the person who knows the time for working in the fields, who, when the proper month comes, gives up beer parties and feasts, and rises at the crying of the cock to go to his garden, caring nothing about the cold and the fury of the sun, his one aim being that *that moment* should not pass him by. If you like kingship and fame, you must be like that. You must be a cultivator of kingship: let your spear be your hoe, use it, and use it intelligently. Where necessary, you must reduce everything to total annihilation, sweep it all away, and never let your enemy escape lest

46

he should afterwards rise up against you. Remove the weeds from your garden of kingship with war, and that is how you will achieve your fame. At Dingiswayo's you will find a place where the spear is put to great use, where braves are greatly loved; and thus, my last word to you, Chaka, is that you must work like a man with that spear of yours, so that the day we meet again you will tell me of the great things which you have done, and of the way in which Dingiswayo regards you.'

When they came close to Dingiswayo's they parted, Isanusi stating that he did not want to meet Dingiswayo because they hated each other.

CHAPTER EIGHT

CHAKA ARRIVES AT DINGISWAYO'S—HE KILLS A MADMAN: THE BATTLE OF ZWIDE

About two months had passed from the day Chaka ran away from home to the day on which he parted from Isanusi; that is to say that those who were mourning for him had already removed the cord of mourning. Dingiswayo, on the other hand, was still busy calling together doctors and diviners to find out where Chaka was; and that shows us that he loved him very much.

Chaka, the day he left home in flight, left as Chaka, a human being like all other human beings, who had his human failings. Today he comes back greatly changed; it is only his flesh that is coming back, only his outer self; as for his true self, that has remained at the place from which he is returning; he comes back with a completely different spirit and a different personality. Even before this, Chaka was an amazingly persistent person who persevered however difficult a thing might be until he reached the very end of it, till he came to the farthest reaches of the desires of his heart, allowing nothing to stand in his way, to keep him from what he wanted. But, in spite of all that he had human feelings, and did not provoke a fight. But now when he saw his own father's children seeking to kill him for nothing, and his father turning into an enemy, he ran away; and when he was out there in the wilderness, his being died, and today he returns with the thought that says: 'I shall simply kill whomever I wish to kill, whether he is guilty or not, because that is the law of this world. I will never have mercy on a person simply because of his pleadings.' Indeed Chaka returns with no human feeling left in him, his sole aim being to kill, resolved that he will settle every dispute and every quarrel with his stick by killing both the accuser and the accused. He returns determined to fight a war that has no end, by means of which he will kill both his enemies and his own people and friends in a clandestine manner. The frightening vengeance of his heart is indeed about to drive him mad.

The sun was already about to touch the tips of the mountains, and the evening shadows lengthened greatly, the cattle already standing in the squares by the folds, and the women already returning with the water from the springs, when Chaka arrived at the gates of Dingiswayo's royal abode. When he came there he sat down in order to be well rested before going in, thereby ensuring that he would enjoy peace and happiness therein. While he was sitting there he heard the men at the king's court chanting in unison: '*Siyavuma*' ('We agree'), while a doctor who was then in the process of divining was telling how Chaka had disappeared, and that he would never be seen again, and, further, that he had been murdered, which was what most diviners were inclined to assert. But one of the diviners affirmed with an oath, swearing by Dingiswayo himself, that Chaka was alive wherever he was, and that he would indeed come of his own accord to his king one day.

Chaka heard all those things, and when he surveyed the village with his eyes, he saw a small group of women leaving the court, and among them he saw his mother, Nandi, who had grown extremely thin, and had become weak like someone who had been ill for many years. And then, when the sun disappeared completely in the ground, he entered the village, and was walking with a sprightly

48

step, feeling light, as a young man should. He greeted the king's councillors. To their questions regarding where he came from and where he was going, he answered that he had come from far away in the south, and that he wished to see Dingiswayo in order to speak to him. When they said he should explain why he wanted him, he said: 'Tell the king and say: Here is a homeless wanderer who wishes to be taken up and protected by you; he is not a human being, but a hare hunted by the hounds, and those who see him simply attack him without a word, so that he has even become brother to the owl; yet he is a male child who has an arm that knows how to carry his weapons, one who can fight in his wars. If the king is afraid that, through me, he will acquire a burden he will never be able to shake off, will he kindly let me know, so that I may hurry on because the hue and cry following me is frightening.'

It was already dusk, so that the people were not able to see each other properly. When Dingiswayo came to Chaka he said: 'Where do you come from? Where are you going? Where is your home? What is your name?'

'My king, I have just recently wandered in the plains fleeing from the spear; I have come to you to ask for protection; my home is at Senzangakhona's; my name is Chaka.' There was complete silence in the court when Chaka began to speak; and when he made that last statement, all the men stood up and crowded around him joyfully when they heard that he was indeed Chaka, the brave after whom their king had been hankering so long. One man among those forming a circle around Chaka and Dingiswayo, began to praise the bones of the dead ones that seek after the living; he praised them in very low tones, constantly throwing side glances at Dingiswayo; and it turned out that he was the one who alone had sworn that Chaka was alive where he was, and that he would one day come of his own accord to his king, and this was truly so.

Instead of answering Chaka, Dingiswayo sent someone to fetch Nandi, Chaka's mother, from her house. And when Nandi came, he asked once again saying: 'Where did you say you came from, young man? Furthermore, where are you going? Where is your home? And what is your name?'

'My king, I have just recently wandered in the plains fleeing from the spear'—Nandi strained her ears and listened intently, and she penetrated the darkness with her eyes to see the person who was speaking—'I have come to you to ask for protection.' Nandi cried piercingly several times, and there was pain in her voice, and she fell down senseless. At that very moment a cry was heard over at the house from which she had been summoned; the other women, her age-mates came running and crying, attracted by a voice they knew well, of someone they had already given up as lost, believing that he had been murdered. Someone spoke over there in the midst of the crowd and said: 'So-and-so could never be wrong!', mentioning the name of this very doctor who was praising his divining bones.

There was a madman in the forest near the cliffs of the Mfolozi River who despoiled the people's property by seizing their goats and cattle. He was like someone possessed by the evil spirits which we hear mentioned in the Scriptures. When the people ran after him to recapture their stock, he would play havoc with them, killing those he could kill, and grabbing one of them, as they fled, and impaling him alive on the branch of a tree, as if he were a butcher-bird. For that reason, the people were extremely afraid of him. On the other hand people in Bokone are generally very afraid of madmen, and even brave men run away without any hesitation when they see them.

On the day following Chaka's arrival, that madman did a lot of damage among Dingiswayo's cattle, as he made them stampede back and forth on those ugly cliffs, while he tried to pick the one he wanted to slaughter. Many fell down the cliffs. He also killed an ox of a beautiful colour, one which drew much admiration in times of festivities, the very one Dingiswayo had doctored in order to strengthen his cattle fold. When the herdboys came and told him later that day, Dingiswayo was greatly saddened, because a few days before that, that madman had caught and eaten an ox of his with beautiful downward-pointing horns, which was the pride of his herd. He was truly at a loss how to kill that madman, besides, among his regiments and his warriors, there was none brave enough to go and face him.

Chaka was present when the herdboys reported to the king, and when he saw that no one was going, he got up and went. On seeing this, Dingiswayo also went with a large contingent of warriors, and he gave them strict orders that no one must run away, and that the madman must be killed since everybody had had enough of him. His heart still sore from all his sufferings, Chaka was desperate, and he told himself that if he killed that madman, that would be good since that act would create peace for him in this village, and would make the king take notice of him; but at the same time, if the madman should kill *him*, that would be a matter of no consequence, since he was already as good as dead on account of the bitterness of the life he was leading. He told himself that that madman, by killing him, would release him from his suffering.

When they came to the forest where the madman lived, some soon began to lag behind. As they passed over the cliffs that were his home, he saw them, and he came out already proclaiming his own praises and waving his spears. The people broke rank and all ran away; Chaka hesitated a while, but eventually had to run also. And then when they came out of the forest, he looked back, and he saw how the madman had scattered the men in their flight, and how he kept stabbing them to death as they ran with no one daring to put up a fight against him, since he was reputed to be possessed of an evil spirit. When the madman came close to him, Chaka pretended to run away, and since that madman was already used to the fact that he was feared by all, and that no one would fight him, he came towards him unprepared for a battle, simply ready to stab, but not to parry; besides which, he observed that Chaka had no spears, and that he was but a tender youth. Suddenly Chaka made a sharp turn, and the madman stabbed the ground, and before he had had time to pull his spear out, Chaka dealt him a mortal wound, killing him on the spot.

That madman was the first person Chaka killed with the short spear made for him by Isanusi.

Dingiswayo saw everything that Chaka did, but he was far off. Then he came, and all the people were amazed at Chaka's bravery, and they wondered just how he had managed to kill the madman for even his eyes were frightening and were like flames of fire; and all the people began to realize that all the things that had been said about Chaka concerning the lion and the hyena of witchcraft, fitted him perfectly. Even as he first arrived, the son of Senzagakhona, he made a name for himself by killing that madman, and all the people respected him.

On the third day after his arrival, Dingiswayo went out with his armies to attack Zwide, for the two of them were constantly fighting each other. Chaka joined the king's regiments like any ordinary warrior under the command of the officers. He went with great joy when he remembered that he had been promised that through these wars he would obtain the kingship he yearned for. He felt happy, not like one going to war where the strong and the brave perish, but a carefree traveller going to joyful festivities where he would meet someone he loved very much; he carried only one spear in his hand, with no spare one, without a club or a battle axe. And on the day they were going to the attack, he cried with impatience as Dingiswayo was praising them, saying that they were delaying too long. When they left the assembly ground, as they approached the outskirts of the village, Chaka was beside himself with joy, and his hand stopped smarting, because it had been itching like the fangs of a hunting dog which was impatient to go to the hunt. He was in the first detachment, the one with the black shields.

As the armies moved closer to each other, Zwide's warriors were singing a *mokorotlo*, a song of men, a song of war, and they were sure of victory; and when the armies were within a short distance of each other, one of Zwide's warriors leapt forward, shouting his praises several times, and he ran swift as a shooting star from one of his home ranks to another, and back again in the same manner; and when he was half-way, he lifted his spear and brandished it many times, aiming its blade at Dingiswayo's army. As soon as he finished praising himself in the midst of that mighty chorus of his home warriors, the battle was joined, and Zwide's men came running.

Chaka's detachment, being in front of the rest, was the first to be sent into battle. When the battle grew too heavy for them, they ran away leaving Chaka all by himself right in the midst of the enemy. When Dingiswayo saw this he sent in two reinforcements one after another, so that Chaka should not be killed. No sooner had he entered, no sooner entered battle, the son of Senzangakhona, than he felled men with his short spear, and he opened up gaps in the enemy ranks; he stabbed with his spear while at the same time fencing with his left hand. All Dingiswayo could see was the black shield of the son of Senzangakhona getting blacker right in the middle of the fray where braves were falling; his brown spear was turning red with the blood of the men he killed.

At mid-day the battle grew too heavy for Zwide's armies, and they fled on all flanks, and as they fled Chaka played havoc among them with his spear. In the end he found that he was once more all alone

52

among the enemies who fell upon him most heavily. Dingiswayo again ordered two regiments to run and cut off Zwide's forward advance so that Chaka should get an opportunity to break free and join his comrades. When Zwide's men first noticed Chaka among them, those two regiments were already near, but were not yet in view. About ten men then rushed at him. Chaka out-manoeuvred them, he turned from side to side with amazing swiftness, and when they thought they had seen him on one side he would already be on another before they knew it, and he was killing them all the while. But because he was alone, they were sure they could kill him even though he had already killed so many of them. Because of this turning from side to side, Chaka stumbled and fell, and before he had risen to his feet again, two men were already descending on him with their spears and clubs. Chaka, in his fright, called the name that was so dear to him, he called it in dire distress, seeing his death close at hand. He shouted: 'Isanusi!' As he shouted so he drew up his legs and kicked the warrior whose spear was already poised above, ready to stab him, he kicked him just below the knees with both his feet even as he lay on the ground, and that one came and fell where Chaka had been when he drew up his legs. When the second man brought down his huge, fierce club, it crushed the skull of his own comrade and splashed his brains out. At that same moment Chaka caught the one who wielded the club, wrestling him from behind, and he threw him down hard and then jumped up and grabbed his spear and his stick.

By then another group of Zwide's men were just arriving on the scene and, believing that it was Chaka who was on the ground, because of their confused haste, they killed their own comrade, and that way gave Chaka a chance to recover his weapons; and before they became aware of their mistake, he had already killed several of them. By the time they realized that they were killing each other, the regiment sent to help Chaka appeared, and so they ran away, one of them carrying Chaka's shield which he had snatched while Chaka was on the ground. When Chaka saw this, he hurled himself forward with great speed, but it was clear that the one he was chasing equalled him in swiftness because the distance between them neither increased nor decreased. To Chaka it was disgraceful beyond description for a warrior to return from battle with his shield or spear captured. This is true also of the Basotho, since a shield ought to be captured only when its owner is dead. For this reason Chaka once more shouted: 'Isanusi!', whereupon that young man from Zwide's stumbled and was thrown forward, and he even somersaulted as he fell. When he tried to get up, he fell down again and even stepped on his own neck. The third time, just as he was getting up from the ground, Chaka had already caught up with him, and dug his spear into him, and he fell down for good. By that time Zwide's men were running helter skelter in their flight.

Since he was not in the battle itself, Dingiswayo was the one who saw clearly the way in which that battle was fought, and better than anyone else how well Chaka performed. We will not tell how pleased he was with Chaka, nor how the women honoured him with their shrill ululations on that day, nor how songs were composed for him: let the reader imagine these things for himself, how it was on that day. What is surprising, however, is that while Chaka was being thus praised and sung, the other warriors did not grow envious, but instead they were the very ones who spoke highly of Chaka, and even suggested to the king that he be promoted to his senior regiments, consisting only of seasoned braves; and indeed the king did so, and also honoured him by making him commander of one of the top-ranking regiments.

That is how Chaka made his arrival known at Dingiswayo's royal village. After only three days he was already known, and counted among the most renowned braves, the king's trusted ones. And now Chaka was happy here at the royal place where a warrior was a highly valued person, and the spear never slumbered.

CHAPTER NINE

NDLEBE AND MALUNGA COME TO CHAKA

Chaka used to tell his mother everything concerning the medicines his doctor gave him. What surprises us so much now, therefore, is that he did not tell her about his meeting with Isanusi and how the doctor worked on him, as well as his promises to him for the future. All he said was that he had met 'that' doctor about whom they had been told, and that the doctor had worked on him, and he told it in a manner which made light of it, simply skimming off the top. Perhaps—we say perhaps because we do not know if this was indeed the reason—perhaps he was afraid to tell his mother the story of Isanusi in its entirety because he believed that Isanusi was a sorcerer, and that his mother would warn him to part company with him, while he, for his part, felt that whether Isanusi was a sorcerer or not was of no importance as long as he could obtain the medicines and the kingship that he yearned for. He had already resolved that, however ugly a deed might be, he would do it if only it led him towards that kingship.

After his war with Zwide, Dingiswayo fought several battles with nations living around the borders of his kingdom, and he conquered them all, after which he halted to rest his armies. When Zwide saw this, he assumed that the reason for that respite was that Dingiswayo's armies had become diminished, and that he was waiting to fill in the gaps with younger men; so Zwide decided to attack while the odds were still thus in his favour. On that occasion he drafted his entire nation—mature men, young men, old men, including even the tenderest youth who was handling spears for the first time, as well as habitual good-for-nothing stay-at-homes. The battle was ordered in the following manner: Zwide was to go ahead and meet

Dingiswayo, and when the battle was joined, he was to retreat and then quickly return to the attack. He was to continue with this strategy with the aim of drawing Dingiswayo to a gorge where Zwide's reinforcements were lying in ambush in the depths of the forests. Besides, on that occasion Zwide had even invited another king to come and help him. When Zwide came to where the reinforcements were hiding, he was to retreat more slowly fighting back with reasonable force, and then when Dingiswayo's armies passed that point, the hidden reinforcements would rise up cutting him off from the rear. Zwide would thereupon renew the assault at once, and the battle would be fought in a tight circle around Dingiswayo so that no one should escape, especially since just below the path of Zwide's planned retreat there were steep drops at the gorge's edge, which no one would dare to descend unless he was deliberately hurled down.

At that very time when Zwide was planning to attack, an event of great importance took place among Dingiswayo's people, even though they were not aware of it.

Chaka went to the river very early in the morning on his usual day, and he bathed and finished washing himself. Just as he came out of the water and started to walk up the bank, he saw two young men, very different in appearance, squatting above the river bank, at the very place he was going to pass. They were completely silent, not saying anything to each other, and were both looking at him. Chaka looked at them, examining them with great care, and he found that they were a different kind of people whom he was seeing for the first time in his entire life, that is to say, a different race of people. One of them had a countenance and a body which showed clearly that he was alert and sharp, a brave who fought in great wars. Chaka realized without a doubt that he was certainly not a man from Bokone; he saw that he came from nations living far away, at the very ends of the earth, nations of powerful giants; yet, among those very giants, he could see this young man playing havoc among the warriors with his spear, felling them and carving out a name for himself among the powerful men of that faraway land. The way in which he was squatting testified that in running, his speed equalled that of a wild beast, that he was a veritable whirlwind. He had strong biceps, and his calf muscles were a tight ball. His eyes were sharp, and did not drop when they met those of another person; they were like the eyes of someone who had grown up amid royalty, among crowds of people, who was accustomed to looking at different kinds of people. He was wearing a neatly made fringe-skirt, a head-dress of porcupine quills, and a copper bracelet round his arm, and it was clear that he was not only a brave, but also a fastidious person in regard to his dressing, a beautiful and refined young man who was much sought after by all the young girls.

As for the second young man, he was a flabby, clumsy thing with big hanging lips and drooping ears which were too big for him, like caves ready to scoop up the wind, or, we should rather say, gossip. His eyes were liquid and were full of treachery and guile to an amazing degree; they refused to look straight into other people's eyes; they were so lustreless that even when they looked at someone they lacked the power to make him feel that his eyes were meeting those of another human being; they were like mere imitations of human eyes. His hair was matted together in long tufts which hung like plaits over his face and the back of his head, exaggerating his ugliness and making him look like a half-wit. His jaws were large, his cheeks sunken, and his chin curved upwards. His arms were disproportionately long, and were muscular but lean, and it was clear that he had the strength of a blind man, and once he caught something in his grip, he never let it go. He had long, thin shanks, and his feet too were extraordinarily long and flat. The shape of his feet and his hollowed flank muscles showed that he was a tireless long-distance runner. His feet were like old dry cow-hides, with cracks on the heels, and even on the soles.

When Chaka looked at them, this second one had his head bowed, but as soon as Chaka's eyes landed on him, this flabby old thing came suddenly alive, and he raised his head and looked this way and that; he grew wild and his ears seemed to grow even hollower than before, and his eyes grew more guileful and treacherous; he strutted about in an agitated manner like an ostrich, and then sat down again. The other young man was holding a spear with a short handle like that of Chaka's and when Chaka's eyes reached him, he slowly wielded his spear like one testing its strength; his face at once became wild, and the sinews in his face and body swelled up, and his eyes turned red. Chaka saw without a doubt that he could not possibly fight against these two, for it would be like lighting a fire which refuses to burn. Then he ran back into the water extremely frightened, and he broke a reed and began to peel it. But just as he was about to call Isanusi, the half-witted one stood up, looked this way and that, stretched out his neck, and then sat down again; then the intelligent one said: 'Chaka, do not trouble yourself about calling Isanusi, we are your friends, not your enemies; we are the enemies of your enemies; come up and hear the news.' When he spoke like that there was a certain authority in his voice which made it impossible for those he commanded not to listen to him, or delay in carrying out his orders; besides the sound of it showed that it was the voice of a leader of men who was accustomed to commanding great armies.

When Chaka heard them calling him by name and mentioning the name of Isanusi who was his own close secret; when he realized that they began to speak to him at exactly the moment when he was about to call Isanusi, and that they were quite aware of what he was doing, he at once believed that they did truly come from his doctor. He walked up from the water with great joy when he heard that these strange people had come to him to be his friends and allies. He greeted them and asked for news without delay in the manner of someone who seeks to know about a place he loves.

'What is the news from Isanusi? Is Isanusi well? How did you know that I was here at the river? And from where did you rise up so early in the morning?'

'News: we have been sent by Isanusi to come and live with you. He is well. We knew you were here because it is your day. We rose up right here in the middle of the veld.'

'But how did you know that I was at this particular river and at this precise spot?'

'We knew because we are Isanusi's servants, who can see in the darkness and in the hiding places, who can hear things that are far, and who are able also to see the thoughts that spring from a man's heart.'

When they began talking, the half-witted one stood up and came and sat behind the other one with his back to him, thus facing in the backward direction. Chaka asked what he was doing and they said: 'Whenever we talk about confidential things we do that so that one can see what is at the back while the other one sees what is in front, so that no one can come upon us unexpectedly while we are speaking confidentially, and thus hear our secrets.'

58

Chaka: 'What is your name?' He was asking the half-witted one.

'Ndlebe.'

'Ndlebe! Why is that so? Or is it because your ears are so large?'

'Because I hear much.'

'You hear much?'

'Yes.'

'What do you hear?'

'All things which an ear is able to hear.'

'Were you also sent to me?'

'Yes.'

'To come and do what?'

'To hear for you all the gossip and secret talks so that you may not be caught unawares by any secret plots against you.'

Chaka was suspicious of this half-witted fellow who talked to him with his head down, refusing to look him in the face, and also about his brief answers which resembled those of someone who was unwilling to talk. But Ndlebe soon convinced him that he had come for the reasons he stated.

'And you, who are you?' he asked the other one.

'People call me Malunga.'

'What do *you* call yourself if that is the way other people call you?'

'*I* never call myself, besides, a person does not give himself a name, it is given to him by other people.'

'What exactly is the business of your visit, both of you?'

'I believe that we have already answered that question: our business is to come and live with you, to look after you and be near you in times of war; besides, a big war is close at hand in which you will distinguish yourself in the eyes of your king more than you have already done hitherto. We will stand by you in these wars: Ndlebe will be your ears and will hear all the news for you; I will be your arm, and will fight for you. But the two of us will only enter the battle when it is already well joined, and well advanced. During peacetime, when there are no wars, *I* shall stay by your side and discuss all your plans with you; which means that when you have an idea in your mind you must tell me, and I shall seek a way in which it may be put into action so that it may be accomplished well in

59

accordance with your wishes. Ndlebe, for his part, will sit in the courtyards of the royal houses, and also near the king, and the people will talk quite freely in his presence without taking any note of him since, as you yourself can see, he is, in appearance, a half-wit. Yet, let me tell you, he is a complete human being with all his faculties. Furthermore, the time for you to return to your home to take over the kingship is near. It is because of all these things that Isanusi has decided that it would be a good thing for us to come here and be near you.'

When Chaka heard that the time for him to go and assume the kingship of his home was near, he simply kept quiet, holding in his feeling of excitement as he imagined in his heart how it would be the day he, Chaka, deserted by his own father, returned to take his rightful seat; of what nature, he wondered, would be his revenge upon his enemies. He concluded that killing them would be too light a punishment, undeserved by such as they.

They walked together up towards the village, and he was asking them, meanwhile, about the war they said was coming soon. He believed everything they told him, simply because it was said by the servants of Isanusi. What is surprising to us is that Chaka did not tell his mother about the coming of these men, except to say simply that he had found himself a fool who would carry his blankets. He did not give her a full account of where they came from and the work they had come to do. Besides, he told her about only one of them, and hid the other. We ask once again what it is about Isanusi, and what it is about his servants, to make Chaka hide from his mother everything connected with them, when in fact it had been his custom to tell her all things in their fullness, both the evil and the good.

CHAPTER TEN
CHAKA CAPTURES ZWIDE

As etiquette demanded, Chaka brought Ndlebe and Malunga before Dingiswayo so that he should know them. He said: 'Since I came here in flight, O King, I have been walking alone; but today two young men from my home have come to join me, both of whom are my servants. Let me correct that and say that *one* of them is my servant who carries my blankets. He is retarded. The second one is my friend who has come to pay me a visit, I am therefore presenting them to you so that you may know them and not wonder who they are when you see them in the village.' They were called and they came. As soon as they appeared Dingiswayo's body shuddered violently, and he even got up on his feet from fright. Then after they left he said: 'Chaka, are you saying that both of them come from your home?'

'Yes, O King.'

'Have you known them since childhood, or have you met them only recently?'

'I grew up with them, O King.'

'I am asking this because one of them is, without any doubt, a half-wit, who is not even fit to carry your blankets. As for the second one, I do not like him at all, he has the eyes of a traitor, and they are full of guile and treachery. You must take him away from here, I'm afraid of him, for he is truly evil. Are you telling me that you have known *him* also from your childhood?'

'Yes, O King.'

On this day we find Chaka for the first time telling a lie, whereas we have known him from his childhood, and as he grew up, as someone who was accustomed to speaking the truth. He began by hiding from his mother the news about his meeting with Isanusi, and even when he told her about these two, he simply skimmed off the

61

top and even applied a thin layer of lies; and now to Dingiswayo he is telling a plain cold lie, without even the tiniest grain of truth. He is sliding slowly away from truth, going we know not where.

'Look well after yourself, Chaka, that friend of yours is harbouring something evil, and will harm you when you least expect it. I am surprised when you say that you have known him since childhood because even his features, especially his face, show plainly that he is not a person from these parts, but a wicked thing which comes from we don't know where. He is a real sorcerer.' As Dingiswayo spoke like that, his body once again shuddered when he thought of the guileful nature which was apparent in Malunga's face.

That evening Malunga said to Chaka: 'I can see that your king detests me, and believes me to be an evil person. For that reason I am returning to my home since I cannot stay in a place where I will be unhappy. I am sure that Ndlebe will be able to obtain for you everything you need. Trust him, and you will see that he is a true human being who is worthy of your trust. If you trouble him, however, he will run away. See that he gets food regularly because, as a matter of fact, he eats a lot. He will carry your blankets for he is a strong beast of burden; he will gather news for you, for he is like a dog which picks up scents, which has a sharp ear; but most important of all is that in war he can expose the secret plottings of the enemy.'

The armies left home to meet Zwide at the border, and they hurried in order to reach that place before Zwide defiled the highways with evil medicines. They met above the plateau overlooking the gorge through which the Mfolozi River flowed. As was his habit, Dingiswayo did not send all his armies into battle at the same time, but held back some regiments so that he could use them to reinforce the weaker ranks. He said that when the warriors first meet and are still thirsting after each other, they fight with blind fury, each one facing only his own opponent, and not taking care to see whether he is still with his comrades. As a result some of them end up right in the midst of the enemy in the belief that their comrades are still close by, and thus get killed unnecessarily. The regiment under Chaka's command was the very first one to be sent into battle.

That battle was fought for a long time, with Zwide constantly retreating and then immediately returning to the attack, meanwhile drawing Dingiswayo's armies towards the gorge and the dense forests. At high noon Dingiswayo charged with all those he had held back, so that they should join the battle with force and throw Zwide's men down the cliffs. At that very moment Ndlebe came to Chaka covered with mud like a dog that had been running hard, his dangling tufts of hair swept backwards and hanging at the back of his head. He was as alert as a dog which had picked up the scent of an animal, his mouth was open, and he was breathing exactly like a dog. He said: 'My master, there is danger lurking here in the forest, you must be on the lookout, and be ready to defend yourself. Zwide has hidden numerous armies in the forest, and this running away of his is no running away at all, but simply a strategy to lure you into the forest so that you may be surrounded and all killed. I advise you to pull back your regiment as if you were resting since it was the first to go into battle, and not to go back to the attack before I return.'

Ndlebe entered the forest and bored his way through till he came out on the other side. When he came there he set the grass alight, for it was winter and the grass was dry and long, a veritable jungle. A slight breeze was blowing, driving the fire towards the place where the battle was raging, and at that moment when Ndlebe set fire to the grass Chaka was standing high up above the gorge together with his regiment, while the battle was in full heat along the gorge's flank, near the forest, and the vanguard of Zwide's army was already level with the place where the reinforcements were hidden. Caught completely unawares, they suddenly saw descending upon them flames burning furiously and moving quickly because of the wind and the denseness of the grass. The reinforcements came out of the forest in a confused hurry to avoid being burnt in there, but it was clear that they could not escape in the homeward direction since the fire blocked the way; they were thus compelled to throw themselves into the battle in order to push back Dingiswayo's armies, and find a way to save themselves. But then it was difficult to force back Dingiswayo's men because they were standing on higher ground. That is where the battle was fought with such fury that corpses piled up in a short time, Zwide's men being driven by the fire from behind, while Dingiswayo's blocked the only corridor of escape, and saw victory close at hand. It was a red-eyed battle that was fought there, each warrior concerned only with finding an opening through which to save himself, no longer fighting for the praises and songs, but for his life. Within a short time the corpses of those who fell there were far greater in number than those of the men who had died earlier in the day.

And while the battle was in full cry Ndlebe came to Chaka and said: 'Now, charge!' When Chaka's regiment appeared Zwide's men thought that Dingiswayo had employed the same strategy as they, and was only then attacking with fresh troops. They turned around suddenly. But then as they did so, they came face to face with the fire, and they saw that its flames were now at their worst, scorching even what lay at a distance from them, and at the time they turned to face it, it was just reaching the forest. The dry trees crackled and made a loud noise when they were consumed by the fire, and, to Zwide's men, that noise was like the mocking shouts of Dingiswayo's warriors. Thereupon they threw themselves down the slopes, some found openings through which to escape, some rushed headlong into the flames and came out scorched or burnt seriously and crippled, some were burnt to death, while others were maimed, but got away with their lives.

There was a cave in the centre of the forest which was known only to a few people. Zwide hid himself in there with a sizeable group of men. The cave was situated right in the middle where the forest was very dense, and a little path like the track of field mice led to it, and went through to the other side. Ndlebe told Chaka where Zwide was hiding, and Chaka then sent a section of his regiment to go and pry him out from behind so that he should run towards him since there was nowhere else to run because of the thickness of the forest; he and Ndlebe hid themselves near the little path. When Chaka's warriors entered the cave, Zwide and his men went out and ran along that little track which led to where Chaka lay in wait. When he heard their footsteps getting close, Chaka took out his spear and held himself ready, and when he looked round he saw Ndlebe on his left-hand side with his battle axe already raised and waiting for them to appear. He was excited, and was very different from that dim-wit of yesterday and the day before; the veins in his body stood out, and he was like a wounded lion which felt the pain in its wounds, and was ready to avenge its blood.

Chaka looked to the right and he was greatly surprised when he saw Malunga already standing by his side with his short spear at the ready. He was completely quiet and his eyes which were blood-red, stared furiously at that narrow little path from which Zwide was going to appear. He stood like a crouching wild beast getting ready to leap. There was no time to ask him where he had come from. Zwide came into view with his people, and they were squeezed so tight that at times they pressed against each other with none able to move forward. Besides, because of the thickness of the forest, it took some time before they saw Chaka, and they were surprised by his presence when many of them were already lying dead on the ground; furthermore, also as a result of this denseness of the forest, they were unable to retreat, or to fight. Chaka rushed on them and killed them rapidly because they were squeezed together so tightly. Malunga stabbed them in the same manner as Chaka, but he even surpassed him in the number he killed, for it appeared that the thickness of the forest did not hinder him in any way. Chaka's warriors who were pursuing Zwide and his men pushed them forward with their spears, while Chaka, Ndlebe and Malunga blocked the passage with *their* spears. On that day Chaka's arm grew swollen from the work of stabbing and killing. Zwide was captured alive and taken to Dingiswayo, because Dingiswayo did not permit a king to be killed. When Chaka looked around, he found that Ndlebe and Malunga were not there any more, and he remained alone with those warriors who had gone to force Zwide out of his hiding.

Ndlebe came to where the battle was still raging, and he shouted in the Ndwandwe language, saying: 'The king has been captured, and Dingiswayo's fresh armies are only now coming into battle under Chaka's command!' Gracious, that was enough to start a stampede! The fire now was considered a minor danger since some might survive it, though with injuries, whereas waiting for Chaka was waiting for certain and total destruction. In their flight, the fugitives pushed each other down the cliffs.

In the end Dingiswayo's army came together and went to the king, and they found Zwide already with him as a prisoner. Ndlebe lay down like a tired dog which had been running a lot. That intelligence which he displayed when participating in the war was gone, and he once again looked as dim-witted as ever. He threw himself down and even rolled on to his back, and in the midst of all those celebrations of victory, to him it was as if nothing had happened. He did not even seem to be interested in knowing how the war had proceeded, thereby proving himself to be a real idiot. Dingiswayo and all his armies were truly amazed at Chaka's strategies in sending regiments into battle, in fighting, and in demoralizing the enemy, because all the things which had been done by Ndlebe were assumed to have been done by Chaka, for no one knew that they were Ndlebe's doing. The women's ululations when the armies entered the village were something never heard before. Dingiswayo came back to his royal place as a king and a conqueror who had scattered his enemies. Chaka's name was spoken in praise by all the women, songs were sung for Chaka, songs were sung about Chaka. Dingiswayo retained his prisoner for a few days and then released him, and Zwide went home in peace just as if he had not been a prisoner, but just an ordinary visitor visiting Dingiswayo on a peaceful mission.

On that day, Chaka was promoted to commander of all Dingiswayo's armies. In many subsequent wars he was sent alone in charge of the armies while the king remained at home; but even when the king was present, he would give the command to Chaka and Chaka would be the one to pass it on to the armies.

CHAPTER ELEVEN
THE DEATH OF SENZANGAKHONA

While Dingiswayo was busy scattering the nations, Senzangakhona for his part was living a very unhappy life since he was the one person who persecuted Dingiswayo in his youth, and actually wished to see him killed. And now when he saw that same Dingiswayo, with his son, Chaka, continuing to rise, and to lay nations low, he was afraid, he trembled, as he thought that Dingiswayo was going to take his revenge on him; moreover, Dingiswayo did not even invite him when he was going into battle, nor did he ask him to look after the village at those times. Senzangakhona's senior wives spared no pains in ensuring that Nandi's name would be wiped off the list of his wives, and that any linking of her name with Senzangakhona's would be on a level no higher than that of a concubine. Mfokazana tried hard to capture the people's hearts. He made people gifts of cattle; his court sentences were light, and he even reduced the amount of labour the people were expected to contribute to the king as in hoeing and weeding the king's fields. He made himself their genuine friend, one who sympathized with them, with the sole purpose that they should think of him when his father died.

Chaka for his part stayed where he was, at Dingiswayo's, troubling no one. He constantly thought about the past affairs of his life. These days he had no sense of frustration as he saw that without doubt he would obtain his father's kingship because all the things which Isanusi had predicted had happened exactly as he had predicted them, and that had made Chaka believe in him unquestioningly. Ndlebe was sitting next to him, sprawled in a careless manner, his mouth half open in a lifeless grin, so that the flies went in and out of it at will. He was drooling at the mouth, the saliva hanging downwards. He looked like a fool of fools, and was, besides, snoring right there where he was sleeping in the middle of the day, looking like a carcase.

As Chaka was thinking these thoughts we have just described, he looked at Ndlebe, and at that very moment Ndlebe woke up, and he scratched himself, ploughing into his flesh with his nails with that half-yawning grin just like a dog scratching itself with its hind leg. He yawned exactly like a dog that had just woken up from sleep, and he looked this way and that, and then began to get up, raising himself with his hands while his loins remained on the ground, twisted. He looked at Chaka and his ears suddenly stood up and became like little caves, and listened, and then he got up and walked away. He walked with clumsy steps like an imbecile, with the strands of his many-plaited hair hanging down on all sides, and his little blanket of dry hide barely covering his hips. When he returned he told Chaka that he [Chaka] had been plotted against by Dingiswayo's paternal uncle and two other men, for the uncle had been greatly hurt when he saw Chaka being raised above him in rank. Chaka reported this to Dingiswayo and it was those plotters who were killed instead of Chaka.

Late afternoon that same day, as the shadows lengthened, Chaka saw Ndlebe stiffen his ears like a dog picking up a scent and off he went in a fine trot exactly like a dog trotting with its nose in the air when it is attracted by a scent, and he went in a westerly direction. The sun set, then it was night, and eventually the next day dawned and the sun of that day even set again and Ndlebe was still gone without a trace. When the third day dawned he returned and he was covered with dew like a wild dog. He signalled to Chaka with his eyes to come to him, and when they were alone together he said: 'I bring you very painful news today, even though I believe that it should make *you* happy. Your father, Senzangakhona, is dead.' Chaka's thoughts flitted sorrowfully from one thing to another, and he shivered, since his father was still very young when he died and was, according to man's self-delusion, as yet far from the grave. He imagined, on this occasion, that his brothers would share their father's inheritance among themselves, leaving him aside. Chaka was not one to entertain grief for long, so he straightway went to tell Dingiswayo while this matter was still fresh.

'I understand,' said Dingiswayo, 'and I'm very sad at the death of my father's subject, but since I do not hear about it through a messenger sent by his councillors or his sons, it is something about which I am, in the circumstances, not able to do anything. You stay calm, and let us see what happens; these are human affairs, they will, no doubt, bring themselves to us.'

Senzangakhona's sons reported their father's death to Dingiswayo when they had already buried him by themselves, and were merely informing him, whereas if he had been notified in time, he would have sent an emissary with his condolences. Besides the report should have been accompanied by a young heifer. The day the mourning cords were removed, which was done sooner than was proper since the sons were impatient to acquire their father's estate, the councillors gathered the nation together and pointed to Mfokazana saying: 'There is the child of your king, take him and look well after him. He has younger brothers, namely Dingana and Mhlangana. Them too you must keep. And you too, children of the king, you must obey your elder brother and respect him, and let him work through you in all his affairs and all his errands.'

The throng said: 'May the cattle increase, O King; keep us well, we are your people! May the rains come!' In that meeting no one ever spoke of Chaka who was denied so much as a footprint's breadth in his father's estate.

In that manner Mfokazana was installed in his father's position, without Dingiswayo having been informed of anything, whereas it was proper that he be informed, as on the day of the installation he should have been present, or have sent an emissary bearing his words, because a king is installed by those who are above him. Mfokazana daily prepared himself for combat like someone who knew that war was near at hand; not surprisingly, perhaps, since he knew that Chaka would never give up so easily a kingship which he had been promised, that he would only give it up as a man would, after trying his best and being defeated.

On that same day Ndlebe came to Chaka and told him about the installation of Mfokazana. Chaka asked whether Dingiswayo knew about this, and Ndlebe said no, he did not.

'I believe you, because Dingiswayo would no doubt have told me. It is highly improper to go into a matter of such importance without Dingiswayo's knowledge; by that act they are putting themselves forward as kings in this place, and not subjects; besides, they failed to report my father's death in a proper manner.'

When Dingiswayo arrived at the royal court, Chaka told him the news. Dingiswayo asked: 'Did you hear this news properly, Chaka, about which you are telling me? I am asking because if so, your brothers have offended me greatly, and besides this is not the first time that they have done that to me.'

'I heard it from one who was there, O King.'

'I am greatly saddened by this act of your brothers; I can see that they have now made a habit of it. Besides, this is a period in which they should still be mourning for Senzangakhona rather than getting involved in the matter of the estate so shortly after his death, before the tears have even dried on their cheeks. At the present time there is nothing I can say because I do not know anything since I have not been told; I shall have something to say the day they inform me. As for you, get yourself in readiness starting this day, I shall send you back to your home to take over your kingship which Mfokazana has stolen. But don't be in a hurry, you are still going to stay another six months here with me, so that you may not profane your father's death by contesting the kingship by war so shortly after his death, with his corpse still warm in the grave.'

At that moment Ndlebe stretched himself out where he was lying, raised his head and looked around, and the saliva dangled making a sickening sight; then he got up and dug his nails into his bare sand-coloured stomach, and then he walked with his head stooping, and went to loiter within the courtyards of the homesteads.

'Chaka, this creature of yours is a real idiot; now he is going to the homesteads because he thinks only of food and sleep, like an animal.'

'It is so, O King, but then I have no other besides him, and therefore I ought to be satisfied with him, even though he is so obviously a half-wit.' Those words made Dingiswayo sad in his heart when he thought how well Chaka had served him, and that he had not yet shown his gratitude towards him. He then gave him a few men as a gift, and then went on to say: 'Moreover, you are to look for a wife, and I shall take care of all your marriage formalities, since I am now your father.'

CHAPTER TWELVE

NOLIWA

Among all his sisters, the one whom Dingiswayo loved the most was the one who came last out of his mother's intestines, the last-born. She looked very much like the girl after whom Dingiswayo himself was born, who had saved him the day he and Tana, his older brother, were in danger of their lives. Those two girls resembled each other like twins, to the very way they talked. Therefore Dingiswayo loved this surviving one more than all his other sisters by far, not so much because she was the child of her mother's womb, but because in this one's face he saw the face of his favourite sister who had died. Her eyes, her cheeks, her ears, her voice, her figure, her ways—all these were exactly like those of the one who had died, who had sacrificed herself for him at a critical time when death stared him in the face. Her name was Noliwa, and she was amazingly beautiful, and crowned it all by having a kind, compassionate heart, which was always well disposed towards other people. All who knew her swore that Nkulunkulu, the Great-Great-One, had used her as an example, so that her exceeding beauty and her eyes that were soft and full of love, should teach his children the beauty and profound love of their Creator, and that through Noliwa they should see the perfection of a woman without blemish, and may thus understand the perfection of Nkulunkulu. It appears that it was because of her beauty that the Basotho came to tell the story of the young woman who was so beautiful that she never went outside, because whenever she did so no one went to the fields, or to other labours, even the herdboys refused to take out their herds, and all ran to her, so that they could feed their eyes on her beauty.

Noliwa loved Chaka exceedingly. When the game choose-the-one-you-love-best was played she never joined in to make her choice, and never became part of the groups playing this game, because whenever it was in progress, Chaka, who was the one who pleased her eyes, would always stand to one side.

When Ndlebe entered the house, he found many girls there, and as he came in, someone said: 'There he comes in, Chaka's half-wit!' Another said: 'There he comes in, Mr Ears, he whose ears are as long as those of a field-mouse, Mr Ears by name and by deed.' When Noliwa heard them say these things, she said: 'Do not laugh at him, he is God's creature. Remember he who laughs at a cripple calls one towards himself, and will give birth to one. Tell me, are you hungry, Ndlebe?' Ndlebe said he was, and then she gave him food, and while he was eating, Noliwa asked him saying: 'Where is your master, Ndlebe?'

'Who is my master?'

'Isn't your master Chaka? Do you serve many masters all by yourself? Is that why you ask?'

'If he is anybody's master, why should he be here at Dingiswayo's, that coward who fled from his younger brothers when they chased him away so that they should remain sharing among themselves an inheritance which belongs to him by birth?'

'Are you serious, or are you joking? If Chaka is not a brave, will there ever be one?'

Ndlebe continued to speak unflatteringly about Chaka, thus drawing out those young people. After some time they began talking about the killing of Dingiswayo's uncle. Ndlebe asked what had led to the plot against Chaka. Then Noliwa said that her uncle had been hurt when Chaka was promoted, and was even more hurt when the young women sang songs of praise for Chaka.

Ndlebe: 'And what made you people sing songs of praise for Chaka, that dog that is no less dead than I, instead of making ululations for true braves and famous princes?'

'To be a prince or a king's child is nothing; the person for whom songs are sung is a brave who is distinguished even among other braves.'

'Do you mean to tell me then, that among the armies and regiments of Dingiswayo's as well as among his princes, the only one you are all attracted by is Chaka?'

The young women all answered at the same time and said: 'It stands to reason!' As for Noliwa, she went beyond those words by saying that a girl could never consider herself properly married if she was not married to someone like Chaka the brave.

Ndlebe: 'Do you want to tell me seriously that even you, the daughter of such a great king as Jobe, would be pleased to be married to such a commoner as Chaka, simply because he once killed a person?'

Noliwa answered that she would be very pleased, adding: 'Besides, Chaka is not a commoner, he is the child of a king; furthermore he is beautiful, he is round-and-smooth, like a well moulded clay-pot.'

'Are you serious, or are you joking? I am asking whether you truly love him or whether you are just making talk?'

'I do not simply love him: I'm afire with love. In truth I am now living in anxiety because I have tried in various ways to make my feelings obvious, but it seems that he simply looks over my head!'

By the time they said these things they were all by themselves. On the evening of that same day, Ndlebe entered one of the royal huts and found them playing the *Senyamo*, a 'lover's preference' game. Someone said to Noliwa: '*Senyamo!*—state your preference!'

Noliwa: 'Upon whom?'

72

'Upon——'

'Ugly thing!'

'*Senyamo!*'

'Upon whom?'

'Upon——'

'Ugly thing!'

'*Senyamo!*'

'Upon whom?'

'Upon Chaka!'

Noliwa's face lit up and beamed with smiles when Chaka's name was mentioned. She looked at Dingiswayo since he was present, and then she said: 'I die utterly! I am unable to give you any idea, to find words to make you understand, the manner of my death!' She said so on purpose so that Dingiswayo should actually hear how completely she died on account of Chaka.

On the next day Ndlebe recounted it all to Chaka: 'Maybe you have noticed, maybe you haven't, but the girls of this village are very surprised and are wondering what sort of person you are that you don't sleep in the young people's hut like all other young men; that you don't go to the dances and the songs; that you don't join the choose-a-lover-game, to choose or be chosen. Do you realize that the people are surprised at you?'

'Their surprise means nothing to me; I don't care whether they are surprised or not.'

Ndlebe continued as if he had not heard what Chaka said: 'Have you noticed that the young girls of this place can hardly swallow their food when they think of you, and that they fear each other's rivalry, each one saying to herself: "I pray that Chaka should not pass me by and be taken by So-and-so?"'

'I don't care about them all, whether they cannot swallow their food or are concerned about each other's rivalry, to me all that makes absolutely no difference. My sole purpose in this village is to work with my spear, to fight Dingiswayo's wars. That's all that I came here for, and that's all that's in my heart. I have no time to think about those girls of yours.'

'You are not telling the truth, Chaka. Just think a little: It is not true that you do not care for them all, because there is one whom you love with an amazing love, whom you avoid simply because you are afraid of her.'

73

'But what exactly have you called me for, Ndlebe? Surely not for this nonsense?'

'I have called you for something important, something that continually gnaws at you, something you love as much as you love kingship, not nonsense as you suggest; and that matter is precisely the one concerning the young girls of this place.'

'Ndlebe, would you really call me for this silly nonsense?'

'You lie, it is not nonsense. Think properly!'

Chaka loved Noliwa exceedingly, but could never see how one belonging nowhere like himself, a homeless wanderer without relations to claim him, could ever marry a child from such a prestigious house, one whom Dingiswayo loved so much besides. He felt that only princes far superior to him in rank deserved Noliwa, and for that reason he gave up even before saying a word, for he was afraid of Noliwa, and was equally afraid of Dingiswayo. Even as Ndlebe spoke those words to him, he did not for one moment entertain the thought that Noliwa could be counted among those who were dying for love of him.

Suddenly in the twinkling of an eye a thought came to him from far away yonder where he had banished it, and said to him: 'Could it possibly *be* that Noliwa is the one who pines for you?' Chaka smiled without talking, and simply looked at Ndlebe, then Ndlebe said:

'Yes, that very one! Don't you love her?'

'Which very one?'

'The very one the mere thought of whom makes you smile?'

Chaka simply continued laughing like a baby, as if he had been told that 'that very one' was already his. 'What is it then about "that very one"?'

'No, you answer my question first: Do you love her or not? I will tell you about her afterwards.'

Chaka simply continued smiling, and then Ndlebe said: 'Now, between the two of us who is the liar? Who is the one who wastes time with nonsense?'

'It's me,' said Chaka bursting into laughter. 'But now tell me, what do you know about "that very one"?'

'The fact of the matter is that "that very one" loves you with a love that surpasses *your* love for her.'

Chaka got up and spun around the courtyard with joy, and kept laughing to himself; and while he was spinning around like that,

Noliwa walked into that very courtyard, and was directly facing Chaka as she entered, and their eyes met. She asked where Nandi was, and they said she was not there; then she went out. As she walked away, her thoughts were floating high as she asked herself what could have made Chaka so happy, a question she answered herself by saying that Ndlebe had no doubt told him about the events of the previous day: 'But could Chaka really be so happy to hear that I love him?'

Chaka remained with Ndlebe in the courtyard, his thoughts swept away as if by a whirlwind, a storm raging in his feelings, which however, was caused by joy. Ndlebe left him alone to twirl around like that until the storm which had captured his feelings had subsided. But even before Ndlebe could speak, it was Chaka who spoke again saying: 'What are you saying, Ndlebe? Are you telling me that "that very one" loves me more than I love her? Which very one?'

'The very one who just came in here. Noliwa herself.'

Chaka once again began to walk around like someone dancing the *motheke-theke* dance, and then when he cooled off again after a while he sat down and listened to Ndlebe's story. But in the midst of that happiness, he became suddenly crestfallen, and deflated when he thought that he was pleased over something that did not exist, that all he had in his grasp was thin air, because Dingiswayo would never agree to let him have Noliwa, but might, instead of giving her to him, indeed chase him away from his place. Ndlebe realized the reason for his disappointment, and then he said: 'That one whom you fear is the very one who will help you obtain Noliwa.' Now he kept quiet and pricked up his ears and they became like little caves, and then he said: 'But these are matters for a later time. Right now I hear the footsteps of those sent by Mfokazana to inform Dingiswayo how he has been installed as king by his father's people. They are near. Go to the council place so that you may hear these matters for yourself and not have to be told by someone else.'

'Are you not coming?'

'I am not after the kingship, you are the one who is going after it, besides I will hear everything even as I remain here in the court-yards.'

CHAPTER THIRTEEN

CHAKA AND ISANUSI AT SENZANGAKHONA'S GRAVE

At mid-day the messengers came to Dingiswayo and gave him their message, namely that the nation had installed Mfokazana in the place of his father. Dingiswayo voiced his outrage saying that Mfokazana always told him things after they had happened, even where they concerned him directly. He said: 'Go and tell Mfokazana that I have heard. However he and those who installed him as king have done wrong because he is not the one whom his father chose to succeed him as king. The son of Senzangakhona who was reported by him to my father the day he was born as the one who would inherit his estate is still alive. I was present on that day. Even the messengers who brought that news are still there, and I know who they are. At no time did Senzangakhona mention the name of Mfokazana.'

The messengers went back disappointed, afraid even to meet the one who had sent them. When Mfokazana heard these words, he sent them again, together with those who had been sent to report Chaka's birth to Jobe, with the message that his father had realized afterwards that Chaka was a bad child who did not obey him, whose mother, moreover, was a witch. It was for that reason that he had chased him away together with his mother.

Dingiswayo answered by saying: 'Go and tell Mfokazana that this is the first time that I hear that Senzangakhona changed his mind and said that Mfokazana was to be his heir. Whom did he tell? Also I hear for the first time that Nandi practises witchcraft. Whom did she bewitch? Tell Mfokazana that even the day Chaka killed a lion, some time ago, Senzangakhona, on sending it to me, confirmed his earlier statement that it was Chaka who would be his heir.'

When Mfokazana heard that, he assembled the nation together and told them that Dingiswayo was depriving him of his kingship and giving it to Chaka. He said: 'Those who are the true subjects of my father will be known today when his little orphan is being robbed of his rights.'

Ever since hearing about Noliwa, Chaka had always wanted to meet her and talk to her. One day they met, but just for a brief while, and they were unable to talk for any length of time; however they exchanged necklaces so that Chaka took Noliwa's and Noliwa took Chaka's. Chaka did this in order to test the people's feelings, especially Dingiswayo's, because if Dingiswayo did not want Chaka to marry Noliwa he would warn her against such a deed. Dingiswayo saw that exchange of beads, and he knew that it was the beginning of a serious matter. He realized that if Chaka should marry Noliwa, he would remain linked to him, and they would be able to help each other in all matters pertaining to their lives, as well as in their wars. This made him all the more determined to see that Chaka should be the king of his home. Yet he did not do this to please him, but because all events pointed to Chaka. He said to his councillors: 'You men who belonged to my father's court, please help me so that I should not make a mistake out of ignorance, for you know that I was away for a long time. Tell me, did Senzangakhona, during my absence, send word to my father that he had changed his mind, and that Mfokazana was now his heir?'

The men who had been councillors during Jobe's reign, denied that such a thing had happened. Then Dingiswayo said: 'Chaka, I was away a long time, I don't know what happened during my absence. However, if your conscience allows you, take your regiment plus one other, and go and take from Mfokazana the kingship of which he has robbed you, and let that contest determine the outcome of this dispute.'

In that battle Mfokazana was defeated and killed. Even though Dingana and Mhlangana were not involved in that battle, Chaka wanted to kill them but Ndlebe pleaded for them. That is something we find very surprising because usually Ndlebe, instead of pleading for someone, would rather fan the flames by suggesting that the person be killed at once, yet here we see him engaged in the strange act of pleading for people's lives, people who are Chaka's enemies besides. Chaka wrought a lot of destruction when he reached his

77

home, but, because he feared Dingiswayo, he was not able to avenge himself as he had wished.

Dingiswayo's sister, Noliwa, on hearing how Chaka had defeated Mfokazana, sent him a beautiful necklace which had been strung with extreme care. By this present she was congratulating him, and also ensuring that Chaka should continue to think about her. Chaka, on his part, continually sent her presents to show that he had much love for her. As we have said, Chaka was afraid to talk to Noliwa because he feared Dingiswayo. But he was also afraid of Noliwa herself, and found it difficult to embark on such a subject with the daughter of such a great king, fearing that Noliwa would be angry with him on the grounds that he misinterpreted her kindness. For that reason he took long to broach that subject.

Malunga was present in this battle in which Mfokazana was killed. As they talked, Chaka asked what it was that Dingiswayo disliked about Malunga to make him chase him away. Malunga answered saying: 'Dingiswayo is wise and has eyes that see more than those of many people. His eyes do not look only at the exterior of a person, but penetrate right into the inner recesses of one's heart. He saw clearly that I was intelligent, and he was afraid that I might capture his people's hearts, and deprive him of his kingship. Little did he know that to me kingship is not important, what I am most interested in is practising as a man of medicine.'

Chaka: 'Malunga, today I live in my own place where nothing can bother me. While at Dingiswayo's I was bound to act according to his wishes, even if it was not to my liking, as long as it pleased him. Today I am in my own place where I do my own will, and for that reason I say, live with me as we had planned, and stop hiding because the one from whom you were hiding does not have so much power here.'

'I am very pleased to hear you speak in that manner, after all that is the very reason why my master sent me here.'

The day came which had been set aside for Chaka's installation into the kingship of his home, and Dingiswayo went as he had promised. Everything was arranged perfectly: the day preceding the one on which Chaka was to be installed was the one on which he was to go to the river for his early morning bathe. On his return from the river, he saw dimly someone coming towards him, followed by two others. It turned out to be Isanusi. That day Chaka had gone to the river much earlier than usual because some of the people attending the installation had already come, and he realized that if he went at the usual time they would see him. We are unable to measure even to the smallest degree Chaka's joy at meeting his doctor after such great things had happened, when his eyes met those of the man who had found him in the wilderness as he lay under a tree tired, hungry, his feet swollen, blundering through the country without even knowing where he was going, and then took pity on him, made a man out of him, made him into that which he is before our eyes today.

'Greetings, Chaka!'

'Greetings, O my master, my father, my king!'

'How is it? Are things going well?'

'Very well, far better than I had expected.'

'The blessings I promised you, are they coming, do you see them?'

'They come in great abundance.'

'Has my word been fulfilled of the day when I said that your troubles would end right there where I found you?'

'It has been fulfilled completely.'

'The spear I made for you, how does it work?'

'*Ao*, do not even talk! Let others speak, not me.'

'Do you think that, with the weapons I made for you, you would be able to wrestle with braves, with mighty warriors whose necks are strong?'

'When I am wielding them, men die in heaps.'

'The ones whom I sent to you, how are they?'

'They are exactly as you described them, and even better. In war they are no less than lions, they tear their adversaries to pieces. In times of peace Ndlebe surpasses even the diviners in smelling out the secret talk, to say nothing about Malunga because he stays at a place I do not even know.'

'In one word, tell me, have the things I have done satisfied you? Has none of them refused to happen the way I promised it would?'

'Your work has satisfied me to the fullest extent, and none of the things you promised refused to happen the way you had predicted. As a testimony to this, tomorrow is the day on which I am to be formally installed in the kingship of my father, I, that homeless wanderer whom you picked up yourself.'

'Very well, Chaka, I am very happy that my work has satisfied you, this will make you believe in me in future, because these things that you have seen, and the things you have achieved, are but trifles, for greater things are yet to come. But you must constantly remember the word which I have repeated to you three times down yonder when I said that the spear I made for you must do its work in the proper way. If you wish for kingship as great as that of Dingiswayo's, and even a hundredfold greater, if you seek the fame for which you were crying, let that spear remain covered with blood, fresh blood, not dried up. Besides, I told you that the medicines with which I inoculated you were ugly, and if you don't kill, they will turn against you and kill *you* instead; thus if today you think that you have killed enough, that you are satisfied with the kingship and the fame you have achieved, that you wish for nothing more, you must tell me at once, this very day, so that I may dilute the strength of the medicines that are in your blood in order that they may not kill you.'

In answer Chaka said: 'Isanusi, when I, Chaka, have resolved to do a thing, I am not able to turn back from it without having achieved its completion. I am still hungry, I am still seeking, I say let the cow's udder swell with milk, my master; I say work with all your strength and all your skill and take me to the very limits of your profound knowledge. As for this spear you are talking about, it will work till it's blunt, till it's covered to its very hilt with men's blood.' Isanusi and his servants laughed when Chaka said that. The questions Isanusi asked were aimed not so much at finding out how things stood with Chaka, but at making Chaka believe in him, and satisfy himself: what he says must happen the way he says it will; that is the law.

When they reached the village, Isanusi and his servants shut themselves up in the house because Dingiswayo had already arrived and they did not want to meet him because he hated them so intensely except for Ndlebe whom he considered to be an idiot, and to whom he paid little heed. When they parted, Isanusi instructed Chaka that the two of them should meet at Senzangakhona's grave at dead of night when Chaka would receive the blessings of his ancestors.

In the depth of night Chaka indeed went to his father's grave alone. As soon as he arrived there, he saw Isanusi and his servants emerging out of the darkness. There at the grave, in the middle of the night, Isanusi worked on Chaka with his medicines with much diligence. Most of the medicines were anointing ones. When he finished, he dug a little on Senzangakhona's grave and made a hollow which was not too deep, and he cradled himself in it and then began to speak in a language which Chaka did not understand. He spoke with much sadness in his heart, his voice full of emotion; he spoke not to Chaka but to those in the grave, and as he spoke the soil of the mound over the grave began to shake and tremble.

While these things were happening, Ndlebe got up and ran in a circle around the grave; as for Malunga, he stabbed the ground often with Chaka's spear, and each time he lifted it, he brandished it from side to side, pointing its sharp edge to the east, and then he would plunge it into the ground. On raising it again he would repeat the same action, pointing its sharp edge westwards, then northwards, then southwards, until he had finished all the four points of the earth. When he finished, he plunged that spear of Chaka's into the soil of his father's grave. Isanusi then kept completely quiet and sat on the grave like a fowl brooding on its eggs; Ndlebe stopped running round and came to stand near Malunga, huddled up like a rain-drenched hen. They were all quiet like that for a long time, and it was frightening there at the grave, enough to make one's flesh creep. Chaka heard something like the sound of a wind blowing far away, and at that very moment Isanusi spoke again with much more sadness than before, and his voice was small and humble, like someone in great distress making a supplication; then he paused, and as soon as he did so Ndlebe and Malunga started at the same time to sing a lament, a song of sorrow, and they sang it with more sadness than those carrying a dead person to the grave.

As they were singing that lament, Chaka heard a voice rising from under the depths of the soil, out of the grave, speaking in that same language that was spoken by Isanusi, and Isanusi continually responded to it. While Chaka listened in surprise, he constantly heard his name being mentioned even though he did not understand what was being said; he heard the name of a great-great ancestor of his being mentioned, and heard him respond; he heard the name of the one who succeeded that one also being mentioned, and he too responded, and so on up to his father, Senzangakhona. Isanusi spoke a little and then said: 'Senzangakhona', and then Chaka heard his father's voice speaking exactly as he knew it, as it was when he was still alive, even though he was speaking in a language Chaka did not understand. He was so frightened that he nearly fainted.

Isanusi spoke and responded to Senzangakhona twice or three times, and then he said : 'Chaka, pick up your spear and your stick and come here,' and when he came Isanusi said: 'Stand on top of me and listen as your father talks to you. You must just listen to what he says, but do not answer; and since you are not accustomed to communicate with the dead and to hear their voices, you will simply receive your father's blessings and then move off and go back to your place.'

Chaka stood on Isanusi holding his spear in his right hand, while in his left hand he held a stick; and then Isanusi spoke again in that same language, and when Senzangakhona answered he spoke in the language he had spoken while he was still alive among the people, which Chaka understood. At that same instant Ndlebe and Malunga stopped singing their song of sorrow, and they came near Chaka where he stood on top of Isanusi, and moved round him, singing a different song; but this time it was a song of joy, of thanksgiving, of someone giving thanks that his prayers have been heard. They sang it moving round him, but not following each other, but rather going in opposite directions, meeting along the way.

Senzangakhona spoke briefly, stating how it was he who appointed Chaka for the kingship on the day he was born, and how he pretended to reject him so that Chaka should know that kingship was obtained with difficulty, and in order that he should hold on to it firmly. He ended by saying: 'Chaka, my child, it is I, your father, talking to you, I am with my fathers and my grandfathers, and it is the desire of all of us that our combined kingship, the kingship of each one of us separately, should fall upon you, and be united there. May you be a powerful king who is not ruled; may you conquer all your enemies. May your shield protect you from your enemies' spears, and may your spear kill; may your nation pay you much respect and fear you. Be a *man*; be a king.'

At that point Isanusi shook himself like a fowl so that Chaka should step off him; Ndlebe and Malunga stopped walking round, and then clapped their hands pointing them towards the grave, and then they kept silent and listened. Then Isanusi spoke and said: 'Anoint Chaka's entire body with the medicine I gave you.' And

82

they anointed him, Isanusi meanwhile speaking unintelligibly in that same language which they did not understand, speaking haltingly like a cackling hen about to lay an egg. When they finished anointing him Isanusi said to them: 'Go home with that child of a king that he may assume the kingship he was given by his father. As for you, Chaka, go and take the kingship and set to work; you are only at the beginning of your task; you heard your father's order when he said that your shield must protect you from your enemies' spears, and that your spear must kill. Go and carry out those orders!' They departed leaving Isanusi at the grave. When he departed he went back to his home as if nothing concerned him any further.

It was early dawn when Chaka left his father's grave, and the cocks had crowed once, and then again, and the mountain chats were already chirping melodiously, and the dawn light was already visible, and the morning star was high in the sky, looking down at him with a face glowing with peace, and seeming to smile as it beheld him the way he was. The wind had died down, and it was perfectly still, as if all creation were paying homage to that moment when Chaka was returning from his father's grave. The three men walked without talking to each other, and without looking back, like someone carrying the sterility herbs; besides, they were walking fast so that the coming of day should not catch them before they reached home; and then when night finally fell to the ground, they entered their house in the village.

Those who saw him when he entered the village say that Chaka, when he returned from his father's grave, came riding on a horse with a smooth shining coat, led by an *intombazana*, a young maiden who surpassed all the maidens of the world in beauty. Many people swear that the *Inkosazana yeZulu*, the Sky Princess, first appeared on that day, and they say further that it was she in person who led the horse upon which Chaka was riding. Others surmise that it was Noliwa, and yet Noliwa had not yet arrived, for she only came after the cattle had been taken out to the pastures, and she came in the company of many people; there was no way in which she could be with Chaka at that time. Besides, that horse which he is said to have been riding is a mystery to us because there were still no horses at that time, for even the two which Dingiswayo had brought with him from the Colony had already died, so that even Dingiswayo himself came to these celebrations on foot. Yet, in spite of all that, those who saw Chaka say he came riding a horse, of that they have no doubt whatsoever.

The second mystery concerns that maiden: the question is where did she vanish since Chaka arrived at the village when the night was gone altogether, leaving no opportunity for that maiden to return unobserved to where she had come from, or to hide; besides, that is the only time we hear any mention of her, after this we do not hear any talk of her except only once, deep into Chaka's reign, when Noliwa herself was already dead.

The third mystery has to do with that horse itself: where did it go because, apart from the two horses which came with Dingiswayo, horses were first seen again in the most recent times, when the white people came.

CHAPTER FOURTEEN

CHAKA IS INSTALLED AS HIS FATHER'S SUCCESSOR

The sun rose on the day of Chaka's installation. Shortly after the cattle were taken to the pastures Noliwa arrived with her group, since she had been unable to come with Dingiswayo. When the throng had settled down, Chaka came out of the house where he had cloistered himself ever since his return from his father's grave in the night. Dingiswayo conducted the affairs of that day, and in all matters, he spoke the truth that was in his chest, not aiming at pleasing anyone, but speaking as only his conscience permitted; after all he had known the pain of a biting conscience, and did not wish to act again in a way that would give him a feeling of guilt. The councillors also spoke. At last Chaka was given his opportunity to address the crowd.

He stood up, the son of Senzangakhona, and he was dark brown in complexion, and was ripe and smooth, rousing admiration in all who saw him. The assembled nation, when they looked at him, saw in him a child of true royal blood born to rule and to reign over other people; and the people of his home felt moved as they remembered how they had rejected him without knowing the true worth of the one they were rejecting, and they saw that they nearly spited themselves by throwing away their king. The armies and the young men, when they looked at him, saw in him a beautiful young man with piercing eyes, with a powerful arm, ready to lift up the spear and the shield; and when they remembered that he was, in truth, the way he appeared, they loved him all the more. The kings, when they looked at him, saw in him a young king, a young shoot of great promise. The young women, when they looked at him, saw in him a gallant young man, more handsome by far than all other young men, one who was without blemish, a true brave, unquestionably superior to all his peers. All who saw him had no doubt this was a young man from a royal house, one accustomed to standing before large assemblies; they saw in him a commander born to lead large armies.

In stature Chaka stood tall, his shoulders higher than those of other people, but he was not lanky because he had a heavy-set body; his shoulders were broad. And yet even though to the eye he seemed so heavy, there was none to equal him in swiftness in running, in jumping, and turning sharply, and in dodging his adversary.

Chaka stood up in the midst of that multitude staring at him as if mesmerized, and then he spoke. He spoke briefly to the people of his home, asking them to receive him honestly with all their hearts, and let bygones be bygones which must be forgotten, so that they might all make a fresh start. He refrained from speaking too long, for fear that he might hurt the fresh wounds in their hearts caused by the recently fought battle in which Mfokazana was killed. Then he went on to talk about Dingiswayo. Here he spoke at great length relating how Dingiswayo had given him asylum, taken good care of him, and made him a human being again. He thanked him with words of praise and with a heart full of gratitude. He went on to emphasize that in rank he was Dingiswayo's subject, and that he was bound to honour and love him because of what he had done for him, and he begged that the king should, even after this day, continue to send him as he wished, and he would go. The king, he said, should use him as much as he pleased, for that is what he would love, since it would show that his king had not thrown him away.

As he spoke thus, Chaka's voice entered the hearts of those who were listening to him, and it was so convincing that even those who had the last vestiges of hatred in them abandoned it and opened the doors of their hearts for him with great joy. When Dingiswayo heard Chaka's confession regarding him, knowing that this was true, he loved him and trusted him all the more. To Nandi all these happenings were like a dream in the middle of the night. Noliwa, for her part, saw in Chaka's face beauty beyond description, which was not of this earth, which surpassed even that told of in fables. She saw in him the very perfection of manhood. The sound of his voice was to her a song more sweet by far than the tones of the stringed calabash or the singing bow. The crowd roared their applause saying: 'May the rains come! We are yours, O King, give us protection!'

On the following day Dingiswayo went back home, leaving Chaka a king in the place of his father. As for Noliwa and the younger people, they spent two more days at that place, and it was there that she and Chaka finally tied up their love affair. And then when all those who had come to the celebrations had left, Malunga began his work of strengthening the royal home with potent medicines, including the houses in which Chaka slept, the cattle folds and everything else that needed to be strengthened. Such was Chaka's return to his home from which he had been driven away.

After these events, Dingiswayo fought several wars alone, without inviting Chaka, so that he should become re-acquainted with his armies, and ensure that they should not, on feeling the heat of battle, open their ranks and leave him unprotected to be killed; nor should they one day conspire with the enemy and kill him. He called Chaka for the first time the day he went to attack Qwabe, returning with countless herds of captured cattle. In that battle the son of Senzangakhona distinguished himself in the eyes of his people who were seeing him for the first time in action. When they reached the royal place Chaka, instead of going back to his own place, stayed there at Dingiswayo's, amid crowds, where the spear never slumbered, where the young men became full of the lust for war when they heard their praises chanted. But he also stayed there in order to be near Noliwa. He spent all the time he was there among the regiments, teaching them all kinds of games; but above all he taught them unity, to act as one man, so that in all things they did there should be none who lagged behind or rushed forward. Knowing Chaka's disposition, Dingiswayo realized that he was reluctant to go home because he craved for war, and so, wishing to please him, he ordered an attack on the amaNgwane of Matiwane, and the regiments went to that war having been thoroughly trained and disciplined by Chaka.

The day before they were to meet the enemy, Chaka filled all the young warriors' hearts with determination, and each one went to war having resolved to fight harder than his peers so that he might distinguish himself in the eyes of the king and of Chaka. The amaNgwane were a very large nation, even though they weakened themselves by continually fighting among themselves, and thus made it possible for the enemy to take advantage of their disunity.

When Chaka finished talking to the warriors on the eve of battle, and went where he was to sleep, close to the king, he found that Ndlebe and Malunga were already there even though he had not called them. Malunga said: 'I have come to you on account of a matter which Ndlede will explain to you. I would not have come, for I have told you that I do not want to fight the wars of someone who hates me; but I have come on *your* account, not his, because even though the glory of victory will be his since the armies belong to him, that is a matter of no importance; as for you, what you will obtain through this war is something you will receive also on the day Dingiswayo dies.'

He asked whether Chaka had already spoken to the armies, and Chaka said he had; and then he said: 'It is unfortunate, because I had wanted to meet you before you marshalled your armies, but it is nothing, you will go again. I have brought you a medicine which you must chew before you speak to the armies, so that by the time you speak to them you have already chewed it, and it is in your mouth. That medicine will work wonders with your troops. It is called sweet-mouth.'

Ndlebe stood up full of life, being his undisguised self, and he said: 'I hear the sound of a great war, which is also but a minor war important only because of a momentous event which will take place in its wake, about which I will tell you the day we go back home.'

Malunga gave him the medicine and Chaka chewed it and kept on swallowing its juice, and then he went back to the armies. In the dead of night he came again to the troops and found some of them sleeping. He roused them and told them that that was not a time to sleep, but a time to be alert because it might happen that the enemy would fall upon them in their sleep. He said: 'My countrymen, I am very concerned, I am unable to sleep or feel peace in my heart. I have already told you that you are going to encounter real men, these ones you will fight tomorrow, and I say to you, you are to go there knowing fully well that you are going to your death. I say, he who is afraid had better go home right now, no one is being forced to stay; but he who decides to stay with us must be one who knows that he will not run away however hard it may be, one who is determined to die with his king or to win victory with him, but never to run away. What I most fear is to see men running away when the battle is too heavy for them, and their king is being captured. Remember Zwide. Those who are afraid, get up and go home!' None stood up. All those who heard him were full in their chests, and they cried, their tears rolling down their cheeks in the darkness of the night; they wondered what kind of war this was about which Chaka spoke with such gravity; they said: 'Where we have been ordered to go, there we will go, though it may be the place of dying.' Their lungs were lifted high with excitement, and they waited for dawn with much longing, wishing that the night would pass so that they might enter into the games, and also having resolved to fight in such a way that Chaka should never again have cause to talk to them in that manner.

As soon as it was light, the battle was joined with great severity. Matiwane's village was at the top of a rise, and the women and the old men were sitting outside the village watching the battle. Ndlebe went by a secret path to the back of the village and quickly set it alight, and his quick feet rapidly took him back to where the battle was raging.

Within a short time, when the amaNgwane heard the heart-rending cries from the village, they looked back, and they saw heavy smoke from their homes which were on fire, they saw their children and their women scattered on the plains and the hills fleeing in all directions, some running towards the forests, others to the ravines, others to the mountains; then their hearts became discouraged and their knees sagged, because a man whose children have been attacked by the enemy at once loses hope. At that point they ran to rescue their children.

Dingiswayo captured all of Matiwane's cattle as well as the small stock. At the place where they slept that night, as he was congratulating Chaka on his ingenious strategies, he repeated once again that Chaka should find a wife, and that he, Dingiswayo, would attend to all the formalities. Chaka answered him by saying that he had no thought of marriage; he stated that there was just one person he loved, but that she was most inaccessible, and he had no hope of getting her, so that he had actually given her up.

Dingiswayo: 'What do you mean by saying she is inaccessible?'

'That is to say she is the child of a very great king before whom I, Chaka, am but nothing.'

'Where is her home? Whose daughter is she?'

'Her home is at ... is at ... is at what-you-call-it....'

'Why do you keep on saying is at ... is at ... why do you find it difficult to talk? Is it my sister?'

'Yes, O King,' his forehead felt hot as he said so.

'Who?'

'Forgive me, O King, I fear even to mention her name, because she is one whom you love very much.'

'Is it Noliwa?'

'Yes, O King.'

'Have you already talked to her? I am not in a position to force her. You may talk to her: let her agree if she agrees, or refuse if she refuses. I want her to do exactly as her heart pleases.'

'If I may say so, she and I have already come to an agreement, O King.'

'O, I see. So you have just been afraid to ask for her hand. Very well. However, remember that if you marry my sister you are the one to give me cattle, because I cannot give you cattle as well as my sister.' The reader can imagine for himself how great was Chaka's joy on that day. Dingiswayo, like the sporting fellow he was, told all the warriors that Noliwa had become betrothed to Chaka, and they were greatly pleased, for they saw that Chaka was now going to belong to them fully, because a head of cattle is a great uniter of people.

When they arrived back at the royal village, Chaka heard that his mother was ill, and then he went on right away without even spending the night there, because his mother was a precious thing to him on account of what she had done for him. When they reached home Ndlebe said: 'I am receiving messages that tell me that Dingiswayo is not going to live for more than ten days from now. Be prepared. That is the matter I said I would tell you about on our return home.'

CHAPTER FIFTEEN

ZWIDE KILLS DINGISWAYO. CHAKA ACQUIRES DINGISWAYO'S KINGSHIP

When Dingiswayo reached home, he dismissed his regiments and dispersed his warriors so that they might go to their homes and rest. Zwide, having felt unhappy in his heart all this time because of the indignity of defeat, attacked Dingiswayo without warning. Dingiswayo only heard about it when Zwide was already at the Mfolozi River; and then he left home with the few warriors at hand and went to meet him, to prevent him from coming into his village. The alarm was sounded and the armies were quickly summoned to come to the king's place to join the battle. The few people Dingiswayo had were tired from the war against Matiwane, and from driving the cattle captured there; for that reason the battle was too heavy for them right from the beginning, with the result that King Dingiswayo was captured. When Zwide reached his home, he killed Dingiswayo,

severed his head, impaled it on a stick and had it taken to Dingiswayo's during the night. The messengers came there and planted
that stick at the council place, and leant his shield on the impaling
stick. And when the people came out of their houses next morning
they were cold with fright when they saw what had been done to
their king.

As soon as Chaka heard that Dingiswayo had been captured, he
tried all kinds of plans to save him: he sent messengers at great speed
to Zwide to beg him not to kill Dingiswayo, saying that he would pay
ransom for his release, whatever Zwide might demand that was to be
had on this earth, but those messengers of his never reached Zwide.
Ndlebe and Malunga were already at the royal village, and they
quickly spread the rumour that Dingiswayo had already been killed,
and yet at that time he had not yet been killed. For that reason the
messengers thought that going to Zwide's was of no further use.
Chaka came with all his warriors with surpassing speed, but when
he arrived at the royal village, he heard the painful news of the death
of Dingiswayo.

The armies had begun gathering at the royal place on the previous
day, the day on which the king was captured, and they continued
gathering until the next day dawned; and it was not only the armies,
but all men who still had strength to fight. Chaka stood there
stunned and lost, not knowing what to do. Because of this death of
his king he found that he had been left destitute and lost, abandoned
by the one he trusted, to whom he turned in times of trouble, and
through whom he had become a human being. He saw clearly that
the people who were not satisfied with his installation in the kingship
of his father would rise up in strength against him, now that the one
who had installed him was gone; and even among the king's armies
he realized that his commands were no longer going to be heeded.

Fearing that the day of his death was now close, Chaka went down
to the river, pulled a reed and peeled it, and then he called Isanusi
with his heart full of sadness. As he went up from the river, he was
even afraid to reach the village, to go among the people; he was also
anxious lest Isanusi should delay in coming until danger befell him.
When he reached the village, Ndlebe came to him covered with
mud, but exceedingly happy. He went into one of the houses with
Chaka, even though he was so full of joy that he was unable to talk,
but simply kept on stroking his battle axe and looking at Chaka

with much excitement. At that time there were heart-rending lamentations in the village, as the people cried for their king who had been killed by a jackal such as Zwide, while still so young besides.

Before Ndlebe had spoken, Malunga suddenly burst in, and he too was very happy, and his joy radiated through his skin. He said: 'Chaka, child of a king, I see that your heart is grieved. But this is no time to be despondent, it is a time for much rejoicing. Those who weep may weep, it is fitting that they should weep for their king. But *you* ought to rejoice because the death of one king is the beginning of the reign of the one who succeeds him and the one who will succeed Dingiswayo is you.' At that point Chaka began to feel his courage returning, and he gathered strength, because he knew that what he was told by Isanusi's servants always happened. Malunga went on to say: 'The day before yesterday I gave you a medicine to be chewed just before you go to address the regiments. It was for precisely this day that I prepared that medicine. The hearts of all the warriors who heard you on that day are clinging to you, and they will never agree to be commanded by anyone else but you. Speak, Ndlebe, I have finished.'

Ndlebe: 'Zwide is on the attack, he is on his way here, bringing a fearful multitude of people; his intention is to kill every man, woman and child so that the Bathethwa should be wiped off the face of the earth.'

At that very moment Isanusi suddenly burst into view among them, and he came in already talking: 'Let your courage rise, Chaka, I have come, and there is no manner of harm that can befall you. Ndlebe, go out and shout and spread the word among the crowds outside that Zwide is going to attack them early in the morning, and that they must get ready. Malunga, run and prepare the armies with medicines in the way you know, and quickly. You, Chaka, undress.'

Chaka's sadness and his fears were banished at once when Isanusi arrived; he was very happy and he undressed gladly, and Isanusi worked on him to prepare him for the important task which he was about to assume on that very night. Even before he finished working on him, the armies outside, on hearing that Zwide was once more on the move, made hurried efforts to find Chaka and to tell him that he was the one to whom they were looking for protection against their enemies.

Then when Isanusi finished, Chaka went out to where he was being clamoured for; and the armies spoke to him in a united voice saying: 'You are Dingiswayo, and all of us bestow on you his kingship and say to you please save us and fight for us, we are your people. We give you Dingiswayo's kingship in this manner with events moving fast as you yourself have no doubt heard. Zwide is coming in the early hours of the morning, and his intention is that not a single one of us should escape. Our eyes are turned towards you so that you may command these armies in the way you commanded them while their owner was still alive; you taught us and we listened and heard. Today we will listen to you not only as our commander, but also as our king. The one little matter we would like to get your word on is that you will truly marry Noliwa, as Dingiswayo had told us that you had asked for her in marriage, and that way we shall truly become one nation with yours.'

It was a time of extreme anxiety and everyone was in the grip of fear, when Dingiswayo's armies appointed Chaka as king, with rumours running wild and rampant, some saying Zwide, whose cruelty they all knew, had already arrived. The reader can imagine for himself what Chaka's feelings were that night, having hankered so much after kingship! His mood changed frequently following the changing pattern of events. He spent that night preparing the armies for the morning's encounter.

Zwide was attacking with a frighteningly large army, having conscripted even the old whose limbs were already too heavy for them, who went only because of their greed for cattle, as well as the very young ones, novices who were handling their spears and going to war for the first time, who were trusting only to the nimbleness and swiftness of their youth to capture the enemy's cattle, since they expected no opposition because the Bathethwa had no king.

When Zwide crossed the Mfolozi-Mhlophe, opposite the Mbelebeleni, Chaka ordered all the seasoned warriors as well as the younger ones to the attack, leaving only the regiments; and since he realized that Zwide's men were far superior to his in numbers, he ordered that the villages be burnt, as well as the sorghum and maize; some men accompanied the women and the children in driving the cattle to a place of safety. The battle raged, and Zwide was forced back to the other side of the river, and then Chaka's people started to follow their king. It was a running battle that lasted three days.

Chaka's aim was to make Zwide's armies succumb to hunger in the end, because in those days they did not carry provisions; that was why he burned the sorghum and the maize so that Zwide's people should have nothing to eat.

On the third day he told himself that hunger must by now have played havoc among the enemy, and he prepared to launch an offensive. On that night he slaughtered many cattle, and there was much feasting among his armies; he slaughtered them with a vengeance so that, if they were defeated, Zwide should have nothing to capture, whereas if *he* won he would capture Zwide's cattle. On that same night Isanusi went to drag evil medicines across the path of Zwide's armies. As dawn approached, Senzangakhona's young man dilated his nostrils, catching the scent of war even while it was yet far off; he threw his eyes into the darkness, and continually walked back and forth with impatience, and the warriors were consumed with war-lust when they saw him in that state. When he spoke to them his voice carried amazing power, so that when he gave his commands, each warrior took a vow in his heart saying: 'I will do it and if I fail, I will die trying to carry out that order.'

The night relentlessly came to an end, and when the sun rose it revealed Zwide's men where they lay covering the entire plateau where they had spent the night; there was nothing to see but people, like the rolling shadows of dark clouds, or endless stretches of dense forests. As soon as the sun came out of the soil Chaka got up, looked this way and that, lifted his short-handled spear which had been doctored with snake poisons, and the commanders of the regiments gathered around him. At once, in the twinkling of an eye, a storm began to rage in his countenance even as they watched him, he turned pitch black, his eyes became red as blood, and from his nose oozed perspiration which was as white as milk, and it stood there in little droplets. He ordered to the attack all the men and the young men not mobilized into regiments, they were the first to fight. As soon as these began to engage Zwide, Chaka attacked with two battalions sending them to the right-hand side of the mountain, and simultaneously with two others on the left-hand side, and all these met at the back of Zwide's armies, encircling them. The frail old men and the unseasoned young men of Zwide's, seeing the enemy give battle contrary to their expectations, ran helter skelter.

When the flanks of those battalions met, Chaka once again raised his spear pointing it at the enemy, and he stood quiet for a long time, looking in their direction. All he could hear was the sound of the spears as they constantly tore into the flesh of the combatants, as well as the groans of the dying as he watched his people dying and being reduced in number. After what seemed a long time he said: 'There is your enemy, the very one that killed Dingiswayo! Go, then, and destroy him!' and then he sent all the remaining regiments into the fray, and he remained only with Isanusi. Chaka had ordered his men on that day not to throw their spears, but to kill spear in hand. The battle now raged most violently, and before an hour had passed, the ground was completely covered with the bodies of the dead; the regiments retreated and then rushed back at each other, and when they retreated a second time, Zwide's slain were equal to those still alive. How effectively Malunga and Ndlebe worked that day! How efficient the spear that stabbed at close range!

As the morning advanced and the cattle began to get used to the pastures, Isanusi could not contain himself any longer, and he left Chaka alone on the side of the mountain and ran into the battle. He grabbed his shield by its handle, and even as he joined the battle, people began to fall at an amazing speed; his servants then came and fought on either side of him, and they mowed down the enemy in a frightening manner. Towards mid-day Chaka ran and joined the battle, and when his warriors saw him their courage rose once more, and they fought like men.

Zwide escaped by sheer miracle; Chaka pursued him until he crossed back to the other side of the river, and then came back. On the following day he pursued him farther right into his village, at Nongoma. The women at this place had stayed behind gathering piles of firewood in order to cook the meat of the Bathethwa's cattle when their men returned; but now when they saw Zwide coming back in flight with only a few of his men, they were badly shaken. And then when Chaka's armies appeared, a great wailing arose at Nongoma, the wailing of the women, the children and the old people pleading not to be left behind when everybody was running away.

Chaka chased Zwide, continually killing his people, and routed him out of his village, and Zwide fled to Pediland where, shortly after his arrival, he died both from fatigue and from shock at seeing that large nation of his not only scattered, but indeed destroyed, in just one day. Chaka ordered that all of Zwide's people, men, women

95

and children, be killed, and only the young men be spared. Then when he returned from chasing Zwide, he summoned together all Zwide's young men who had escaped, and he incorporated them into his armies, rather than kill them.

When the battle of that day began at sunrise, Zwide's men were countless in number. Chaka started the day with ten regiments without counting the men and the youths, and Zwide with seventeen regiments without counting the men and the youths. A regiment consisted of two thousand people, yet when the sun set on that day all of Zwide's regiments had been turned into corpses, and only three of Chaka's had survived; that is to say that more than forty thousand people died on that day.

When the sun rose on that day there was no nation greater than Zwide's in strength and in the number of its people, but when it set that large nation had been wiped off the face of the earth, and its villages had been turned into ruins.

I do not believe that there was ever a human being whose life was as full of mystery as that of Chaka. Dingiswayo's life was full of darkness and secrecy, but these could be unravelled and be made intelligible; but Chaka's life has been cloaked in dark mystery until this very day. Just a few days before he was trembling one evening when he heard the report of the death of Dingiswayo, his protector, and he was afraid he would be assassinated or deprived of the kingship which he had worked so hard to obtain. Yet that same night found him active, going from here to there, surrounded by large armies which had appointed him king and commander, being the only one they considered suitable among all those crowds of people. The following day found him in command of all the armies, commanding them as his own, and not as someone else's property; and now as today's sun goes towards its setting, he is a king, a victor who has just scattered a nation greater than his own in strength; as it goes to its setting, he is the king of kings, and the nations tremble before him. To show how other nations trembled in fear of him, Matiwane, on hearing how Chaka had routed Zwide whose nation had been so large, took to his heels and only stopped when he reached the Maloti mountains.

CHAPTER SIXTEEN
THE NEW NATIONAL NAME

Isanusi and his servants were sitting with Chaka, talking about the past events in his life. Isanusi said: 'Things have changed a great deal now, Chaka; you are Chaka the king, you are no longer like Chaka that lonely homeless vagabond whom I picked up under a tree. A few days ago you called me because you were in the grip of anxiety, but today those whom you feared are the ones who live in anxiety, in fear of you!'

Chaka: 'It was not without reason that I was so afraid; times were bad, and there was much uncertainty when I called you. But tell me, where were you at the time I called you, and how did you manage to arrive on the evening of that same day when your home is so far, far away as you yourself have told me?'

'When you called me I was already on the way because I had already divined that you would be faced with serious problems this month or, let me say, on that very day.'

'Who told you since Ndlebe and Malunga, the only people who know where you live, were here with me all the time?'

'I am Isanusi the Diviner, remember!'

At that point Chaka simply scratched his head in embarrassment, and then changed the subject, saying that Zwide was a coward to have killed Dingiswayo because he, Chaka, had sent word that he should not be killed for he would pay his ransom. Isanusi asked: 'Where would you have obtained so many cattle since you don't have any that belong to you?'

'I would have taken the very ones belonging to Dingiswayo, and paid his ransom with his own cattle; and if they were not enough, the people would have to pay a levy in order to ransom their king.'

'How did Zwide answer you?'

'He never answered me to this very day; I arrived here at the royal village to be met with rumours that the king had already been killed, even though I have since heard that he had not yet been killed at that time.'

Ndlebe and Malunga spoke at the same time saying: 'Your messengers were stopped by us, and it was we who spread the rumour that Dingiswayo had already been killed, even though at that time he had not yet been killed.'

Chaka was greatly surprised when he heard them confessing this, and he asked their reason, and they said: 'You will remember that we are here on *your* account, we have come here to obtain kingship for you, and we want you to acquire it soon, after which we would like to obtain the cattle for our payment and return home. However, if your messengers had reached Zwide, perhaps Dingiswayo might not have been killed; which is to say that you would not yet be king. But now you *are* a king with no one superior to you, while you are the superior of others, even though you have not yet reached kingship of the stature that Isanusi tells us you are craving for. Today, however, we promise ourselves that things are going to be much easier, because the decision is entirely in your own hands.' When Chaka heard these things, he was greatly surprised at the way in which these men had dedicated their lives to serving him.

Isanusi: 'I understand that you are betrothed to Noliwa. Tell me, do you want to marry her?'

'I love her with all my heart, and I will marry her. But also I am bound to marry her, even if I did not wish to, because I have promised Dingiswayo's armies that I would.'

'But if they had not bound you with that promise, what were you going to do?'

'I would still have wished to marry her because I love her, and, after all, they spoke to me in that manner after I had already become betrothed to her.'

'If I were you I would not marry. Marriage splits kingdoms apart, because it always leads to quarrels in one's house. You may remember the quarrels in your own father's house. The children of one man fight, instead of loving each other, and blood flows as they kill each other. The best thing is that a person, especially a king, should marry when he begins to go grey, so that he will die of old age by the time his sons become young men, thus preventing such incidents as took place among the sons of Jobe, and also in order that there should be only one king, and not many, because if a king has many sons, the kingship of his heir is correspondingly weakened. But these are your own affairs which do not concern us at all, and we were merely making a suggestion.' Isanusi spoke these words like one who was merely jesting, yet they became a seed which began to grow in Chaka's heart, especially since he had never really been very fond of women.

Isanusi continued, saying: 'Chaka, I shall soon be going away, I don't have much time because I always have many engagements. You will remain with my servants: trust them and they will trust you, love them and they will love you. Ndlebe's most important role will be to sniff out the gossip and the secrets for you; there is no evil plot that can be hatched and take root without him knowing about it, even if it were to be discussed in an ant-bear's hole, I swear. Malunga's main duty will be to prepare your armies with medicines when you are going to war; he has the right medicines for that purpose, and your armies will never suffer defeat, not even on a single day, if they have been doctored by him. But before I depart, I want to ask you only one question, and you must answer me suitably after giving thought to the matter, and without feeling rushed. The day I found you in the wilderness yonder you were crying for the kingship of your father which had slipped out of your grip because of your stepmothers; secondly you wanted fame. I have now obtained those two things for you. Afterwards you said, if I could make you a king of the stature of Dingiswayo, who is not ruled by others, you would be very happy, and then I said to you that if you wished, I could make you a king even greater than Dingiswayo, and now this has happened. My question is this: Are you now satisfied, or do you still want something beyond that?'

'I understand your first question, Isanusi, and I will answer it in a moment; the one I do not quite understand is the second one, because you ask as if there were still something greater you could obtain for me if I had greater aspirations!'

'That is so.'

'Are you saying that you are able to obtain for me blessings greater than the ones I have already received, and greater kingship than I already have?' Chaka asked in surprise because a kingship surpassing his was unknown in those days.

Instead of answering immediately Isanusi showed a disappointed countenance, and he looked at Chaka with sadness and said: 'What is painful to me is that it is now several years that I have been working with you, and in that time I have never on a single occasion deceived you by claiming to be able to do something I could not do; yet in spite of all that you still talk like someone who does not know me.'

'Forgive me if I have offended you, I spoke those words purely out of surprise. And now therefore I say, work, master, and take me to the very limits of your wisdom and your strength.'

'Are you, then, still seeking kingship and fame greater than those you now have?'

'Yes.'

'Very well then, I have heard you; but you realize, of course, that the payment due to me is also getting bigger: for a kingship such as your father had, and which you have inherited, you owe me a full fee for my professional services as a doctor; for a kingship of the stature you have now obtained, that fee is doubled; for greater kingship than this, it is three times that fee. It is a high fee, even though to a king it is but nothing.'

'Payment is nothing to me, there is nothing I would spare as long as you take me to the things I desire.'

'I shall leave instructions with my servants to arrange these matters for you. I, for my part, will tell you the entire truth, and that is, that there is a sense in which it is quite difficult to obtain the kingship you want, such as will give you territory so big that, if a man started from here where you are, as a young man going to the ends of your empire, he would walk until he grew old before he returned. It is quite difficult, because the medicine for obtaining that must come from you, not from me; and perhaps you might be unable to procure such medicine and place it in the hands of us, the doctors. If you are afraid, there is, of course, nothing I can do.'

'What sort of medicine is that which I, Chaka, would be afraid to give you if I knew where to find it?'

'I say that it is difficult because if you want such a kingship, every time you go to meet the enemy, your warriors must eat food mixed with medicines containing the blood of someone you love most dearly, one who is constantly in your thoughts, who is in your heart day and night, whom you love more than all the people in this entire world. It is by means of the blood of such a person that you can obtain the kind of kingship I have just described: I know no other way besides that one. I know of one king in my country who strengthened his royal city with the blood of his first-born son when he was seeking a kingship of this nature, and he fortified the city gates with the blood of his last-born son; which meant that he was left without children. Now you may ponder over this matter, and then tell me what is your wish.'

Chaka tried to answer, but Isanusi stopped him with a wave of his hand, and insisted that he should think seriously first and not be in a hurry. Then he moved away from him, and returned after a while, and said: 'Have you given this matter your most serious consideration?' Chaka agreed. Then Isanusi said: 'Speak then, so that we may hear what you have decided.'

'I, Chaka, do not ponder long over a problem. I have decided in favour of the kingship you have just described; I only regret that I do not have any children, I do not know whether the blood of my mother or of my brothers would be suitable. If it is suitable, I shall let you have it so that you may mix those medicines of yours.'

'But among these whom you have mentioned there is none whom you love with the love I have just described, that one you have left out. Please think of that one, and then tell us your truest wish.'

'Apart from those, the one whom I love is Noliwa....'

'Very well then. Think well and decide which you will choose: the kingship you now have which you may enjoy in the company of Noliwa, and the one which surpasses it, but without Noliwa. To make this quite clear to you let me tell you that there *is* a kingship which surpasses what you have by far, but you cannot obtain it without killing Noliwa, you, Chaka, with your own hand.' Isanusi laughed and said: 'Today, Chaka, we are teaching you witchcraft, how sorcerers kill their own children or their parents in order to ensure that they shall be efficient in their sorcery.' Isanusi once more laughed like one who was joking, and then he said once again to Chaka that he must think about the matter for that whole day and give him an answer in the evening.

Chaka, when he was all by himself and thought about Noliwa, and about the kingship just described, found that Noliwa was as nothing, and he further told himself that in a kingdom so big he would, without a doubt, find many beautiful girls, or even one more beautiful by far than Noliwa. For that reason he decided to make her the most efficacious component of his medicines. As soon as they met that evening Chaka said: 'To tell you the truth, in this world there isn't anything I love other than kingship, war, and commanding armies. Therefore I will give you Noliwa in order to remove any stumbling block from the path leading to my kingship. I have considered this matter and concluded: the medicines will be mixed with Noliwa's blood.'

Isanusi and his servants were quiet until Chaka finished speaking. Only then did Isanusi say: 'I believe, Chaka, that you heard me when I said I am not binding you to do anything, but am leaving the decision entirely up to you, because we doctors simply give a person the medicine he wants, even though it may be one that kills. *We* are mere barterers, accepting no responsibility; we are mere traders, we want cattle for our medicines, and it is the person we serve who must choose the medicine he wants. You must understand that there is neither force nor compulsion; you are to act according to the wishes of your own heart.'

'I have heard you well, you have told me the price of that kingship, and now I am deciding on my own to buy it myself, because I like it.'

But in spite of that, Isanusi refused to have the work begun immediately, saying that Chaka had not yet weighed the matter carefully enough; and then he gave him a full year in which to let his thoughts settle, so that he should not change his mind when the work had already been done, when it would be of no further use. But Chaka pleaded, saying that that time was too long and should be shortened, so they agreed on nine months.

When Isanusi was on the point of leaving he said: 'Here is a little matter which I nearly forgot to mention: since the name of your nation is so ugly why don't you abandon it, Chaka, and find yourself a beautiful one with a pleasing sound, one suitable for a king like you and a nation such as yours?'

'Such as?'

'You can find one for yourself; do you think that even national names must be obtained from doctors? These are matters for the kings to decide. However, this one you have now is disgraceful.'

Chaka agreed that the one they had was ugly and disgraceful, and at that very moment, there was a low rumbling of thunder to the west, in the direction of the Maloti mountains where it was raining at that time. Chaka heard that rumbling and took note of it; Isanusi also heard it. Then Chaka looked up in the sky and began to laugh, saying at the same time: 'You speak the truth, Isanusi. Today I shall find for myself a beautiful national name, which no nation ever had before.'

'What is it?' asked Isanusi. Chaka laughed loudly until the tears streamed out of his eyes, and yet as a rule he was not a man who laughed a lot. He then said: *'Zulu! Mazulu!'* (the sky, people of the sky). Isanusi and his servants broke into fits of laughter and then Isanusi asked: 'Why do you choose a name like that?' 'Mazulu! It is because I am big, I am like that same cloud that just rumbled, before which no one can stand. Likewise, when I look upon other nations, they tremble, and the one upon whom I pounce is wiped out, like Zwide. Zulu! Mazulu!' All of them laughed once more, greatly surprised; and we too are surprised and wonder how great were the desires and the impudence in the heart of this Mokone that he compared himself to the greatness of the heavens! 'Zulu! Mazulu!' Isanusi went away repeating that name over and over.

Before the men who had served in the war had scattered and gone to their various homes, Chaka told them the new, beautiful-sounding national name which he had found for them, namely, Mazulu. He said that now they had conquered all their enemies, and that was why he had chosen for them that beautiful name.

All the men and all the regiments applauded loudly, an indication that they were happy with the new name.

We have already mentioned that Chaka, while he was still at his home, was the subject of evil gossip, and was said to be someone who was not quite like other human beings, and that he had been sired by a *tikoloshe*, an evil genie, and that that was why Senzangakhona chased him away together with his mother. Now that he was king, the people once again began to talk about him, but this time they were saying beautiful things. The beauty of his face, and his impressive tall stature, and his heart that was afraid of nothing, as well as the manner in which he marshalled the armies in war—these things were taken as an indication that Chaka had been sent by the gods among the people; it was said that the heart that was in Chaka, and the spirit that was in him, were not those of ordinary mortals, but were the heart and the spirit of Nkulunkulu himself.

On the evening of the day on which Zwide was vanquished, the talk in the mouths of the regiments and the young men and the women went like this: 'None but Chaka could do that! Those who would fight him had better first fight with the gods and conquer them, and then only should they dare to face him!' We have also told about Noliwa. And now there grew around these two people who were about to get married, the legend that they were the messengers of Nkulunkulu.

When Ndlebe and Malunga heard this, they confirmed those rumours, saying that Chaka had been sent by Nkulunkulu to come and teach his children the art of war, and their statements were easily believed, because those thoughts were already there in the hearts of the people. Chaka's spear also helped to confirm that belief because its handle had been made from timber that had been fortified with medicines of witchcraft, and was thus full of evil power, and it performed wonders. The national name Mazulu also strengthened the belief that Chaka was not a mortal being. Chaka and Noliwa were worshipped, and people knelt before them, and this pleased Chaka, but Noliwa for her part was embarrassed because she knew that she was just a human being who was like all other human beings.

The matter of their wedding became a big problem because it was not clear who would be in charge of the festivities, and who should receive the *bohadi* cattle, since all those who were suitable for these duties were in their graves. For this reason the wedding was delayed, and that delay pleased Chaka because of his plot with Isanusi.

CHAPTER SEVENTEEN

THE REFORMS AND CHANGES
BROUGHT ABOUT BY CHAKA

Before we proceed further with the story of Chaka's rule, we ought to describe briefly the state of the Bathethwa nation when Dingiswayo came and took over the kingship, and where it stood at the time of his death.

Dingiswayo arrived and became king at a time when his nation was in pitch black darkness, when the men simply sat at home without doing any work, and were therefore unable to acquire cattle. He came and changed all that. He brought together those who knew how to tan skins and to make blankets from skins and hides, and he built for them a workplace where they did their work, where these skins were sold, and that place soon turned into something like a super-store where blankets were sold. He did the same for the carvers of wood and horns, and he encouraged them in their trades by giving prizes to those whose work was superior to the rest; and that way the nation was greatly inspired to engage in trade, and not only to produce goods, but also to work neatly, with an eye to beauty. Even the farmer who produced more sorghum than others over the seasons was given a prize in recognition of his excellence in farming. Dingiswayo even opened up a trade route leading to Delagoa Bay, where trade flourished. The women also strove to mould beautiful pots, ones of which they were proud, because they were eager to win prizes. He also tried hard to instil in the nation the spirit of human compassion, so that they might refrain from attacking each other for no reason; here, however, he failed, and it was clear that he was teaching them something that was above their understanding by far, something strange and unknown to them. The land basked in the warmth of peace and of plenty in the days of his reign; and Chaka assumed the kingship when the affairs of the nation were in that state.

After changing the national name, Chaka brought together the young men from Zwide's scattered nation, as well as those from nations who owed allegiance to him, and he said to them: 'Today you have no king of your own any more, nor are you any longer a nation; besides, you deserve to be killed because you killed my king, Dingiswayo, who always treated you with compassion, but I will not kill you against your wishes. I place before you two alternatives so that you may choose for yourselves: if you give up your national name as well as your language, and join my regiments, and become Zulus, then you shall live; if you refuse, then I will kill you all, and that no later than today, in fact at this very moment, as soon as I have heard your answer.' They found it the easiest thing on earth to decide to join Chaka's regiments so that they might live. Chaka mingled them with the Zulus, especially so that they might become Zulus in their hearts; and he then chose some of his headmen to keep watch over Zwide's country.

Chaka, right from his childhood, did not have many wishes; his desire was for one thing only: kingship and fame. Now he is very famous and he is a great king. Is it possible that he will be satisfied? Never! Now his greed has been aroused, and he is in search of something which even he himself does not know. Now Chaka was able to decide on matters of war without anything standing in his way, he alone having the power to do as he wished. He looked upon all the nations to the north, up to places which even he did not know, and he longed to see his kingdom stretch till it reached those very places which he did not know. He looked upon those nations settled along the sea and stretching to the south, and he saw the villages and the hamlets; great kings and small, the country adorned with villages built on the foundation of peace, and he smiled to himself. He cast his eyes beyond the Maloti mountains and looked towards the west, and he saw the nations of the Basotho and the Batswana living peacefully, not troubled by anything, and then he laughed and even talked to himself saying: 'My kingdom will begin right here where I am, and spread along the breadth of the earth, till it reaches its very ends. There will be but one king, not many, and that king will be me!' And when he said so, he was filled with overflowing joy, and his youthful blood raced in his veins, and he wished he could change everything at that very moment. At that time his thoughts were so preoccupied with kingship that he even forgot about Noliwa.

In the first place, Chaka built for himself a royal city which was called Mgungundhlovu (great as an elephant), in recognition of the frightening power of its owner.

Chaka built this royal city south of the big river called Mfolozi, that is to say where the Black Mfolozi was already joined together with the White Mfolozi, to the north of the Mhlathuze River. He chose this site because of its abundant water supply so that a city of that size should be adequately supplied; and also for its large forests, so that timber and firewood should be obtainable close by; and finally because of the natural beauty of that place.

Basotho kings are used to building their villages on mountain tops or on the flanks of the mountains or near natural fortresses such as a rocky ledge. Chaka, on the other hand, built his city on level, but slightly sloping, ground.

It was a city of immense size, unequalled among all nations past and present in sheer bigness and the number of its inhabitants, as well as the power of its owner. It was circular in shape and was built as follows:

A great road, wide enough for crowds of people, armies or cattle to walk in it without being squeezed tight, divided that large city in half, running from east to west. A second road, identical with that one, divided the city from south to north. Those two roads were perfectly straight, and were built with much care, showing that their owner was a very particular person. There were many other smaller roads running through the city, and we are simply singling out those two because they were used by the king and by crowds of people.

In the centre of the city was a large, well-paved and firmly stamped down square. That is where the regiments held their games; that is where the regiments which were about to go out to battle received orders from the king, and saluted him; that is where the regiments returning from war met the king in order to greet him and give him an account of the campaigns they had just concluded, and also in order that the king might see how many of them had come back. That is where the captured cattle stood so that the king, as well as the assembled people, might see them. Cattle came to this square in large numbers. It was in that very place that important national festivals were held. It was in that very square that many momentous events in Chaka's reign took place, and all the high points in his life were celebrated there as they happened.

To the east of that square, but on the southern side of the eastward-bound road were the king's trusted men as well as his councillors and his doctors; that is where Ndlebe's house was situated. Close to that spot stood the cattle fold of Chaka's own cattle, which comprised milk cows, slaughter cattle, race oxen, and also cattle chosen for their beauty, to be displayed on festive occasions, that is to say those which were outstanding in the beauty of their horn shapes and their colours. These were prized cattle and well trained so that they knew their praises and recognized their herders.

Near this fold was a large enclosure surrounded by a pole fence; this enclosure was the king's court. It had two entrances where two or three fully armed warriors stood guard night and day, and no one could enter, nor could anyone go out, without their permission. When Chaka was present in the court, everyone who entered had to shout greetings, with his spear and shield and cloak left with the guards at the entrance; he would then have to prostrate himself, and come forward creeping on his stomach; and then when he was half-way across the court, he would have to shout the royal greeting '*Bayede*'; and then at the conclusion of his greeting, his forehead had actually to touch the ground, and he would have to lie stretched out like that without any covering on his body till it should please the king to accept his greeting, and to allow him to stand up, at which point he could once again drape his cloak around him. It was at this very court that Chaka received kings through their emissaries, and that events of extraordinary magnitude took place.

At the second entrance to this court stood a very high sentinel post on top of which the village sentinel sat day and night so that he might see anything coming towards the city while it was yet far off, and shout a warning to the councillors to pass the word to the king: 'I see a person, or several people, coming from such and such an approach.' And at that very moment one or more people would be dispatched to go and meet the strangers while they were still a long way from the city, and find out who they were and what their mission was; and anyone who might by chance arrive at the city gates without having been seen and met was killed without any question. On his return, the runner would tell the king who the strangers were and what brought them there, and at that point sentinels at the city gates (not the gates to the royal court) would be informed so that the strangers might be allowed to enter, and only then would they be escorted to the gates of the court.

No one was allowed to enter the city at night except the king's runners and messengers; but even they had to make signals, known to the sentinel sitting on his post, with lighted wooden torches, and only then would the sentinel tell those on night guard duty inside the court that such and such a royal runner was coming, and then they would go and inform the king, and then he would give the order for the guards to let him in. The runner would then sit there in the court until the king was pleased to recognize his presence, and sent to know what his message was.

From the court there was a wide enclosed walk in which four men could walk abreast, which led to Chaka's own personal dwelling called 'Ntukulu' (great house). Anyone who dared to walk there without having been summoned by two different messengers, was killed with a death more painful by far than that of the spear. Ntukulu was big, exactly as its name says, and its walls consisted of stout poles planted in the ground over which there was a thatch. Only a few people entered this house; it was the king's own abode where no one entered, and therefore the things that took place there were not known. The handful of people who were known to enter there were Ndlebe, Malunga and Isanusi, and just a few others. It was in this house that the king's medicine pot and the little royal stone were kept. Ten warriors guarded it night and day, when Chaka was present and when he was not, even when he was away in battle; and they were fully armed.

Behind that house of the king's was a long row of houses in which the king's women lived. But Chaka had no wife, he never married. Instead he chose for himself the most beautiful girls in the nation, who were well built and smooth and brown like the cannabis seed; the ones with beautiful bodies and perfect poise, and he kept bringing them into those houses. He called them his sisters, which meant they were ones with whom he could have no carnal contact, and yet they were the very ones whom he continually visited; he ate the young fruit of other men's daughters, picking the very flower of their youth, and then when they became too worn out to please him, he would pass them on to his councillors, if they were still alive. We shall tell later of the way in which many of them met their end.

The second and third sections of the city were occupied by the people living in the royal city. The fourth section was allotted to the city regiment, as well as to the young men of the court whose duty it was to execute those who were condemned to die.

That large city was encircled by a fence of poles which were planted in the ground, and at every entrance were warriors who refused anyone entry or exit without the king's permission.

When Chaka's kingdom was already firmly established, he did not pay his regiments regular early morning visits as he had done before. During the night he used to walk in the city to see whether the watchmen were keeping proper watch, and then he would return to his house at early dawn; and then, when the sun began to get warm, he would come out of his house with Mbopha and his group of men walking in front of him to escort him to the court, so that the people might know that the king was coming. Then all those in the court would get up, and as soon as Chaka appeared, they would greet him with the royal greeting, with their heads bowed close to the ground until the king received their greeting.

On leaving the court he would go to the cattle fold, at milking time. When the calves were let loose for suckling, the cows would bellow, others belched, while their herders chanted their praises. Often they were deliberately made to sleep without being milked by the herdboys so that they should bellow a lot on the following morning. At that same time the shepherds and goatherds would also let the lambs and the kids go to their mothers, and in the midst of that din of the sheep and the cattle, the chief herdboy would then praise the king indirectly through chanting praises appropriate to the cattle, which go: 'Mooing bovine, fit to bellow in the royal village, if it bellows in a lesser village it is not fitting ... god with the wet nose, who causes quarrels among the nations!' And then he would end by saying: '*Bayede*, O King! The cattle of Zululand praise you, they greet you, you who are the heaven that gives rain and pastures. The sheep and the goats of Zululand praise you, you to whom they owe their existence. All the living creatures of Zululand praise you, you who were belched forth by a bovine, who are belched forth by a bovine!' Then Chaka's heart would be filled with joy to overflowing when he was being praised even by the animals of the veld.

When he left this place he would go to the square where the

regiments were, in order to greet the people of his city, or rather to be greeted by the people of his city, and by the city regiment. The greetings he received here in the square were extremely pleasing since they were performed in the presence of everybody, in a place frequented by all the people of the city.

Afterwards the king would visit Ntombazi, the city sector occupied by his 'sisters'. The greetings from this section of the city surpassed all others in sweetness for they were made out of love, and their words were meant to flatter:

Mntwanamuhle, Mhlekazi
Uteku lwabafazi bakwaNomgabi!
Ababelutekula behlezi emilovini!

(Beautiful child, Most Excellent One!
Sport of the women of Nomgabi!
Of which they made fun as they basked in the sun.)

He was praised in that teasing manner: *Uteku lwabafazi bak-waNomgabi* means 'Sea of the women of Nomgabi'; *Ababelutekula behlezi emilovini* means 'Which they fondled, or played with, while they lived with happiness, contentment and peace in their hearts'.

Before we end our description of this city, we should state that Chaka was in the habit of walking in this section disrobed of his skin kaross, wearing only his fringe skirt. This he did at the request of his 'sisters' so that they might feed their eyes on his beautiful body, because Chaka was a strikingly beautiful man. He was taller than anyone in his entire nation, yet he was not lanky, since his height was offset by a heavy frame. From his feet to his head he was without blemish, a truly handsome and dignified man.

Even on the battlefield his men, when wounded and about to die, would request the king, as their last wish, to disrobe so that they might admire his body for the last time, and thus die in peace; and he would, indeed, do as they asked.

At the time in Chaka's life which we are describing here, there was truly no king on earth whose people loved him as much as this one. On days of national festivities, it was the custom that, before the people dispersed to their homes, the king would disrobe, so that the nation might conclude its festivities by admiring the body of their lord.

Chaka also built many military villages because so many people could not all stay in one place. He released Dingiswayo's regiments saying: 'As for you, I have trained you enough, and you may now take your rest; I shall call upon you when I am ready to go out to attack.' He put the remaining ones through a rigorous training programme; he taught them fighting strategies: how to attack, retreat and then suddenly renew the assault; he taught them how to dance smartly, moving in unison with no one going too fast or too slowly: they turned and threw their bodies to one side all at the same time. He taught them some beautiful war games which were impressive to watch. Above all he taught them obedience, so that when they were given orders they did not answer back, nor did they ask the reason why, but simply did as they were told. He also composed many beautiful songs and praises, which made the warriors weep when they heard them, for they roused in them strange emotions.

Every day he got up at dawn, earlier than the fowl resting on its perch, and the first cock-crow would find him already among his regiments which he had stretched out into straight lines, or bunched up in a tight group around him. Malunga also got up at early dawn, long before the dawn light reddened the eastern sky, and since Chaka had no wife, he would be the one to carry the king's personal medicine pot. Every morning he went to examine the cattle which were slaughtered for the regiments, and he would add potions to that meat so that those who ate it should obey their leader with unquestioning obedience; and then he would add another medicine which hardened their hearts so that they should be completely devoid of mercy.

Secondly, Chaka abolished circumcision, saying that it was useless, and that it served only to waste the time which the boys could have spent learning the art of war. He therefore had two types of regiment: ones comprising mature young men, true wielders of the shield who had fought in the wars, and the others consisting of boys who were being taught how to fight. As soon as a male child began to grow strong, he would at once be taken to the regiments where he would be taught true manhood. Day after day that child would not see his parents or come in contact with women; instead he would be in the company of other boys from morning till evening. Their speech was all about war, their conversations were about war, their songs and praises were about war, their games were about war, even the manner of their eating was related to war. That is to say that all the things they heard, all the things they saw, all the things they did, were matters pertaining to war, because they did not see anything but the spear, the war axe, and the shield; and they expressed their pride through acts of war. Thus were all the male children of Zululand brought up in a unique way calculated to harden their hearts; they thought of nothing but blood, because he who knew best how to kill was the one who was considered to have gone through his initiation, and become a man. These boys looked with joyful anticipation to the dawning of their day when they would become the objects of admiration in the eyes of the nation as a whole, that is to say the day they would be sent out to their first encounter; and on the day they went out to attack they would go with great eagerness, like dogs that had been denied meat for a long time, while at the same time being kept away from hunting, and, because their teeth were itching with the desire to bite at something, would tear up the goats and sometimes even bite people. With that viciousness did they go to battle, unable to distinguish man from woman, or young from old.

That was Chaka's second act.

Thirdly, Chaka refused to let his troops marry, saying that marriage was suitable only for people of mature age. He also argued that when people are dying in the heat of battle, the married man thinks of his wife and children, and thereupon takes to his heels, which is a shameful act. A bachelor, on the other hand, fights with resolution to kill or be killed, till he attains victory, for he is aiming to be honoured by the young women's songs. However Chaka did not deny them marriage for good, but promised them that the regiment which distinguished itself over all the others in its fighting prowess would be released first from the bonds of bachelorhood, even if it had not been long in that state; furthermore the *bohadi* cattle for their marriage would be provided by the king himself. If, however, there was no regiment which distinguished itself, they would be released in their order of seniority, beginning with the first one which would be released at a certain time according to the king's wish. Besides, such regiments would have to find their own *bohadi*.

Another thing, if a warrior outstripped his comrades in his regiment, he could be promoted to the next regiment; and if he continued to distinguish himself, he might even be made a commander, or be released as an individual from the vows of his regiment while the rest of his comrades were still far, far behind. That meant that the time a warrior served before his release was not determined by someone else, but by him personally according to his performance. In the space of one year he could begin from the most junior regiment and make his way swiftly through to the senior one right at the top, and thus get out of the bonds of bachelorhood, with his *bohadi* cattle provided by the king, besides being given cattle to begin a new life fitting for such a one. The reader must remember that among all the things that are held in high regard by the black peoples, there is none held dearer than marriage; very often when other things are being evaluated, marriage is kept apart from them, for marriage is life itself. That will make us understand more clearly the extent to which Chaka's warriors exerted themselves in their eagerness to qualify for it. To set an example for his regiments, Chaka remained a bachelor till the day of his death.

That was Chaka's third act of great significance.

Fourthly, until Chaka became king, each warrior carried a whole bundle of spears, all of which had long handles, which were hurled at the enemy; some also carried war axes or clubs. Chaka abolished all these things. Each warrior was given only one spear with a broad blade and a short handle, so that it could not be thrown, and he was given strict orders never to throw it at the enemy, for it was made for stabbing at close range, and that was how it was to be used. In order for this spear to work efficiently, the combatants had to be close to each other. Under those conditions its results were devastating, it tore the victim's flesh in a most frightening way, and the wound it inflicted was a gaping gash, which was always fatal. Furthermore, each warrior was strictly enjoined to bring it back with him on his return from battle, and never to come back if he did not have it with him. Besides, he was also to bring one that he had captured from his fallen opponent. Such captured enemy spears were smelted and beaten out afresh, and were reserved for the boy regiments when they reached the stage of being able to handle spears. Each spear had to pass through Malunga's hands so that he could strengthen it with medicines of herbs and snake poisons, in order that it should kill at once whoever was stabbed with it.

Chaka, after changing the national name and choosing for himself the pleasant sounding one of Zulu (Sky), also desired to find a beautiful greeting which would complement that national name of his, whose sound would be pleasing to the people's ears.

One day when he finished the army games, he assembled his regiments together, and he also called together the people of his city and he said to them: 'My children, at night as I lay asleep, Nkulunkulu sent his chief messengers to me. These messengers said that I should teach his nation, the Mazulu (the Sky People) a beautiful, sweet-sounding greeting, one showing the great respect with which the nation should greet its king who has been placed by Nkulunkulu over all the kings of the earth and all the nations under the sun and the moon, so that they should pay homage to him and worship him.

'You, my children, will grow with me, and rule with me, you will be respected by all nations exactly as they respect me. Nkulunkulu says that if you obey me with true obedience and carry out my orders to the fullest in the same way that I obey him and carry out his orders, your children will witness greater things than these that you are witnessing now; and as for you, the day you go to the place where all must go, he will send the *Nkosazana yeZulu* (the Sky Princess) to come and meet you so you may go to him in person and rule with him like people who have listened well to his commands.

'The greeting I have been told to teach you is BAYEDE. It is a greeting with which you will greet only me, and no one else; even in jest, you must never say to another person '*Bayede*', because merely to say that will be your death; you will pronounce that word only when you greet *me*. Nkulunkulu says I should tell you that if you should fail to respect this greeting in the way he is ordering you, lions will tear you to pieces, your cows will always miscarry, your women will never be heavy with child, your fields will fail to yield crops, the rains will cease to fall, and your enemies will rise up against you.

'I say to you, my children, respect this command from Nkulunkulu.' *Bayede* means *he who stands between God and man*, it means *the junior god through whom the great God rules the kings of the earth and their nations*.

After all those things Chaka reformed the military dress and the embellishments of his warriors, because he wanted his regiments to be neat, he wanted them to dress alike, and each regiment to have its own distinctive dress by which it would be known. People wore sandals in those days, but Chaka forbade his warriors to wear them, saying that they prevented them from running swiftly. Besides these things, Chaka taught his nation proper respect, and the manner in which they were to address him. All the men and all the regiments were taught the greeting of respect; he taught his councillors and his advisers (even though he never listened to any advice) the manner in which they were to counsel and to address him.

The warriors greeted him by saying:

Bayede, baba, Nkosi yamakhosi!
Wena Ngonyama, Ndlovu-ayiphendulwa!
Wena owakhula silibele,
Bayede, baba, Nkosi yezulu!
Wena omnyama, owavela wasiphatha ngetahu!
Wena ongangendlovu,
Wena odl'amadoda,
Wena onzipho zingengezebhubesi!
Wena ongangezulu eliphezulu,
Wena Zulu, siphathe ngetahu!
Bayede Nkosi! Bayede Baba! Bayede Zulu!

(*Bayede*, O Father, King of Kings!
You who are a Lion, Elephant-never-to-be-answered!
You who grew up while we dawdled,
Bayede, Father, King of heaven!
You, O Black One, who appeared and ruled us with compassion!
You who are great as an elephant,
You who devour other men;
You whose claws resemble those of a lion!
You who are as great as the sky above,
You Zulu, rule us with compassion!
Bayede, O King! *Bayede*, O Father! *Bayede*, O Zulu!)

The men of the council woke up in the early hours and went to the court so that they should be able to greet the king; and as soon as he appeared they would stand up as one man and remain on their feet; Mbopha, their leader, would say: 'The sky is clear today' (that is to say the king is happy), and they would respond by saying: 'If the sky is clear, we shall enjoy its pleasing warmth'; and then they would greet the king in unison: '*Bayede*, O King! You whose warmth is like that of the sun which makes the seedlings grow. Greetings to you, O our Sun!'

Or Mbopha would say: 'The sky is overcast today' (the king is not happy), and they would answer him saying: 'If the sky is overcast, we are happy because it brings us the blessings of rain', which meant that many people would be killed.

The young women, the king's 'sisters', greeted him by saying:

Sakubona Mntwanamuhle, bayede Mhlekazi
(Greetings, O Beautiful Child, *Bayede*, Most Excellent One)

or:

Bayede, Nkosi
Uteku lwabafazi bakwaNomgabi
Ababelutekula behlezi emilovini,
Bayede Zulu!

(*Bayede*, O King!
Sport of the women of Nomgabi
Which they joked about as they basked in the sun,
Bayede, O Zulu!)

Chaka had only one purpose in mind: war. Therefore all his conversations, his expressions of beauty, leaned towards that one purpose. So the beautiful traditions which brought good to the people, which had been initiated by Dingiswayo, fell to the ground because all the men had been drafted into the armies, and the women worked for those armies.

Here we now reproduce the praises of King Chaka, in Zulu, which we were able to obtain:

USHAKA (NguChakijana kaMsenteli)

UShaka ngiyesaba ukuthi nguShaka,
UShaka kwakuyinkosi yaseMashobeni,
Uteku lwabafazi bakwaNomgabi;
Ababelutekula behlezi emilovini.

Babethi UShaka kayikubusa
Kayikuba yinkosi
Kanti kunyakana uShaka ezakunethezeka.

UDlungwane woMbelebele,
Odlunge emanxulumeni,
Kwaze kwasa amanxuluma esibekelana.

Umlilo wothathe kaMjokwane kaNdaba,
Umlilo wothathe ubuhanguhangu,
Oshise izikhova zaseDlebe,
Kwaze kwaye kwasha neziseMabedlana,
Izinkomo zawoSihayo zamlandela
Wakhangela enzansi namaDungela,
Kwaze kwalandela nezamaFongosi
Ezazisengwa yindiki lakwaMavela.

Izulu elidume ngenhla komuzi eKuqobekeni,
Lazithath'izihlangu zamaPhela,
Lamudl' uNomhlanjana ezalwa nguZwide,
Lamudl' uMphepha naye ezalwa nguZwide.

Indlov' ethe imuka babeyilandela abakwaLanga,
Yase idla uDayingubo ezalwa nguZwide,
Yamudla uMpondophumelakwezinde emaPheleni,
Yamudla uMthimona ezalwa nguGapa.

Inkonyane ekhwele phezu kwendlu kwaNtombazi,
Bathi iyahlola kanti yibona abahlolayo;
Indlovu ebuyise inhloko, yadl'amadoda,
Indlovu ekhal'isemiThonjaneni;
Izulu elidume ladl'izihlangu zamaPhela,
Abafazi imikhubulo bayishiy'izinqundi,
Imbewu bayishiy'isemanxiweni,
Abafazi abanendeni banyekeza.

KwaSomdombana udle izimfe zambili
Kwayisimanga ikhambi laphuma lilinye,
Akayi nasebandla, akayi nasemaduneni,
UnjengoVimba wakwaMangwekazi.

Igawu abathi beliluma bebeliphimisa
Bakhumbul'amagawu abebesi
Umlunguzi wezingoje, izingoje zilunguzelane.
Ngoba walunguz' ingoje yomfowabo.
Unyaluthi olumnyama lukaHlayukana,
Balukhotha bengakayi enyangeni abakwaZulu.

Umbebe kamame, beba simuke,
Abanye basemhlane kanina babelethwe,
NgabawoMbuzo, ngabawoNsele,
NgabawoSichusa sikaDingankomo
Intethe egolwe ngomkhonto kwaMalandela,
Intethe ethe ukusuka yajubalala.

USHAKA (By Chakijana Son of Msenteli)

(Shaka, I fear to say he is Shaka,
Shaka was the king of Mashobeni,
The joke of the women of Nomgabi
Which they bandied about, sitting in contentment.
They said Shaka would not rule,
Would not be king
Yet that was the very year Shaka inherited a life of comfort.

Ferocious one of the armies at Mbelebele
Who unleashed his fury within the large villages
So that till dawn the villages were tumbling over each other.

Fire of the dry tinder, of Mjokwane of Ndaba,
Fire of the dry tinder scorches fiercely
Which burned the owls at Dlebe hill
And afterwards those at Mabedlana also burned
And the cattle of Sihayo and others followed him
And he looked down towards the maDungela,
The cattle of the maFongosi then followed also
Which were milked by the demented one of Mavela's place.

The Sky that thundered above the village at Kuqobokeni
And took the shields of the maPhela regiment
And ate up Nomhlanjana begotten by Zwide
And ate up Mphepha also begotten by Zwide.

Elephant which, on leaving, was followed by the people of Langa,
Whereupon it ate up Dayingubo begotten by Zwide,
Ate up Mpondophumelakwezinde among the maPhela warriors,
Ate up Mthimona begotten by Gapa.

The Calf that climbed upon a house at Ntombazi's place
And they thought he was portending evil whereas they were the
    ones who were portending evil.
Elephant which, on turning its head, devoured the men.
Elephant which trumpets while yet at miThonjaneni.
Heaven that thundered and ate up the shields of the maPhela
So that the women left the sprouting crops while still short
And left their seeds in the deserted villages;
And expectant women were forced to give birth.

At Somdombana's he ate two sugar-canes
Yet surprisingly only one chewed refuse came out,
He does not even go to his court, nor to his personal bodyguards,
He is like Vimba from the place of Mangwekazi.

Strapping young one whom they bite only to spit out
As he reminded them of the strong-muscled cubs of lions
Peerer over precipices, so that the precipices may peer at each
    other
Because he peered into the precipice of his brother.
Black sorghum of Hlayukana
Which the people of Zululand licked before going to consult the
    doctor.

My mother's little one, climb on my back and let us go,
Some others are already carried on their mother's backs,
They are the ones of Mbuzo, the ones of Nsele,
They are the ones of Sichusa of Dingankomo,
Locust which was trapped with a spear at Malandela's
Locust which from the very start soared ahead.)

CHAPTER EIGHTEEN
THE DEATH OF NOLIWA

The number of months set by Isanusi for Chaka to consider his proposition came to an end and found Chaka's mind unchanged, as he stood steadfastly by his word of the year before. As we have stated, there was a delay in Chaka's marriage, since there was no one to receive the *bohadi* cattle, yet at the same time Noliwa could not simply be taken without *bohadi* like a homeless vagabond of a woman. Yet in spite of that Chaka continued meeting Noliwa until she became pregnant. During her pregnancy, Noliwa became infatuated with Chaka and would always cry whenever she did not see him.

Chaka, too, loved Noliwa very much. If Chaka ever loved a woman with true love, we believe that Nandi was the woman upon whom that love was lavished. All beautiful and worthy things which a true wife might do for her husband, and which Chaka ever experienced he received from Noliwa. And even as he betrayed her like that and planned her murder, his conscience ate him up and gave him no rest; it told him he had strayed from the straight path of human compassion. Yet, because of his desire for kingship, he suppressed it and pushed ahead, and walked about carrying death on his shoulders.

The way Ndlebe and Malunga carried out their duties had already begun to convince him that they were truly leading him towards the kingship he wanted, and so, even though it was as hard as swallowing a stone, he pressed on and made his heart strong.

Malunga told him that the time Isanusi had set had already passed but that Isanusi had no doubt done this on purpose so that Chaka should let his mind settle on his decision. Then Chaka said: 'But this delay of Isanusi's is beginning to puzzle me because I am all ready to go out to war; we have been sitting for a long time doing nothing, and our spears are going to end up being consumed by rust.'

Malunga: 'But, according to the way I have already worked, you cannot go to war without the blood of the one you love, but that is Isanusi's responsibility, not mine; even if you have weighed the matter and decided to spare Noliwa, there is nothing that *I* can do; it is Isanusi alone who can undo what I have already done; it is he who has the knowledge of the going and the coming, of the doing and the undoing.' Chaka heard and understood that there was still time to be merciful and to spare Noliwa, and his feelings were in turmoil.

On the evening of that same day Isanusi arrived and joined them in the house where they were all by themselves, and he came in already with a question on his lips: 'How is it, Chaka? Have you chosen to live with Noliwa as your wife as was decided by Dingiswayo, his nation, and yourself, or have you chosen the kingship?'

'I, Chaka, do not know how to speak two things with one mouth. What I have spoken I have spoken, Isanusi.' Isanusi was quiet for a long time with his head bowed; at last he lifted his head and said: 'Gracious me! Greetings, I beg you, my countrymen. How is it, Malunga? Have you done your work as ordered?'

'I have done my work and finished, Isanusi, and we are waiting only for you who are the completer and the perfecter.'

Isanusi: 'Have the warriors already been given their medicine without their knowledge?'

'They have been made to swallow it, Isanusi.'

Isanusi: 'Have the spears already been beaten afresh and strengthened with medicines in the proper manner, like the spears of the warriors of my country?'

'They have been beaten and strengthened, Isanusi.'

'The medicines for churning the potion, are they ready?'

'They are ready, Isanusi; everything you ordered me to do I have done in accordance with your orders, and I have finished.'

Isanusi turned towards Ndlebe and said: 'Ndlebe, what tasks have you performed since I went away?'

'I have prepared the people's minds, those of men and women alike, so that they should feel that every deed performed by Chaka is good for no other reason than that it is performed by Chaka who has been sent by the gods among the people. Furthermore, I have secretly given them the *boreba*, the medicine that dulls the mind, so that even where they might have had doubts, their minds should react without intelligence, they should be dull, and lack awareness of what is going on; they should look upon Chaka, and even think about him, the way they would think about Nkulunkulu.'

Isanusi smiled and said: 'You have worked well, and in a matter of great importance too.' Then Isanusi asked Chaka again the same question he had asked him a while before, and Chaka gave him the same answer as he had done. Isanusi once again kept quiet for a long time, and was troubled like a judge who passes judgement without wishing to pronounce his verdict against someone he loves, but who is compelled by the evidence to do so, and indeed to impose a heavy sentence on him, which is something he would much rather not do.

After a long time he said: 'Think well, Chaka. What has been done by my assistants can be undone, whereas that which I shall do with the blood of your wife, Noliwa, is something that even I cannot undo even if I wish to. That will be the ultimate seal. For this reason it is necessary that a person should understand what he is doing while there is still time, so that he should not afterwards regret when regret is of no further use. The day I left here I told you that today we shall teach you the ultimate in sorcery. And that is true, because we doctors are sorcerers who surpass other sorcerers. If you decide in favour of the kingship, you will be transformed into someone else, you will be like the kings of my country. But, I ask you once again, and do answer me with the truth that is in your heart, having fear of nothing, not even that I shall say that you have troubled me over nothing. What do you choose for yourself, Noliwa or the kingship?'

Chaka: 'The kingship!'

At once, in the twinkling of an eye, Isanusi's face lighted up and brightened, the trace of unhappiness which had clouded his countenance fled and made way for joy, and he said: 'You have answered like a man; I like people of your calibre. I cannot get on with someone whose mind is fickle; I was simply testing you with my questions so that I should know the depth of your feelings; but I can see now that you are a man, for when you have spoken you have spoken. You are a king, and you have answered me like a king. On this day I have learnt exactly what kind of person you are, and I shall work for you with a more willing heart than I have done hitherto because I know your true nature. Through Noliwa's death many things will be revealed to you, and even if you are not aware of them in the beginning, that awareness will come with time; you will even come to know that there is no death, there is no dying.

'When a person is said to have died, he is not dead, he is merely transformed, the breath of life having left this covering of flesh and migrated to another land which shines more gloriously than the sun, and he goes and lives there exactly as he had done before, as you yourself can indeed testify to some extent because you heard for yourself your own father's voice when he spoke to you, and it was exactly as you had known it. He who has worked hard in this world will reap a rich harvest there; one who has done nothing here will receive nothing there, because everything a person does in this world the sun takes with it when it sets and carries it to that great land of the living whom *you* regard as dead, and refer to as *the dead*; and all these things will wait for him there, growing and increasing like cows which calve repeatedly. But the deeds of him who has worked little do not grow, but rather diminish and become less, just as it is with someone who has sown little, for the handful of sorghum which he obtains at harvest time is lost in the soil of the threshing floor, instead of filling large grain bags, and he remains a piteous figure, with his hands grasping nothing but air.

'At this very moment you are about to be counted among the strong, yea, among the strong whom even now I see where they are sitting covered on all sides by the glory of their works, men whose brows sweated when it was time for sweating, who worked like true men. At this very moment you are about to be counted among those kings who resemble the kings of my home.' Isanusi's heart was moved so that he fell silent just when he was on the point of revealing to Chaka the secrets of the world beyond the grave. Chaka listened to these matters with his heart's desires keen and sharpened and goading him on to attain quickly the kind of kingship described to him.

And then after a long while Isanusi finally said: 'You are a man of understanding, Chaka; truly there are not many like you for recognizing the right moment; for there is a time in the life of a human being which he must seize at once or else forfeit numerous blessings which will never come his way again till he is buried in the cold earth; whereas if he is alert and vigilant, he will receive blessings which will never again slip out of his grasp. Such was the time when I found you sleeping under a tree: If you had not made your choice like a man on that day, where would you be today?' (Chaka said in his heart: 'Where, indeed, would I be?')

'At a moment such as you are facing today, you knew how to choose the road you would follow, as well as the way you would live in this world. Consequently by the time you die you will not even know the ends of your kingdom. But the most important thing is that, when you reach the land of your fathers you will find that your renown as well as the glory of your kingship will have been multiplied tenfold, and they will be yours for ever and ever; because there is no dying there, and no death, and the people live for ever, and they live in the manner in which they lived in the present world.' Isanusi was quiet again for a long time. Then he pulled Chaka by the hand and they went outside, and then he looked up and pointed at the stars: 'The number of your warriors will surpass in number those stars that you see in the heavens. Among the nations you will shine like the sun when it is not covered by the clouds, at whose rising the stars fade away; so too will all the other nations vanish and cease to be when you come into view, because Noliwa's blood is going to bring you riches which will be a wonder to behold.'

The reader can imagine for himself the state of Chaka's thoughts when so much fame and glory were being predicted for him, and he knew that the one predicting them spoke nothing but the truth in all things. In spite of that, however, things were left as they were for a few more days, waiting for the day Chaka would go for his bathe in the river, for that would be the day on which the work would be done.

On the following day when Chaka returned from playing games with his armies, he found that Isanusi and his assistants were away, having gone to the fields and the forests to find medicinal herbs. He went into Noliwa's house and found her alone with her personal attendant. On that day when Chaka looked at Noliwa, he saw that she was a deep brown colour, surpassing even the cannabis seed in ripeness; her complexion was clear, and her beauty overflowing. Her black-and-white eyes were gentle. Her voice when she spoke to Chaka, her beloved, made him forget the war songs and the praises which he had thought were so beautiful; it was clear as crystal, and was soft and full of truth, and without guile or deceit. But above all these things, her eyes! They were eyes which revealed a message which said: 'I am yours with all my being, Chaka; I am yours in life and in death.' Her beauty on that day left Chaka dumbfounded, unable to say anything, and he simply stood there in utter confusion. He rubbed his eyes and looked the other way, and when he looked at Noliwa again, it was as if her beauty had kept growing, and was truly like the beauty of a woman who was beloved by Nkulunkulu and was chosen by him to come and demonstrate to the people the very perfection of womanhood. A storm arose in Chaka's chest, a strange whirlwind which swirled and raised much dust in his heart, and he went out.

When Isanusi came he spoke even before Chaka said anything, saying: 'You are a true man, Chaka: I saw how mixed your feelings were when you saw Noliwa, but you controlled yourself like a man, and a king, because a king ought not to be fickle and change his mind from one day to another.'

When Chaka's day drew near, Noliwa suddenly took ill; she did not feel well on account of her heaviness, and that which she was carrying was causing her unease even though she had not grown so 'big' that the people would notice her. On the evening preceding the day he would go to the river for his early morning bathe, Chaka went to Noliwa holding a thatching needle, and he found her sitting alone with her personal attendant, in order to keep away from crowds. When he came in the attendant went out. There was a wood fire burning, and its flame lit that little hut quite brightly.

Chaka came close to Noliwa and started playing with her and kissing her. He asked her where the pain was. Noliwa said: 'Chaka, my lord, your face has an unhappy frown, and your voice too has a stabbing, painful sound. What is the matter?' Chaka said there was nothing the matter, except that he had been annoyed by some idiot during the warriors' games. They kept talking to each other in that manner, and kissing each other, and then suddenly Chaka covered Noliwa's mouth with his powerful hand, and he stabbed her with the needle in her armpit, and then he turned her over, with the stabbed armpit facing upward so that the blood flowed back inside the body. Noliwa, when she was about to die, turned her eyes backwards twice or three times, and then said: 'Chaka, my beloved, you who are now my father, you who are Jobe, you who are Dingiswayo, you. . . .!' The little flame of her life went out and her pure spirit flowed and went to Dingiswayo in the glory above. When Chaka saw her eyes roll backwards, he was greatly frightened, and he trembled, and then he ran away. As Noliwa died, Chaka felt somewhere inside him, in his chest, something falling down like a heavy stone, and settling heavily on his heart.

He ran outside, but his vision was blurred, and he could not see; he saw one thing only—Noliwa's face and her eyes rolling back, when she was about to die. His ears were blocked and he was unable to hear; he heard one thing only—Noliwa's voice just before she died. And when at last his senses came back, he found himself already with Isanusi in the house, and Isanusi was congratulating him, saying: 'At this very moment your name has been entered among those of the kings of my home, and the highest ones, at that.'

The poor young girl who was with Noliwa when Chaka entered was killed; it was said that she had not reported when Noliwa was seriously ill so that she died without anybody knowing; and Ndlebe spread the rumour that she was the one who had bewitched Noliwa. Isanusi had already taken whatever it was he wanted from Noliwa, which *we* don't know, and had used it in a way known to him alone. On the dawn of the following day he went with Chaka to the river, and Malunga and Ndlebe were present also. When they left the river, Isanusi for his part went directly back to his home.

So it came about, the death of Noliwa, the daughter of Jobe, the sister of Dingiswayo, the wife of Chaka.

CHAPTER NINETEEN
THE KILLING OF THE COWARDS

After Noliwa's death Chaka underwent a frightful change both in his external appearance and also in his inner being, in his very heart; and so did his aims and his deeds. Firstly, the last spark of humanity still remaining in him was utterly and finally extinguished in the terrible darkness of his heart; his ability to distinguish between war and wanton killing or murder vanished without a trace, so that to him all these things were the same, and he regarded them in the same light. Secondly, his human nature died totally and irretrievably, and a beast-like nature took possession of him; because although he had been a cruel person even before this, he had remained a human being, his cruelty but a human weakness. But a man who had spilt the blood of someone like Noliwa, would understandably regard the blood of his subjects exactly as if it were no different from that of mere animals which we slaughter at will. This was Chaka's act of greatest magnitude in preparing himself for the kingship he so much coveted; and with Noliwa's blood he had branded himself with an indelible mark which resembled that of the kings of Isanusi's home. We are unable to measure Nandi's grief when she heard the report of Noliwa's death, because she loved her very much, and regarded her as no less than her daughter-in-law.

After such preparations, Chaka attacked Buthelezi's and Qwabe's territories just to try out his own strength, and also to put his untried young warriors to the test and see how they would perform. He went out with armies which were more than twice the strength of Dingiswayo's. In the whole of Nguniland there was peace and prosperity, and the land was warm and the nations lived in great contentment when Chaka took to the road with his armies to go and bring that peace in the world to an end..

It is perfectly understandable that in those two battles some ran away, some lost their spears, some threw theirs, and some returned without having captured any from the enemy; that happens among all nations, people kill each other, people capture loot from each other. In these two battles Chaka attacked only with the new regiments and held back the older ones; and among those new regiments there was only one which stood its ground and continued fighting even as the others turned and fled. Even when the enemy was making a concerted assault on them, threatening to wipe them out, they stood firm without giving an inch, until Chaka sent reinforcements to help them push back the enemy. Some few others were in the habit of making a quick retreat when they felt the heat of battle, and then turning back quickly for a fresh assault; but this particular one remained unshaken.

There was a young man in that same regiment from whom Chaka

never removed his eyes. When they were ordered into battle, this young man went with his eyes deep-set, way back in their sockets, and he held his spear high with a backward thrust, and grasped his shield by its handle, with his chest pushed out like that of a bird swimming. And as soon as they met the enemy, that young man who was of a lean physique became transformed and he held his shield close to him, grasping it by its thong handle, and his spear stabbed with an upward thrust rather than downward. His performance in those two battles was exactly like Chaka's when he was still a warrior. His name was Mzilikazi.

When Chaka returned home with his armies, he called all the grown up men and women to the royal place at Mgungundlovu; the armies comprising young boys were also summoned; which means that he called together his entire nation and assembled it outside the city walls.

When everyone had come, he went there ushered by Mbopha, leader of the king's courtiers, and followed by the young army which had acquitted itself so well in those two battles. Mbopha was reciting praises as he walked, telling about the profound wisdom of the king, and the justness of his verdicts. When Chaka reached the assembled multitude, he raised his little spear which contained medicines of witchcraft, and there was dead silence, then he called all the regiments which he had taken out to battle, and he ordered them to stand to one side. When they were there, he said that each warrior should produce his own spear as well as the one he had captured from the enemy warrior he had killed. Those who had them showed them, and those who did not were told to stand apart from the rest. Those whose spears were captured by the enemy were also told to stand by themselves apart from the others. After that he called those who ran away from the battle, and their spears and battle dresses were taken away from them, and they were also made to stand to one side. Those who had thrown their spears were also called and made to stand by themselves.

The commanders of the regiments stood near the king, crowding around him. Chaka looked at them and then he looked at the people he had commanded to stand to one side in the midst of the assembled crowd, and then he raised his spear which had killed nations of people, and there was dead silence; the commanders strained their ears in order to hear what the king's wish might be, and the king said: 'Let the Nkandle and Myozi regiments come to the front.' The commanders of these regiments ran at once and fetched them and made them stand in the centre of the crowd; and then Chaka raised his voice and said: 'All you who are present here, open your ears and hear me well; open your eyes and see, and be witness to the deed that I shall perform, and the law I am going to lay down by the example of these ones here. Do you see these people?'

The crowd: 'We see them, O King.'

Chaka: 'These are cowards who ran away from battle, and yet I had instructed them very strictly that no one in my armies should ever do such an ugly thing, because he who runs away disgraces our name, Mazulu, which means those who are invincible; besides this running away of theirs is already an indication that one day the Mazulu will be defeated. These are people who deserve a very heavy punishment.'

Malunga was suddenly heard from somewhere in the crowd saying: 'The king's command must be obeyed by each and every warrior, because he who does not obey the king's command is failing to obey the command of Nkulunkulu himself who sent the king here to come and teach his children, the Mazulu, the art of war, and thus deliver them from their enemies.' Chaka turned about often, looking on all sides, and the people trembled, because when he was angry he turned into a veritable wild beast. He looked at these two regiments which stood in the centre of the crowd, and then lifted his spear and pointed it at those who had run away. He did this without uttering a word. In the twinkling of an eye the warriors fell upon the condemned like wild dogs charging into a flock of sheep. Those thousands died and became food for the vultures right there at their home, not in battle, but within view of their parents, within view of the young women and the children, and they became exposed as cowards who surpassed all other cowards.

After they had been executed, there was dead silence. At that time Chaka was so angry that he was foaming at the mouth; and then the king's courtiers, the men appointed specially to advise the king, said: '*Ao*, how great his wisdom! This deed will ensure that there will never again be any cowards in Zulu's empire! No warrior will ever again turn his back on the enemy!' They spoke these words with their heads bowed to show how overwhelmed they were. About twenty of Zwide's people who were now under Chaka's rule cried when they saw these people killed, among whom were their own children and their brothers. Then Chaka ordered that they be brought to him, and he would comfort them in their grief.

When those killed had been carried to a place outside the crowd, Chaka once again raised his spear, and he instructed the commanders to summon forward the Dinare and Dilepe regiments. When those two regiments came, the people understood that the killing had not yet ended, and they were greatly frightened, because it was the first time that they had ever witnessed such a massacre. Ndlebe was moving about in the crowd, spotting those who were crying and bringing them to the king to be comforted for the death of their children.

'These whom you see here now are cowards just like the first group; they are the ones who threw away their spears which I had gone to great pains to have forged and strengthened with the potent medicines of Zululand.' Someone shouted in the midst of the crowd and said: 'It is obvious that they threw away those spears because they were running away.' Chaka paced this way and that, then he stopped and looked around; he raised his spear and pointed it at them while maintaining his silence, and at once the vultures swarmed up in flight above as the warriors brought them more food.

The king's men: 'How great his understanding! The spears of Zululand will no longer be lost, and the king's efforts will no longer be reduced to naught through people throwing away their spears on purpose as they run away.'

Chaka raised his spear a third time, and when the people saw it all things turned as dusty as the earth, they saw grey. He said: 'Those whom you see now are those who returned from battle without having captured any enemy spears; that is to say that they did not kill anyone.' A voice shot out of the crowd: 'If they did not kill, it is clear that they had gone there simply to increase the volume, but were afraid to go into the heat of battle, where warriors stabbed each other with their spears. They are cowards.' Two or three princes from nations which had been destroyed, said: 'O King, let the lion withdraw its claws and tread on its paws; your spear has killed, it is enough; have mercy on them, great master!' Chaka said he had heard them, and he bade them come to him; the spear nevertheless pointed to the very ones for whom the plea had been made, and the vultures rose again as more food was brought to them. They indeed were full already, and were leaving the rest for the scavenging hyena which, out of fear, never comes out to eat while the sun is shining.

The king's men: 'Oh, how great his understanding! It is a deep pool that goes down endlessly. Among the Zulu armies, no warrior will ever again go to war simply to increase the tumult!' They signalled to each other with their brows to prove to the king how overwhelmed they were by his unequalled wisdom.

Chaka once more lifted his spear, and passed word to the commanders, and two more regiments were brought into the midst of the crowd, and the people were dead with fright. 'These are the ones who threw Zulu's spear at the enemy whereas it was made to stab at close range, and that way they have thwarted the instructions that go with the medicines with which they were fortified....' His mother, Nandi, came while he was speaking in that manner, and threw herself at her son's feet and said: 'I implore you, O King, do please hear me. I say, let the lion tread on its paws, O Zulu, it is the first time that they have wronged you, and they have seen the enormity of their crime. They will repent, and will fight your wars, O father.' Chaka was utterly silent. Nandi, for her part, remained prostrate. Then Chaka said: 'Just because of my mother, since she is my mother who bore me, who fetched me from Nkulunkulu and brought me into the world, I forgive you, don't do it again.' Chaka then told his mother to leave and go home, he had heard her prayer.

When Nandi had left, Chaka called out saying: 'The sentencing of the warriors is now over. I told you to open your ears and listen, and open your eyes and see; and you have heard, and you have seen. All of you who are present here, including you boys, be warned that the penalty for whomsoever shall do even a single one of these deeds, is death. I have called you so that you may hear for yourselves and see for yourselves. My law has to be obeyed completely, not outwardly only, but in the heart also, because I shall consign him who carries it out only because he is bound to do so, to that place over there (pointing to where the corpses had been thrown).

'I end by saying, open your ears once more and listen; open your eyes once more and see clearly. You saw these ones when they cried. That crying meant that I had done wrong in my judgements; and to say that I, Chaka, have erred is a great wrong. Besides, that crying will weaken the hearts of my warriors in battle when they die unmourned, and will make them run away. Now I am going to teach them the proper way to cry for their children, besides I have said that they should come to me for comfort, so that I can make them forget the death of those for whom they are mourning.' The commanders listened with great diligence, and then he said: 'You must gouge out these eyes of theirs which are overflowing fountains, and thus only will they forget their children who have done such great wrongs.' In the twinkling of an eye their eyes were gouged out, and they were let loose outside the crowd and it was said that if they knew how to find their way back to their homes, they were free to do so; if some should fall down the cliffs, then so be it.

The king's men: 'Not since the creation of all the nations has there been a man whose judgements equal those of this one! He testifies by his words, he testifies by his deeds too that he is one sent by Nkulunkulu.'

Chaka lifted his spear one more time and said: 'These ones you see here now are those who give free rein to their tongues. You heard them for yourselves. They will spoil my warriors by making them believe that there will always be someone to plead for them.' He paused, and then he said: 'You must pull out by their very roots these tongues of theirs which babble so much; you must not cut them for fear they might start sprouting again. Only that way will they stop meddling in the affairs of kings when they chastize their subjects.' In the twinkling of an eye, those people's tongues were pulled out, and they died.

The king's men: '*Siyakubonga, siyakudumisa*, Zulu (We thank you, we praise you, O Zulu)! Your judgements are just and they are without favour. Your eyes see deep into people's chests, they reveal things which are hidden to others! Your ears hear the plots which are hatched in people's hearts! All your deeds testify, O Zulu, that you are no mortal being, but the servant of Nkulunkulu, you are the Heaven which is towering over us all.' If any one of them had spoken in a manner which did not please Chaka, the penalty would have been death.

Chaka shouted for the last time: 'I hope you have seen for now and for always, I hope you have heard for now and for always!'

The regiment which had refused to retreat even when the battle was hot was given the entire loot which had been captured from Qwabe's and Buthelezi's; the cattle were given to them to become their property rather than for immediate feasting by the regiment. Chaka took not a single one of them even though they were so many. In addition to that, this regiment was promoted immediately to join the senior regiments who were called to active duty only when there was real danger, which meant that the time for them to qualify for marriage was very close. Mzilikazi was elevated to the rank of commander of that very regiment, and was also given the privilege to choose for himself one hundred cattle from the king's herds, and also select their bulls. That was how Chaka rewarded his braves.

On that one day the people who were killed were counted in tens of thousands. That is how cowardice was banished from Zulu's domain, and from that day the Zulu warriors went to war understanding in full the saying: 'A boy-child is an ox apportioned to the vultures.' They went to war understanding that they were not the children of their parents, but of the king; they went with the resolve to win or else die there rather than be killed like mere dogs, at home, before the eyes of the women. From that day on one Zulu warrior was equal to ten of the enemy, and could put them to flight. The day they went to the attack again Chaka's command to his armies was: 'Go, my children, and work with diligence and come back victorious, with a lot of war spoils; otherwise don't come back.'

This was only the beginning of Chaka's numerous massacres. Those who witnessed the events of that day had nightmares throughout that night. They grew thin because it was the first time that the people had ever witnessed such a deed.

CHAPTER TWENTY

CHAKA INVADES THE SOUTH: MZILIKAZI

Soon after the killing of the cowards Chaka sent an expedition southward. He finished off the remnants of the Maqwabe, and then fought with the Mafuze, Bathembu, and the Machunu. Those were the first nations to be scattered by Chaka with his combined forces, made up of local and drafted foreign armies. He killed them without mercy and set their villages alight together with their crops; but instead of returning home with his enormous booty, he stopped there for several months. While stationed there, he went on the rampage, slaughtering people, while incorporating the young into his armies.

When he left there he continued south, crossing the Thukela, and he scattered the Mabomvu and Bakwamachibisa. He had those people's cattle and small livestock driven homewards while he himself pressed on. By this time there was often no need for him to fight because the people dreaded him so, that whenever they saw his armies advancing, they immediately ran away. Afterwards even the mere mention of his name was enough, and whenever the alarm was raised that Chaka was on the march, the men would immediately forsake their villages and flee. His fame spread far and wide: whenever there was a group of men the talk was always about Chaka, in the courtyards the women's talk was about Chaka, in the pasture grounds the herdboys' talk was about Chaka.

These nations which were fleeing from Chaka destroyed the weaker ones who were in their path, took away their cattle and their sorghum—everything. Other nations on the onward path, which had not yet heard about Chaka, blocked the way and fought against the ones who were fleeing from Chaka; that is to say that those who were running away were attacked from all sides, by Chaka from the rear and, in front, by the people of the country through which they were running. But since they had to flee from Chaka, they joined together into a large army, and they easily trampled over all the little nations which stood in their way, venting their rage on them. All the nations joined the stampede of the southward flight, and they killed each other with such viciousness that sometimes they waded through the blood of the slain. Often when Chaka came upon the people he found them already broken, tame and lacking the strength to fight, and he would simply finish them off. Those whom Chaka killed with his armies were far outnumbered by the victims of those fleeing from him. And that was the beginning of the *difaqane* and of the wandering bands: it was through Chaka that these things began.

In these wars Chaka killed all the married people, the old people and the children, that is to say the older people who had become accustomed to being ruled by their own kings and could never be changed into true Zulus; and as for the children, he killed them for fear that they would be a hindrance and become a pitiful sight when their parents were no more. All the youth had their lives spared on the calculation that they would soon forget their original homes and become Zulus at heart; the girls were made into slaves who served the armies, and among whom those armies would find wives when released from their bond of celibacy.

Wherever Chaka had passed clouds of smoke were to be seen from the villages he had set alight in order that the people should have nowhere to hide; smoke could be seen also from the fields as he set fire to the crops so that those who escaped should die from hunger. Yet in spite of that, a few still managed to escape, and Chaka, in his anger when he realized that there were some people who were hiding where he could not reach them, killed their dogs so that they should not continue hunting for them. That way, he assured himself, they should die and be completely wiped off the face of the earth. Whether they died by the spear or from hunger mattered little to him so long as they were dead.

Ahead of Chaka's armies the land was beautiful, and was adorned with villages and ploughed fields and numerous herds of cattle; but upon their tracks were charred wastes without villages, without ploughed fields, without cattle, without anything whatsoever, except occasionally some wild animals. Wild dogs and hyenas roamed about in large packs following or flanking Chaka's armies, and stopping wherever they stopped in the knowledge that that way they would obtain food without sweat or labour, provided free by someone else. The land became wild and unfriendly and threatening; the smell of death was upon the earth and in the air. The fields lay fallow for lack of people to plough them, because the moment someone dug his field, Chaka would see him, and that would be the end. Where villages once stood was utter desolation, the ghostly sight of which made one's hair stand on end.

It was at that time that, on account of hunger, people began to eat each other as one eats the flesh of a slaughtered animal; they hunted each other like animals and ate each other; they started because of hunger, but afterwards continued with their cannibalism out of habit. The first cannibal was a Zulu called Ndava, who lived near the place where the city of Durban now stands. And then after a few years the persecutions and sufferings from the east climbed over the Maloti mountains and entered Lesotho, and there too cannibals came into being because of hunger. This is the worst of all the evil things of those days, and that too arose because of Chaka, originator-of-all-things-evil.

When Chaka reached Mathuli's place, he turned back, and he gathered together the cattle of the nations he had scattered, and placed them in cattle posts in that very land which now had no inhabitants; all the black ones were kept together in one cattle post, and so too with the yellow, the fawn-coloured, the red-and-white, and so on. When he reached home, he released his old regiments from their bonds of bachelorhood, and he gave them the cattle which were to provide them with livelihood; he also gave them the young women who tended the fields and cooked for them, and thus fulfilled his word when he said that he would arrange the marriages of such regiments. He gave them what he had taken from other people.

The day Chaka returned from the south, where were the Maqwabe, Mafuze, Bathembu, Machunu, Makhuze, Bakwamachibisa, Mabomvu, and Bathuli? They had been wiped out from under the sun, and had gone where Zwide's nation had gone. On his return only animals could be seen in the veld, but there was not a single human being to be seen; they had all been wiped out, finished, no more.

It was at that time, when Chaka was returning from the south, that Moshoeshoe's messengers came to him with tributes from their king who, through the mouths of these messengers, announced that *he* was not a king, but was Chaka's subject, adding that he knew of no other king than Chaka. Chaka received those gifts with joy, and never thereafter entertained any thoughts of attacking Moshoeshoe. Instead he decided to make him his subject-king in whose land his armies, deployed to fight on this side of the Maloti mountains, would camp. He was very flattered by Moshoeshoe's words, and he repeated them often in his heart, saying: 'Moshoeshoe says he knows no other king besides me! So, the people have already begun to say that I am the only king on earth, even though I have done nothing yet, for these recent events are but trifles! How then will it be the day I accomplish my purpose as I have conceived it? What will they say on that day!'

Chaka once more went to make war. This time he attacked the Mangwane of Matiwane who were now living right up against the Maloti. He scattered them with ease; in fact, they fled even while Chaka was still on his way. In their flight they fell upon the Mahlubi of Bungane (Pokane), fought and scattered them, so that the Mahlubi were the first to climb over the Maloti, something they did under great pressure since the Mangwane were hot on their heels. In order that the reader may understand how extreme was their suffering during that flight, we should state that the fugitives left behind their aged as well as their children, indeed even their wives and their sisters, when they were overcome by fatigue on the way, because there was no time to do anything about it. That same Matiwane was the fox that caused much trouble at Thaba-Bosio. The *difaqane* in Lesotho began with the coming of those Mahlubi and Mangwane.

After this war, Chaka did not go out to battle in person any more, and his regiments and their generals went by themselves, while he remained at home. Mzilikazi (Moselekatse) was by now at the head of all of Chaka's commanders, with Manukuza as his next in command. Moselekatse was the one who led the armies in many of the expeditions to the north, and on every occasion he brought all the spoils to the king; but, even though Chaka gave him quite a large share, he could never satisfy his greedy heart. The most important problem, however, was that Moselekatse did not want to be ruled and to have to do somebody else's will instead of his own, to fight for someone else instead of fighting for himself, to bring the spoils to someone else instead of capturing everything for himself, to bring renown upon someone else instead of bringing it upon himself, and to place the garland of kingship on someone else's head instead of his own. He felt a great sense of grievance, telling himself that his efforts were as useless as the sweat of a hunting dog which was always sucked up by its fur. Secondly, Moselekatse was already grown up and was a mature man who yearned much for marriage, whereas the king had not yet thought of releasing him from his duties as a commander. For these reasons he decided to establish his own kingdom far away from Chaka, where he could run his own affairs.

One day he was sent again to the north to go and destroy a petty king and capture all his cattle. Moselekatse went and did as he was told, and on the way he found an excellent opportunity to talk to the troops under his command: 'Men, what are we going to gain by working with such diligence for Chaka, and exposing ourselves to death for his sake? He will never make us kings, and, besides, he does not give us our fair share of the war spoils; we capture the cattle at the cost of our own blood while he sits at home with his many women, and yet when we get back home he chooses the miserable-looking ones and gives them to us while he keeps for himself not only the largest number, but also the best-looking ones. Here we are today, with our hair beginning to turn grey, yet we have not yet been given permission to marry. He has his women, but we shall only be released when we are no longer much use, and marriage is no longer a pleasure. Furthermore, Chaka kills us. Besides, Chaka is a human being just like all other human beings, he is no miracle, he is no god, what he does we can also do; he has taught us how to fight and that is enough. We are now able to part from him, to throw off the yoke of servitude from our necks, and create a kingdom all our own where we shall be kings and princes. How do *you* view this matter which I am talking about?'

The troops agreed with him since they were tired of the endless marches and endless wars in which most of them succumbed to disease and hunger and the enemy's spear. Yet they also cautioned him saying: 'If Chaka should know our plan, we shall become food for the wolves in no time at all. If we are truly serious, we ought to proceed straight ahead now on our flight, and not go back to him any more.'

But Moselekatse drew their attention to certain things: 'In the first place we must have wives, and they must be Zulus. That means that we have to go back home and fetch the young women of our regiment, because we cannot take as wives the dogs of foreign nations. They too are grown women now and they are crying for marriage, and will understand at once that we are making them into human beings by taking them out of their bondage. As regards Chaka's anger, you should remember that among all his armies, the most efficient and best trained are those ones which are under my command; his warriors will come to us with very little hope of victory because they know me well, and besides I know that even Manukuza has had enough of this heavy yoke.'

Among these regiments of Moselekatse's, a warrior who fell by the spear in the heat of battle was considered fortunate by his comrades for having died in the manner expected of a male child from Zululand. They had grief in their hearts, and were moved to tears as they wondered when *they* would come to an honourable end to their suffering.

When he came close to Zululand, Moselekatse sent some of his people secretly to go and smuggle out some young women, and at the same time he sent messengers driving an ox with a beautiful yellow colour to Chaka to inform him that he was near but was unable to travel fast because of the large number of the cattle he was bringing back with him. Unfortunately they drove that ox too hard and it became tired on the way, and they slaughtered and ate it. Ndlebe told Chaka that that was a lie, there were no such cattle coming, and that Moselekatse had decided to turn against him. Chaka, in his anger, sent numerous troops under the command of Manukuza to go and kill Moselekatse and all those with him; but Manukuza, instead of fighting Moselekatse, found an excellent opportunity to escape. He fled with those armies and went far away beyond the Zambezi, where he established his own nation, the Machakana. That very Manukuza was the father of Gungunyani.

The young women of Moselekatse's age group trilled their ululations when they heard his invitation, and they said: 'We have long been asking when such a hero would come forward! We suffer under Chaka's rule, and we all grow old without knowing the joys of marriage.' The women of those days were strong and could run fast. Moselekatse thus departed with young people only who had no children to slow down their progress. He climbed over the Maloti mountains in the same direction taken by his own people, the people of Zwide (towards Bopedi). He found the nations of the Basotho, the Batswana and the Bapedi living in peace with their weak little spears, and he played havoc among them with the Zulu spear which stabbed once and killed. He destroyed the nations in a manner never known before. Whenever he came into a village he killed the men, the women and the children, but incorporated the young into his regiments. He burned the villages and the crops, and would also burn the grass in the fields where he camped for the night. This meant that between him and Chaka's armies which came in pursuit, there was not a single person, no cow, no animal, and not even a grain of sorghum or of maize, nothing to eat, only charred ruins all around. For that reason Chaka's armies which were chasing him were not able to go far because of hunger.

Moselekatse ran on in that manner destroying all the little nations among whom he passed, until he reached Kudumane in Botswana; and it was through him that the Masarwa and the Bakgothu came to know Chaka's name, even though they were taught it in a cruel manner, by being killed. Afterwards he migrated to Bulawayo in Inyathi. That is to say that the conflagration which had been lit by Chaka in the east, crossed the Maloti through Moselekatse, destroyed those in the centre while just singeing those in the extreme west, leaving them as casualties. There is nothing that will survive the path of a wild fire, and so both the Mokone and the Mosotho died, both the cow and the lion.

When he saw his armies returning without having killed Moselekatse, and he heard, besides, that Manukuza had defected with his armies, Chaka was extremely angry, and he ordered the commanders of the armies which had gone in pursuit of Moselekatse to be burnt alive in a blazing wood fire; he said that was the kind of death they deserved since they had deliberately allowed his enemy to escape, and it was obvious that they themselves had already become corrupted by that evil spirit of rebellion.

CHAPTER TWENTY-ONE
CONCERNING NONGOGO AND MNYAMANA

Chaka's thoughts were in turmoil, and his anger was almost driving him insane when he saw how Moselekatse and Manukuza had defied him. From that day on his spear destroyed the Zulu with the same viciousness as the enemy, making no distinction. Furthermore, from that day Chaka never again promoted anybody to the position of commander; instead he would appoint a person to lead the armies when they went out to attack, and then demote him when they returned home, and then the next time he went to war again he would appoint a different person. His heart was full, and he was choking with rage, and he killed many innocent people for fear that they would do as those two evil ones had done.

In those days spears were obtained with great difficulty, for they were made from ironstone which was very tough indeed. Just around that time people far away near the Zambezi, as they were digging ochre, unexpectedly discovered a stone which was easier to work with in making spears. News of that stone gave Chaka the pretext to kill many people who had done no wrong, while cleverly disguising his intent.

There was one outstanding brave who worked for Chaka with all his heart, and without any evil motives, and all of Chaka's armies were very fond of him. His name was Nongogo. When Chaka saw how his armies loved Nongogo, he was seized with envy, because he wanted them to worship him alone. So he called Nongogo. On arriving at the king's place Nongogo left his spears outside the city walls as was proper, and as soon as he came in view of the king he shouted his praises:

Bayede Nkosi yamakhosi
Wena Ngonyama enzipho zibukhali
Wena odla amadoda.
Bayede baba!
Bayede Zulu!

(*Bayede*, O King of kings!
You, Lion with sharp claws!
You who devour other men.
Bayede, father!
Bayede, Zulu!)

And then he threw himself on the ground and crawled on his stomach with his face close to the ground, which was the manner in which Chaka was greeted. He crawled on till he came near Chaka, and he stood there ready to do to the king's utmost satisfaction anything whatsoever which he might command, no matter how difficult it might be, or else die while attempting it rather than come back having failed.

And when he was near, Chaka said: 'Take two hundred warriors and go where I bid you. I understand that in some country which I do not know, yonder to the north, there is iron ore for making spears which is both easy to obtain and easy to work with. I am sending you on a secret scouting mission to find out if this is indeed so, and also to bring these stones. You must also study the method used to mine and smelt it.'

The manner in which Chaka spoke made Nongogo realize at once that Chaka was cleverly sending him to his death; he was sure that someone had slandered him before the king. He returned from the king with a very sore heart and went where he was being sent, to a place he did not know. He was also unhappy at the small number of men the king gave him for this mission.

On the way many nations fought against him, killing his men, so that he even sent messengers to Chaka asking him for reinforcements; but Chaka refused, saying that the men he had were enough. Nongogo pressed on until he reached that place and brought back that stone. During his return journey, one day he had to fight a furious battle. He had found himself surrounded, at sunrise, by a large army. The Zulus had then stood back to back in a circle and defended themselves like men. By the afternoon, there were more of the enemy killed than remained alive, while Nongogo was left with only ten warriors to whom he continually shouted words of encouragement, urging them to line the ground with many enemy warriors before they fell down, so that they should go down like the true sons of Chaka. The enemy were in no doubt that they could kill all those Zulus and finish them, but it was obvious that, by the time the last Zulu went down, they would probably themselves have only one man left, and that would not be any use; and so they left them to go their way.

Nongogo and the ten were afraid to go back by the same road they had taken on their outward journey, and so they went west in order to avoid meeting any people. They went through deserts where most of them died of thirst, and only Nongogo and one other man escaped. Those two trudged on with their feet swollen and their soles cracked, and they were weak from hunger and thirst, and fatigued by the journey and by fighting. Nongogo's entire body was covered with sores, and he would most likely have died first, but his strong will kept his soul within his flesh till he was able to present himself again before his king. They came into Zulu territory unable to walk properly, barely able to touch the ground with the soles of their feet. They were so emaciated that many who had known them as they had been before would never have recognized them now. Indeed, so wasted were they that even the animals of the veld did not take any notice of them. A lion would come and sniff at them and then pass on unconcerned; the hyena would also sniff at them and then go its way, because they were no longer people, but mere skeletons.

On the eve of their arrival they could see the royal city at a distance; they saw the regiments at their games, healthy, vigorous young men in their prime; and at that sight Nongogo's companion cried when he thought that, even though they loved Chaka so much, he cared nothing for them. He cried also when he pondered over the troubles they had been through, to which most of them had succumbed. The sun set before they could reach the city, and so they slept again in the open. That man fell asleep for ever, and did not see the rising of the next day. Nongogo got up at sunrise and shook off the dew that had lain on him, and when he looked at his friend he saw that there was white dew on his eye-lashes and on his upper lip, and his eyes had rolled backwards; his face was turned in the direction of Mgungundlovu, the royal city. His life was a thing of yesterday. And now the weight of the entire grief of their journey became the burden of Nongogo's heart alone, and his eyes became dim and he could not see clearly, and his ears were blocked and there was a throbbing ache in his heart; his legs and knees shook and he was unable to walk.

When the afternoon shadows began to lengthen, he arrived at the city, and he passed through the city gates with no one saying a word to him. He went to the king's house which was near the council place and he asked to see the king and was granted permission. And as soon as he came within Chaka's presence, he mumbled some indistinct words because even his jaws had become stiff, and then he crawled on his stomach to go to Chaka, and his spear had not even been taken from him as required by law. When Chaka first saw him he was extremely frightened, because he resembled the *tikoloshe* he once saw at the river when he was bathing, and he wondered why it was visiting him on this day, in broad daylight, and in full view of all the people.

When Nongogo came to Chaka he stood up unsteadily, unable to keep his body erect. Chaka took a quick look at him, and he realized that the spear he carried was a Zulu spear. And then he looked at Nongogo and saw that his blanket was in tatters, and his body was full of open sores oozing pus. The blood from those wounds and from his travel-torn feet had left a trail as it dripped, right up to where he stood, next to Chaka. Nongogo took his spear and gave it to Chaka, and then he produced the little stone he had been sent to look for, and he gave it to Chaka also; and then, maintaining complete silence, he removed his tattered clothes, and his wasted body was seen in its entirety by Chaka and the men of his court.

Nongogo mumbled: 'I have tried to fulfil your command, O King.'

Chaka: 'Nongogo! Is that you, Nongogo?'

Nongogo: 'It is I, your servant, O King!'

All the men were surprised and silent because the Nongogo of former days whom they knew as a tall, handsome young man, stood shapeless before them, like something dead.

Chaka: 'Where are your men?' He asked this in anger when he realized that Nongogo had come back alive from a mission from which he did not expect him to return. Nongogo told about his

145

journey right up to the end, and then Chaka said: 'Take this dog and destroy it! He has killed my people and now he is fabricating a lot of lies here! Besides, I had ordered him to bring enough ore back to make many spears, and now here he is coming back empty-handed.'

When the executioners came close to him, Nongogo spoke again, and this time his voice was clear and could be heard well when he said: 'Chaka' (not King), 'many people believe that you are not a human being resembling other people, and today I'm convinced this is true. I have carried out your very difficult orders which no other person could have done, yet the reward I receive at your hands is death. But...' he did not finish what he was saying. Chaka, in his anger, stabbed one of Nongogo's executioners to death and told them they had delayed in carrying out his command. The remaining ones grabbed hold of Nongogo and took him outside, but when they reached the place of execution, they found that all belonged to yesterday.

Some of the men of the king's court were so overwhelmed and moved when they saw the state Nongogo was in, that they forgot to express their admiration of the king's wisdom and the justness of his verdicts. They too were killed because it was said that their silence meant that they were critical of the king's action.

That is how Nongogo's secret mission ended.

While Nongogo was away in the north, Chaka had become suspicious of yet another one of his commanders, called Mnyamana. So he said to him: 'There are cattle in Swaziland which are as good as mine; they are just sitting there. Go and bring them. Take your regiment to accompany you. Go!' When Chaka spoke in that manner, the one who was sent knew very well that things were not going well for him.

During his journey there, Mnyamana was trying to think of a way to capture the cattle. When he reached there he hid his people in the forest, and they began to study the forest paths and the Swazi fortresses, and they also observed the grazing grounds of the cattle. By some strange luck, the Swazi armies went on an expedition to the north, and while they were gone Mnyamana captured all the cattle. Messengers were dispatched to carry the alarm to the men, but by the time they arrived Mnyamana had already left their country, with its difficult terrain, its forests and rocky ledges and caverns and was in the plains where one Zulu warrior was equal to five of the enemy. The Swazi gave up and abandoned their cattle. They were gone for good, but by the time this happened Mnyamana, the commander of the Zulu army, had lost an eye in a skirmish.

When he arrived at the royal city, he was greeted with joy. Chaka, however, was cross because he had already heard that Mnyamana was coming with countless herds of cattle. He wondered how he had obtained them when he, Chaka, had personally failed many times to capture them even with the backing of all his armies. He said: 'So you are back, Mnyamana?'

'Yes, O King.'

'Where are the cattle I sent you to fetch?'

'I have brought them, O King, here they are.'

'Where are your men?'

'They are there, O King, and are tending the cattle.'

Chaka kept quiet for a long time looking for an excuse and then he said: 'How did you capture them?'

Mnyamana explained.

'You dog! You stole the cattle of the Swazi whereas I had not commanded you to steal them, but had told you to take them in a fair fight! Execute this thief who is afraid to meet the enemy face to face; he has given me a bad name because other nations will think that I live by stealing, not through skill in war, which is the occupation of men.'

The executioners took him and sent him on to the other world.

That was the reward which Chaka dealt out to his braves and to the commanders of his armies, a bitter reward. These matters of the killing of Nongogo and Mnyamana brought about a bitter feeling of dissatisfaction among the commanders and generals, and even among the regiments themselves, because a commander was killed together with those under his command. The people's hearts began by slow degrees to feel unhappy about Chaka's rule when they saw that his spear did not spare even those who had served him so well. Dingana and Mhlangana noticed this spirit among the people from the moment it began to grow, and instead of calming them down, they secretly fanned the spark in order to encourage this incipient jungle fire.

CHAPTER TWENTY-TWO
THE DEATH OF NANDI

Chaka sent a strong contingent of his armies to the north far beyond
St Lucia Bay to go and destroy the kings of those places and capture
their cattle. But those armies were decimated by a severe disease
endemic in that country, and they died in thousands and returned
empty-handed and harassed by death all along the way. Then
Chaka decided to take some armies near to that place so that they
could develop immunity and only attack thereafter; but before he
did so, he sent another expedition to the south where the Pondo
came upon them unexpectedly and killed them in large numbers so
that they returned home with nothing.

When this army reached home, Chaka became very angry, and he
caught hold of its commanders and burned their eyes with a red-hot
iron, saying that those eyes of theirs were useless, else how did it
happen that the Pondo caught them so unawares! The senior commander was burnt alive. All these things were done in the presence
of the army which had been dispatched to Pondoland. When all this
was over, that same army was dispatched to the north on the very
day of their return. They thus went on that new mission still tired,
without having had a chance to rest, and thus the vicious diseases of
those northern territories killed them in large numbers. On that
occasion it killed approximately thirty thousand people.

As the armies were leaving home, Chaka asked Malunga what
had gone wrong that the Zulu armies came back empty-handed like
that. Malunga said: 'I believe it is because you who are Zulu himself,
hardly ever see people die in large numbers, and your hand does not
kill as often as it should. You only experience these things indirectly
by being told of them. Yet, as you know, a dog which has been given
drugs to make it long to bite, if not allowed to hunt, will end up
tearing up the goats and the people. And so it is with a person who

has been inoculated with such strong medicines as you have! If he does not kill, those medicines will turn against him and kill *him* instead.'

This was exactly what Chaka wanted to hear, since he was a man who loved to see blood flowing. He collected together all the women who had been captured in the wars, as well as the Zulu widows whose husbands had been killed by the diseases of the north and by the wars, and he said: 'The doctors say that it is because of the sorcery of these people that the armies come back without anything, and that they succumb so much to disease.' It incensed the Zulus very much to hear that it was because of these foreigners that they carried the shame of not having captured anything, and thus they killed beyond the order and the measure set by Chaka.

Chaka had chosen for himself from within his nation extremely beautiful girls, healthy-looking ones whose youthful blood gave colour to their skins; houses were built for them and they were fed well with meat, and their complexions glowed even more. He continually visited them, picking the fruit of their youth, and then when their breasts fell and they were considered to have lost the bloom of youth, he would pass them on to his councillors. Some of these very ones with whom he had lived in this manner, were also killed on that day. As Chaka thus plundered other men's daughters, he instructed his trusted man, Ndlebe, to see to it that every single child born to those young women should be killed on the very day of its birth, so that no child fathered by him should ever survive. When those women cried for their children, Chaka said: 'It is fitting that a woman should cry for her child, and since it is painful to separate a woman from her young child, I will permit you to go where your child has gone.' And so saying, he would kill them. The pain in the hearts of the mothers of those children can only be fully understood by other women. Ndlebe's large ears helped him to perform that task of killing the children begotten by Chaka.

Nandi had already talked a great deal to Chaka suggesting that he should take a wife for himself to bear him children who would be his heirs, and that by doing so he need not deprive himself of that harem of his. But Chaka refused and said that he did not want children. Because of her desire for a grandchild, Nandi abducted one of Chaka's women, a girl from Qwabe's village who was pregnant, and hid her until she gave birth. When the woman at the place herself returned to Chaka, the child remained at the place where she had been hidden.

Eventually Nandi could not control herself any more, and wished to see the child fathered by Chaka, and then she fetched him from his hiding place. When he came, he was treated just like a strange child who was visiting his relatives there. Ndlebe soon knew the whole truth, and he told Chaka who then kept a close watch on his mother, and saw that she loved that child very much indeed. One day Chaka came suddenly upon her mother while she was off her guard, playing with the child, and he asked her what made her so interested in that child. Nandi said she was merely holding him. Then he asked her to put him in the centre of the courtyard, and then he came close to the child so that his shadow fell on him, and as soon as this happened that child died immediately. That was how Chaka knew the children he had fathered.

His anger now rose like foam in a boiling pot. That evening he went to his home, and he asked his mother why she persisted in giving him children when he did not want them, and then he killed his mother in the manner in which he had killed Noliwa. When Nandi died, Chaka once more felt as if something was pressing hard on his insides, exactly as on the day he killed Noliwa.

Early next morning people began to hear that Nandi was no more, and then Chaka threw dust over himself and he bawled saying: 'Oh, oh, my mother is dead O! Oh, oh, from other homesteads there is smoke rising, but none is rising from my home O!'

On that day Chaka outdid himself completely. He sent Ndlebe to go around the royal city to spot those who were not mourning with the king, and then he said the fact that they did not cry showed that they were the ones who had bewitched his mother, because a deceased person is not regarded as an animal whose skin is simply pegged out on the ground to dry. Some people, afraid they would be killed, threw snuff and dust in their eyes so that tears should come out, and the spear should pass them by. Chaka sent out people to stand at all the roads leading to the royal city to observe those who were walking slowly in coming to the king's palace, and those who were not crying as they came. All these were made to stand to one side near a little cliff. He slaughtered cattle in tens, and those who ate the meat or any other kind of food, were also told to stand by that cliff because they continued to enjoy food while the king was mourning. That regiment which had been sent to stop Moselakatse in his flight was fetched, and it was said that all these calamities were happening because of it, because it had failed to carry out the king's orders; they too were made to stand by that cliff, having first been deprived of their spears.

Chaka commanded that all the relatives of Nongogo should be brought to him because Nongogo had spoken evil words to the king the day he died. By 'his relatives' was meant all those who shared the same clan name as he. They too were made to stand near that cliff. Chaka had once been plotted against, and was even wounded with a spear during some festive occasion; and today all those related to the one who had stabbed him were collected together and also made to stand by the cliff. The cliff was now almost full, but he issued one more order, that all of Moselekatse's relatives be brought, that is to say all those who had been ruled by Zwide. They too were taken to that same cliff.

Now Chaka commanded his regiments to kill all those people who were on that cliff in order to remove the curse from his nation; and when the regiments came near, there arose a sorrowful wailing among those dying or about to die. Some prayed for mercy, pleading that they had been delayed in arriving because they came from far; some died with curses in their mouths, caring nothing any more. As the regiments were killing the condemned, Chaka came to the cliff to witness the slaughter, and the wailing of the dying made him feel good.

On that day the vultures ate till they could do no more than just stare at the food; the hyena ate till it just lay down; but it was not even noticeable that they had eaten anything. The smell of decay grew, and the stench was beyond description. The little fountain which was near that cliff had to be abandoned. The corpses were thrown in the chasms of that cliff, into a ravine called Donga lukaTatiyana.

After that Chaka said that his mother ought now to be satisfied where she was because he had sent her off with a large escort of people with whom he had made a mat for her, and that there were numerous people to make fire for her. On the other hand, Chaka was already tired of his mother's interventions on many occasions when he wanted to kill people.

Chaka filled this place, Donga lukaTatiyana, twice with the people he killed, that is to say, on two separate occasions.

This incredible amount of killing, which even made the wild carnivorous animals get accustomed to staying close to the villages, frightened the Zulu people as well as the regiments when they saw the spear laying waste the home people instead of the enemy. The people's hearts turned away from Chaka altogether, and his commanders were also complaining a lot. He was indeed proving himself to be unlike any ordinary human being as Nongogo had said.

A few days after these happenings, Isanusi came to Chaka. He had not taken this journey specifically to visit Chaka, but was on his way elsewhere and decided to stop briefly. Chaka told Isanusi how his kingdom had grown, and that there was now only one king in the world, and that was he, Chaka; and also that his warriors were now as numerous as the stars. Isanusi said he was very pleased to hear that kind of report. He told Chaka to stand firm and carry on with his efforts, and then he added: 'I have made it possible for you to obtain all the wishes of your heart. Be prepared then, so that the day I return from where I am going, you should be ready to give me those few heifers to reward me and my assistants for our services.' Chaka asked when he would return from where he was going, and he said: 'I am not able to tell you exactly because one can never predict the duration of a doctor's visit, sometimes he is delayed much longer than he had planned because of the people's demands for his services. However, I shall try to come back soon.'

When he parted from Isanusi Chaka began to inspect his cattle and to pick out the ones he would give to Isanusi, and they were greater in number than any ever paid in fee to any doctor. He kept them to one side, and they waited for their new owner to come.

CHAPTER TWENTY-THREE
THE UNQUENCHABLE THIRST

The events in Chaka's life were overwhelming because they were so numerous and of such tremendous import; they were like great mysteries which were beyond the people's understanding. But since it is not our purpose to recount all the affairs of his life, we have chosen only one part which suits our present purpose. And now, as we draw our narrative to a close, we shall first remind the reader of some things which have already been told.

With the spear made for him by Isanusi Chaka killed without mercy, thus winning himself instant fame as well as great kingship. With the armies of his great empire he invaded the south, and he laid everything to waste without pity or compunction, yet those who fled from him far surpassed him in the numbers they killed. And so it was too with his invasion of the north and in all the wars that he fought. When we count the people killed by Matiwane when he was fleeing from Chaka, those killed by the Batlokwa of Sekonyela, those killed by Moselekatse, as well as those killed by Chaka at home in Zululand, together with the infants who were killed at his bidding, we find that the number is overwhelming indeed. And when we add to it the deaths of Noliwa, Nongogo and Mnyamana, and of Nandi and Chaka's women, we find that the greatness of that number is now frightening. In order to comprehend this fully, we should use the example that the number of people killed by him in the ways we have described, is equal to the number of the Basotho, counting every man, woman and child, multiplied three or four-fold. Imagine them all being killed!

It was through Chaka that the *difaqane* came into existence, the time when people ate each other, and stole or took by force what belonged to others; it was also the time of the homeless wanderer, something that had not been known before. It was through him that cannibalism first came into being, this thing which is uglier and more despicable than all others, when people hunted each other like animals for the sole purpose of eating each other.

In those days, that is to say when King Chaka was in the very middle of the years of a man's life, the time when life is most enjoyable, when he who has been working begins to taste the fruit of his labours, when he sees the cattle and the goats he has earned beginning to multiply, and the people enjoying their milk; the time when he watches with satisfaction as the children of his loins are running around and playing; at that very time in his life King Chaka began to suffer untold pain in his soul. He suffered even though he was a king, instead of enjoying his large kingdom and enormous wealth which were the longings of his heart. Chaka was a king of kings, and the renowned of the earth paid tribute to him, and came to him crawling on their knees or on their stomachs, their heads bowed low. Where he sat, there was always a young warrior shading him with his shield, and his courtiers were continually declaiming his praises, acclaiming him and greeting him with salutations which were greatly flattering, which were spoken with much respect. Yet, in the midst of all that adulation, he began to suffer extreme pain in his soul.

The number of his warriors was equal to the stars in the sky, and no king before him had ever had so many; but even more important, they were invincible, and they fought against the winds and the storms till they conquered them, to say nothing about other human beings. He ought therefore to have been happy in the knowledge that all these things had come into being, and were of the nature they were, because of him. And yet, in the midst of all that wealth and all that glory he began to suffer pain and a gnawing sense of discontent in his soul.

What, we may ask, was his heart yearning for now? What was the object of its whimpering? What was it hankering after? What was it that he could wish for and be denied? But, in the midst of all these things, his heart lacked peace and contentment, nothing pleased him any more, his thoughts were in turmoil and were not able to calm down and to make firm decisions. Chaka was a warrior who saw much blood in his growing up, blood that was spilt by him personally; now that he no longer went to war with his armies, therefore, he longed to see people dying by his own hand. He craved to witness death. Whenever he did not see that spectacle he became truly sick, and he desired that as his armies were shedding blood in battle, his right arm should remain steeped in gore here at home.

To still the throbbing in his heart, he called for a big feast, and as the people were enjoying themselves, he kept his eyes open for those he might find an excuse to remove from this world, by means of whom he might quench the thirst that was burning inside him. Some were killed right there during the festivities for, it was said, they sang out of tune or danced out of step, and thus spoiled the king's feast. Now since people do not have the same strength in their chests, those who feared to be killed for singing out of tune kept quiet so that their voices should not be heard; but that very silence of theirs became the misdeed for which they were killed, for it was said that they despised the king's feast. In these modern days, when a sermon is moving, people often cry; even in those days of darkness also, good dancing and singing did often make people cry, especially the elderly who were no longer able to participate in the games. On that day also many people's hearts were moved when they saw those uniformly adorned warriors, each division having its own dress, and when they remembered what they themselves used to be like in their days. They wept then. Some induced their weeping artificially, and said they were crying because they were moved by the king's feast.

Chaka asked what was the cause of their weeping, and they explained, and then he said: 'It amazes me that you are moved to tears by watching my warriors at their games, and not by *me who am a wonder*, by me who created all these things; you are not moved by my person, you are moved by the beauty of a garment not by him who is wearing it, and who made it, and by that act you are despising me.' When he spoke those words, he raised his little spear and pointed it upwards, and those poor people were killed, and yet they had acted under the mistaken belief that the king would be pleased that they were moved to tears by the magnificence of his feast. The people who were adept at the games, and the ones with beautiful voices who sang most tunefully, were also killed, for it was said that they made the people cry and usurped the glory of his majesty. And now the people were at a loss to know what it was that might please the king since the good singer, the bad singer, and the one who kept quiet were all killed alike. These ones we have just told about were the ones who were killed during the day, in the middle of the festivities.

When the night was advancing, when the people turned in for the night, Chaka took his regiments and killed the majority of the people who had come to the festivities at his own invitation, saying that they had been plotting against him; and the menials of the king to whom that task was entrusted, carried out this order quietly, and hundreds of people simply disappeared in the middle of the night, and were no more. And now his heart began to feel happy, and things began to look normal again, and he was able to derive some joy from them, now that he had done this deed; he could taste his food again, and that painful thirst which had seized him was diminished, and he felt like a human being again. He repeated such acts many times to douse this heat that seared his insides. The reason for arranging the feast was that he should be able to kill the people easily when they were all gathered together in one place.

CHAPTER TWENTY-FOUR
PAINFUL DREAMS

From that day Chaka never experienced again the joy and the happiness he had once known. He often had painful and frightening dreams which disturbed his sleep, and which he could never remember when he woke up. A few days passed after the feast, and then he had a dream. He dreamed that he saw himself from his childhood to the day he met Isanusi, and when he reached that point, he woke up from his sleep on account of the painful nature of his dream. He fell asleep again, and when sleep came, he dreamed that same dream, and when he came to his meeting with Isanusi he woke up again. Three times in that same night he dreamed that one dream, from a certain point to a certain point, but the most amazing thing was that he kept waking up when he reached the point of his meeting with Isanusi, even though we are at a loss to know why it was that suddenly he was afraid of his dealings with Isanusi who was his closest friend.

When he woke up the third time he did not sleep again, but he sat up instead until sunrise. By this time, however, he had forgotten what his dreams had been about, and all he remembered was how painful they were.

That morning found him extremely worn out, his heart was blackened, and he desired nothing. He flared into a temper when people simply talked to him or greeted him. On the following night, the moment he put his head down he dreamed that same dream again. He woke up, and then he left and went to the house of his most beautiful woman whom none could equal, a girl with an extremely beautiful carriage, a figure of unequalled charm, and a beautiful complexion, whose skin glowed with the blood racing beneath it, the champion of all the young women of Zululand. When Chaka entered her room, her face was to him all coarse and pimply and not smooth as usual, and even her voice sounded hoarse and jarring, and jabbed his ears most painfully. He walked away from her in the middle of the night without having obtained the comfort he was looking for. He went from one to another, but found each one the same as the other, or even worse; but he avenged himself by killing some of them that same night, because they had failed to soothe his aching heart.

Believing that his condition was caused by witchcraft, he decided to leave the city and go into the veld and stay there till Isanusi should come to strengthen him and his city also. What is surprising, though seemingly unimportant, is that it never occurred to Chaka to tell Malunga and Ndlebe his frightening dreams, even though they were with him all this time. Chaka left home taking with him two regiments, one called the Ma Chaka and the other Dinotshi, and he went a little way to the south and stationed them there, since his regiments were never congregated in the same place; besides, he was taking a new regiment to a place called Dukuza, and the other two were simply escorting this one, and would go back with him. He went there under the pretext that he was taking the new regiment but knowing in his heart that he was running away from something which pestered him and gave him no rest night and day, urging him to try to find peace and rest in the veld, far away from the people.

Chaka arrived at Dukuza where he was taking that new regiment called the Dukuza, and on his very first night there he had a dream more painful than the ones he had had thus far. He dreamed that he saw himself asleep, and a spear was piercing his heart. He was startled to a painful waking and he grabbed his spear and his shield, was on his feet at once, looking about, but he found that all was perfectly still, and all the people were sleeping peacefully. He laid down his head once more because his eyes were heavy from lack of sleep for several nights on end. But once more, as soon as sleep came, he saw a Zulu spear piercing his heart. This wrenched him awake most painfully and he scrambled to his feet and stood there looking this way and that. He found once again that everything was perfectly still, nothing stirred, and the people were all asleep and snoring. Then he decided not to sleep again, but started pacing up and down to dispel his sleep; he was extremely frightened and trembling as he marvelled at the strangeness of his dreams.

At last he squatted on the ground to rest and flex his knees which were weakened by fright; and while he was squatting like that, a jackal cried over in the middle of the veld, far away from the camp. Chaka jumped up when he heard it for it was like the hue and cry of people running in pursuit of him. He stood up, and once more paced up and down in the darkness of the night; and while he was pacing like that, a hyena screamed and once again he was severely jolted as its cry penetrated his heart, and it was like the alarm raised by the one who was holding the spear which he saw stabbing his heart. Towards dawn, a dog pierced the sky with its howling far away among the caves, and it was a dog belonging to people whom Chaka had scattered and destroyed, killing even those who had come to him of their own accord to plead for peace and for the fighting to come to an end. The howling of that dog reminded Chaka of the cruel acts he had perpetrated against the people of that place. To him, it was as if that dog was crying for its owners who had been killed so mercilessly even as they begged for their lives to be spared; and now, it seemed,

158

that dog had remained in great sorrow that made it cry unceasingly as it wandered about without even knowing where it was going.

Chaka was very angry when he saw other people sleeping while *he* was unable to sleep, and he killed nine men on that same night stabbing them fatally so that they died in their sleep right there on the ground where they lay.

We should have mentioned that that place where Chaka was on that day was where, at the beginning of his wars, he had killed off all the people in a clean sweep, so that dogs ran wild there in large numbers and were troublesome to people who chanced to walk through that area. They became as vicious as hyenas, and roamed in large packs. Where large villages once stood there were now dangerous places for a man to traverse, which made one's hair stand on end.

When he recalled his deeds and heard these cries of the night, Chaka was seized with incredible fear and he wept bitter tears. But, instead of helping his pain subside as tears usually do to a heart swollen with sorrow, his crying only aggravated his grief. He stood up and walked about in an agitated manner throughout the night, some unknown force inside him driving him relentlessly. When the red light of dawn began to appear and the other people were waking up he dropped off in a doze which was brief and heavy, and only made his head ache.

He woke up only after the sun had already risen, and he called Malunga in order to tell him what had happened; moreover on that day he had not forgotten his dreams. However, Malunga was nowhere to be found, and no one knew where he had gone, even though by sunset of the previous day he was still there. He called Ndlebe, but he too was nowhere to be found, and the people told him that Ndlebe had decided to go back to the courtyards where there were lots of meat, and besides he was going to watch over the king's women. And now Chaka realized that things had reached a difficult pass, for here were his servants simply walking out on him without his permission. He choked with rage as he wondered why they disappeared on the very day on which he most needed them, and desired their help and advice.

When the sun set on that day it left him in dire grief, with not a moment of rest as he paced about unable to stay in one place, as if there was water boiling furiously in his stomach. His eyes sank deep in their sockets, receding far to the back; and sometimes they bulged out and drooped like those of a drunkard whose lungs had been consumed by liquor. He became faint and weak, and was a pitiful sight indeed. His head swam and countless images flitted through his mind, and he saw them dimly; the only thing that stood out bright and clear was blood. His body would become hot and perspire profusely at one moment, and then grow ice-cold at the next. He continued to pace about and was an object of pity; he resembled a horse suffering from an intestinal fever which runs this way and that without seeing where it is going, yet driven mercilessly by the sickness inside it. He walked back and forth in agitation, finding no place to rest, and was like a horse from the Zambezi that is seized with madness when it has been struck by the sickness of that land, which makes it run about and bite itself, tearing the flesh from its body with its own teeth, unable to control itself since it is compelled by its sickness, and rousing pity and compassion in the hearts of those who see it. Chaka was exactly like that, and those who saw him were sure he was ill.

When the last rays of the sun disappeared, he left with about ten men, true braves whom he trusted, who, he had no doubt whatsoever, would lay down their lives at the place where he died, and their corpses would be found with his. He went with them and found a spot to sleep some distance away from the three regiments, which would be cool being far away from the evil tracks of other people.

His younger brothers, Dingana and Mhlangana, were on their way to attack the kingdoms to the north in accordance with his orders, but they returned half-way, on the pretext that they were ill. They arrived at the royal city shortly after Chaka left, and then they sent their greetings and also informed the king of the reason why they came back. When Chaka heard the news, he quickly dispatched a messenger to fetch them, hoping that he might find solace and his inner pain might cease when he saw his brothers. And so his eyes were fixed on the road until sunset, and every time he saw something moving there, he would hope that it was his younger brothers. Dingana and Mhlangana had long noticed that the people had already had enough of Chaka's rule, and this was fully confirmed when they were on the road with their mission when they saw that the warriors were no longer sure what they were supposed to do or not to do. This was why they went back, so that if they could find a way, they would kill Chaka and take over the kingship. Chaka waited for them in that manner, little knowing the secret plan in their hearts.

CHAPTER TWENTY-FIVE
DONGA LUKATATIYANA

The sun set, and the evening shadows formed and deepened. It grew dark, and the people went to sleep. Chaka immediately fell into a deep sleep because his brain was tired; and as soon as sleep came, his painful dreams which crept on him like spirits more evil than the *tikoloshe*, visited him again. He had a dream, and on that night his dream stretched out and proceeded further. He dreamed that he saw his king, Dingiswayo, and all his praiseworthy deeds as he tried to instil the spirit of humanity into his people, and he saw himself destroying all those beautiful deeds; and then he woke up, and he walked back and forth to scatter away his sleep, and he cast his eyes often on the road in the middle of the night looking out for the coming of Dingana and Mhlangana, his younger brothers. Since his knees were tired, however, he had to sit down, and as soon as he did so, he fell fast asleep and immediately began to dream.

In that dream he saw himself from his first meeting with Isanusi until the time he was installed as king; all his deeds passed slowly before his eyes, even though he wished they could pass quickly. He saw all his wars; indeed he saw them even more clearly than in those days when he was actually fighting in them; he saw the dying of those who were killed in them; he saw the nations as they scattered before him, fleeing and eating each other in the process; he also saw all the deeds he performed as king. He saw Nongogo's scouting journey together with all its hardships and its sufferings, and he saw also how he was executed; and in the same manner he saw the story of Mnyamana. He saw very clearly how each individual was slain in the killings of those many innocent women captured during the wars, and of the infants.

Then when he came to the killing of his 'wives', he felt such pain that he woke up. He tried to stand up, but was unable to do so. He tried to scream, but his mouth was stilled. Something pressed him down to the ground. At last he gained some strength and was able to get up, and he heaved himself up and reached for his spear. He stood on his feet, and threw glances this way and that, but he found that there was perfect stillness, and all his men were asleep except three who were on guard but a little distance away, keeping watch in accordance with the king's command.

Chaka realized now that the time of his death was near. His one regret, however, was that he was out in the veld, far away from the people, and that therefore there was no way in which to perform the ritual of killing as his own life came to a close. Nevertheless he devised a plan. He went to those watchmen of the night and said: 'What time of night is it, you watchmen?'

They said: 'It is the depth of night.'

He spoke to them about that illness which was consuming him and said that he was being bewitched by the Dukuza regiment, and that he ought to destroy it. He sent a messenger to fetch it from the other regiments. When it came he split it into two, and he sent one half to the little villages around the Mvoti River with an order to kill all the people there and let not a soul escape for, he alleged, they were the people who were bewitching him. He divided the remaining half into three groups and posted these at three different places and told them that, if the people from those villages should pass by them in their flight, they should kill them all. And then he called MaChaka when the others had already left, and he told them where each little group was stationed, and he instructed them to kill them, and those three little groups were killed easily because they were so small in number. That is to say, that Chaka killed Zulus by Zulus, without them being aware of it.

When the section which had gone to the villages came back, the MaChaka Regiment attacked them, and as they were fighting

Chaka went to the Dinotshi Regiment and sent them to the attack saying that the enemy was upon them; *they* soon realized, however, that these were other Zulus and they stopped right at the beginning.

There is nothing so beautiful and praiseworthy as when a person sees himself doing a beautiful and useful deed. On the other hand there is nothing as painful as when an evil man sees himself performing his evil deeds. It is very hurtful when a person thinks of his ugly deeds, but when he actually sees himself performing them at exactly the same place and in exactly the same manner as when they actually happened, the pain he experiences is one which nobody can adequately describe to another person. Therefore we are unable to describe the severity and the throbbing of the pain which Chaka's dreams caused him when he saw himself in the act of performing those ugly deeds.

There was a gorge near the royal city which had very deep ravines. A little way above it, opposite the city, was the fountain from which the people obtained their water. This was the gorge where Chaka killed the people he had condemned, who were then thrown into its crevasses. This was the place which the vultures and the hyenas had at last begun to frequent. This was where the cowards were killed, as well as all those whom Chaka killed during his lifetime, including the occasion of the mourning of Nandi's death. Eventually the adjoining fountain was no longer used after sunset or before sunrise because of the evil ghosts haunting it; and as the killing continued, the fountain was in the end abandoned altogether as the evil spirits refused to let anyone use it. Even today no one crosses that gorge after sunset, because that is the abode of the spirits which failed to reach their destination, the home of Zulu. The name of this gorge, together with its ravines, is uDonga lukaTatiyana (Tatiyana's gorge), even though we do not know its original name, because this one came into being during Chaka's reign.

We have said that Chaka sat down to rest his tired limbs, and he fell asleep instantly and began to dream again. He saw himself at home at Mgungundlovu; he was looking over that little gorge called uDonga lukaTatiyana. He heard a strong wind which blew with the force of a hurricane, followed by a deafening clamour of many people. And then suddenly he saw, inside that gorge, the people whom he had killed milling about in rage, while others were looking at him with pity, without saying anything. He saw *uHili* whirling about in there saying over and over again: 'Chaka! Chaka!! Chaka!!!', and then gnashing his teeth. He also saw all the evil spirits gathering in that place, as well as his friend, the King of the Deep Pool. And all these were looking towards him.

While Chaka was still looking at this spectacle in his dream, Isanusi and his servants arrived. All three of them stood dead quiet. They looked like people who were happy to see him. Yet theirs was not the normal happiness of human beings, but resembled that of someone who had conquered his enemy and was getting ready to strike the final blow. They were like people who were glad that that particular day had arrived at last. Isanusi said: 'Chaka, today I have come to demand my reward; I told you, the day I passed here, that you should get yourself ready while I was gone, and that you should give me that which belongs to me without hesitation or argument just as I have worked for you diligently and with precision, so that you obtained kingship and honour and riches and fame in great abundance.'

Even though these were not evil words, they caused Chaka untold pain, for he realized that Isanusi was counting the milling multitudes in uDonga lukaTatiyana as comprising his kingdom as evidenced by the fact that he was looking at them as he spoke. And when he heard those words, he jumped up in his sleep and fell on top of one of his men, killing him. He woke up, and he looked this way and that, trembling all the time, and all that he noticed was that the night was about to pass; beyond that he saw nothing, and was only conscious of the fact that he had been dreaming.

The sun came up, and with great difficulty he held himself steady, and he got up and conversed with the people; yet even as he spoke to them they were conscious that he was no longer the Chaka they knew. He stood up, the lion of Zulu descent, fearless beast of the wilds, but he stood up sapped of his strength, unable even to raise his mane. He stood up, the great elephant, but he stood up tremblingly, drained of all his strength, gasping like an ox suffering from the *mmamotohwane* disease, with its ears drooping besides. His beautiful body, his broad shoulders, and his heavy limbs, all rolled over and lumbered slowly, wearily and shakily, refusing to do as he wished. He stood up unsteady on his feet, yet so fearsome that whenever he as much as raised his hand as if to strike someone, that person died at once with his mouth open just like the beak of a bird. Death, strong as the male calf of a bovine, had seized him, but he could not see it; it had come, but he was unable to run away from it, or to fight it! That very same death which in his boasts during the days of his greatest glory, he claimed the Zulu armies had fought and conquered, and buried deep in the ground, that same death had come today, but he was unable to release himself from its grip.

When the sun rose that day the Dukuza regiment was no more, having vanished with the night, and only a portion of the MaChaka remained. There was only one regiment which remained intact, and that was the Dinotshi. Chaka told the men who were there with him to choose for themselves fifty cattle from each of the groups he had separated by colour, saying that that was his token of gratitude to them because they had served him with such devotion. But while they were busy selecting them, he sent a charging mob of young warriors to go and kill them, alleging that they were the ones bewitching him because as he lay ill, even before he died, they were already helping themselves to his cattle.

CHAPTER TWENTY-SIX
THE END OF CHAKA

The sun came up, and it rose higher, and when the cattle began to get used to the pastures, Dingana and Mhlangana arrived. By then they had already been among the surviving regiments, because these were camping some distance away from Chaka, about a half hour for a swift runner.

When his brothers arrived, Chaka felt a surge of new life from his excitement, and he jumped up as if he was seeing them for the first time, and as if they brought him cool waters with which to soothe his pain. The aches and affliction that he had suffered also subsided and gave him a chance to talk to them. Chaka had already been much weakened by his fretfulness and the unsettled nature of the thoughts in his troubled heart; yet, despite his weakness, he had not grown thin. He conversed with them for the greater part of that day, asking them about their expedition, and they in turn explaining all the things he asked them. Dingana soon realized that Chaka had indeed lost much strength, and he resolved to accomplish his evil design on that very day on which they met.

At mid-day Chaka's illness once again rose up, and when the afternoon shadows formed and stretched away, the pains became so very severe that they gave him no time to converse with his brothers.

At that very time Moshoeshoe's messengers arrived, bringing him crane feathers which he used to decorate his armies. He took them and admired them; but the aching of his heart once more rose up against him. His deeds once more passed before his eyes; and of all the people he had removed from the earth before their time, the one he saw was Noliwa, and she was in that same hut where he killed her, and he also heard her voice as she uttered those last words: 'Chaka, my beloved, you who are now my father, you who are Jobe, you who are Dingiswayo, you . . . !' And when he heard those words, and even saw Noliwa's face, his head swam, and his entire body was bathed in sweat. He now understood Isanusi's words much more clearly than when he first heard them, as he said to him: 'At this very moment your name has been entered among those of the kings of my home, and the highest among them, besides.'

When Noliwa's apparition vanished, Nandi's came into view, and as soon as their eyes met, Chaka tried to scream but his voice would not come out, and he simply sat staring blankly at the crane feathers, and to all appearances he was looking at them, whereas in fact he never even saw them. Nandi was at that same place where she was when her son removed her from the earth; and during all this time Noliwa's voice kept ringing in his ears.

When those had vanished, he saw uDonga lukaTatiyana crammed full with the people he had wiped off the face of the earth with Nandi standing on one side and Noliwa on the other; and while he was looking at them, Isanusi appeared from far away together with his aides, and he heard a voice coming from that multitude mocking him and saying: 'Chaka, murderer of your own brothers, the blood of your own father! Murderer of your own wife, companion of your heart! Murderer of your own children, your very own blood! Murderer of your own mother, she who gave you birth!'

Dingana observed that Chaka was dreaming, and then he signalled to Mbopha with his eyebrows so that he should get closer since their time had now come; he glanced back at Mhlangana, and he too came closer. Dingana came nearer to Chaka as if to admire the feathers, and then in a flash he stabbed him so that his spear sank into his body and appeared on the other side; Mhlangana stabbed him in the back, and his spear came out in front, while Mbopha's entered on the side; all those spears met inside Chaka's stomach, and at that very moment Isanusi appeared before Chaka to demand his reward.

When he felt the spears enter his body, Chaka, instead of fighting back like a man, as he used to, turned around slowly and woke up from his waking sleep, from the daytime dreams he dreamed with his eyes wide open. When he began to turn around, his pains ceased and his face smoothed out and assumed its normal appearance, and Dingana and Mhlangana knowing him as they did, ran helter skelter. And then Chaka said to them: 'You are killing me in the hope that you will be kings when I am dead, whereas you are wrong, that is not the way it will be because *umlungu*, the white man, is coming, and it is he who will rule you, and you will be his servants.'

Chaka died riddled with wounds, far away from his home. When the sun had set his corpse was carried to a little rise in the open plains so that it should be devoured by the beasts of the veld. On the following day the people went early in the morning to see what remained. They found that Chaka's body was still intact, but had instead turned as green as moss. They found many animal footprints all around Chaka's body, and they were utterly amazed that even an animal like the hyena, which is more greedy than the pig, had not eaten it in the night. They went and told Dingana, and he went with them to the corpse. As they came near, a flight of crows flew away from it, and they were sure they would find that they had dug out his eyes. But they found them both intact. A great fear descended upon them all, and they trembled, and Dingana ordered that the body should be buried quickly lest it should, by some unknown chance, rise again.

So it came about, the end of Chaka, son of Senzangakhona.

Even to this very day the Zulus, when they think how they were once a strong nation in the days of Chaka, and how other nations dreaded them so much that they could hardly swallow their food, and when they remember their kingdom which has fallen, tears well up in their eyes, and they say: 'They ferment, they curdle! Even great pools dry away!'

Ka mathetho
(End of the Tale)